MOSTLY SHATTERED

URBAN FANTASY ROMANCE

MERELY MORTAL
BOOK TWO

MICHELLE M. PILLOW

MICHELLEPILLOW.COM

ABOUT THE BOOK

Fall deep into book two of the spellbinding new first-person POV romantic urban fantasy series by NY Times and USA Today bestselling author Michelle M. Pillow.

I'm the mortal outcast in a powerful magical family, and danger is my constant companion.

The man I love doesn't remember me. My adoptive brother's ghost won't let me live in peace. And my uncle is dead set on marrying me off to the worst supernatural suitor.

If that's not enough, there's Constantine—an irresistibly dangerous master vampire who claims I'm part of an ancient prophecy. He's tempting, seductive, and makes me feel like prey. Being on his radar is a hazard I can do without.

As the balance between my mortal life and the

supernatural realm blurs, I'm thrust into a whirl-wind of family secrets, deadly enemies, and treach-erous alliances. The clock is ticking, and I must accept my true calling before the shadows swallow me whole.

Will I rise to claim my destiny or be consumed by the dark forces hunting me?

Perfect for fans of urban fantasy, paranormal romance, supernatural mysteries, forbidden love, enemies-to-lovers, power struggles, and heart-stopping twists. This is a must-read for anyone craving more than a little danger in their love stories.

MAILING LIST

To stay informed about when a new book in the series installments is released, sign up for updates:

Sign up for Michelle's Newsletter

michellepillow.com/author-updates

To my dear friend, Mandy M. Roth, who is a talented author in her own right. Thank you for always being there for me. Readers, check out her Grimm Cove series (shameless promo plug for an awesome person). You won't be sorry.

FROM THE AUTHOR

Though this book can be read as a standalone if you really want to, the author recommends reading this series in the order of publication.

ONE

I'm not a stalker.

I may be *stalking*, but I'm not a stalker.

I like to think of it as watching, but if I were honest with myself—which I'm not sure I want to be in this case—I'm dwelling on my pain. There is an ache inside of me, deeper than breathing, harder than death. I had everything that mattered. For one tiny moment, I had it—hope, normalcy, Chinese food with a man who loved me and the birth mother who accepted me.

Then I lost it all.

I want so badly to be normal.

I watched my adopted brother, Conrad, shoot and kill the man I love. Paul died in my arms. Have you ever had someone you love die in your arms? I keep reliving that horrible second when his breathing stopped.

I trusted Conrad more than anyone in the world, and he betrayed me.

It's a long story and one that I don't particularly want to talk about, but it is in my head, churning my thoughts, haunting my nightmares, and filling my bones with a hollow emptiness that eats away at my very core. Even now, if I close my eyes, I feel Paul being ripped away from me. My skin literally aches to hold him again. I want so badly to go back in time, to that moment in the hotel room when we were naked and alone and hidden from the cruel super-natural world.

It's not fair.

I fucking hate this.

I'm not being dramatic. At least not in this case. The pain is real. It breaks my heart, over and over again.

I wish someone would stab me in the chest so I don't have to feel it.

Our entire relationship seems like a bad halluci-nation because here I am, sitting on a bench, watching Paul and his daughter, Diana, play catch with their new retriever.

I fight back the grief of loss and close my eyes, even as I know I'll see the flash of his death tormenting me. In some ways, I need to see that moment. I need that reminder and that pain. Otherwise, I'd get up from my bench and I'd go to him. Then he and his daughter would both be in danger again.

It's best they don't remember.

"Paul," his name forms on my lips, but I don't call out.

He looks in my direction, and for a moment, I can't breathe. I will him to recognize me, to remember that alternate timeline when we were in love before magic screwed everything up.

He doesn't.

Of course, he doesn't. Some magic can't be reversed.

It was such a short time that we were together, but I can't move past the idea of us.

I can't see Paul's eyes, but I remember the soulful light brown vividly. He's had a haircut recently. The brown waves are tamer than when we were together. When I close my eyes at night, I can still feel him against me, and I hear his whispering voice. It's faint and far away, but I do everything I can to hold on to it.

"Dad!" a distant shout washes over me, followed by laughter.

They're so much better without me.

I don't want to admit how I tracked Paul and Diana to a dog run near the East River, just down from Central Park and my Upper East Side home. Let's just say being in a wealthy, supernatural family comes with some perks—even when you're the only mortal blood relative.

Diana takes off running, and their dog chases her.

I'm the only one who remembers that other life. Well, me and the asshole ghost of Conrad, who has decided his new favorite thing is making my life a living hell. I used to think that Conrad and I were close. We were both mortals being raised in a magical family—the odd kids out. My parents adopted him from foster care when I was five.

My father had an affair with a human, Lorelai, and then brought me home to his wife to raise. I can't say I blame Lady Astrid for having deep—if not highly suppressed—emotions about that scenario. Finding out my origin story as an adult sure explained a lot about my childhood.

I pick up the notepad on my lap to continue writing. In the digital age, handwriting letters is old-fashioned, but it feels safer and more private than email. Yes, I know magic protects my phone from hacking, but I've been having trust issues with everything lately. As I try to concentrate on what I've already written, I hold the pen at the ready while I read to myself.

Dear Lorelai,

You won't remember this, but we met a few months ago. I'm your daughter, Tamara Devine. A little while back, the woman I thought was my mother, Astrid, told me the truth of your existence, and I hired a private detective to find you. I always wondered why I wasn't like the others in my family. Now I know. It's because you aren't like them either. We're both human.

I came to your house in San Francisco. I saw the altar you made for my protection as you kept tabs on me my entire life. I know that you have loved me all these years. I know how you and my grandfather, George, kept in touch before he died and how you traded with trolls for the amulet necklace he gave me for protection.

I take a deep breath, feeling the grief. Like Paul and Diana, Lorelai is not dead, but she is lost to me. My life has become a series of losses. Sending this letter might be crueler than not.

I have a lot of confusion and guilt when it comes to Lorelai. I can imagine what it would have been like to be raised by her as a human in a normal house having mortal problems. It's a fantasy I visit often—going to Lorelai's for family dinners with Paul as my husband. Diana is our daughter and I love her like my own. The only drama is that someone over-cooked a pot roast and maybe a storm knocks out the power for a few minutes.

Simple. *Normal.*

I want it so badly.

The guilt comes when I think of my parents. To be normal means to reject them and the life they gave me. Davis and Astrid Devine are not perfect—far from it. I think that comes from being so powerful. As magical beings, they have a lot of responsibility to the supernatural community. I know that much of how they raised me was for my protection. And, I hate to admit it, but as much as I long to be normal, there is that little girl part of me that longs to be as powerful as they are. That is what I used to daydream about, having magic and belonging. That is until I got older and told myself that I needed to put away childish fantasies.

There is a rift inside of me, like two sides of the coin battling it out—supernatural versus normal, mortal versus immortal. I feel pulled in both directions. And there are times that I want them both equally.

My grandfather, George, was a remarkable man who treated me with kindness and love. I think about him every day and feel the ache of his absence. Growing up, he was my only steadfast supporter, always making time for me, even though I was a mortal in a world filled with magic. His presence was a warm shield, allowing me to navigate my childhood without ever making me feel like I was less than.

"You are a delicate butterfly in a world of fiery drag-

ons," he would say. *"The world needs butterflies, Tamara, as much as it needs dragons. Probably more. We all have our place."*

Even now, I hear his voice in my head, and it comforts me.

I touch the small pouch tucked away in my pocket that holds the amulet. I can't help but imagine that the stone is a physical representation of my life. Like me, it's mostly shattered—here but broken with a few shards missing. It will never be what it was.

I will never be what I was.

I can't wear it, but I carry it with me. The once red stone is now a fragmented green. The magic is completely drained, no longer able to stop any death that comes for me.

Until three months ago, I didn't even realize the story my grandfather told me about it being enchanted was true. Then, it saved my life a bunch of times before killing Conrad in an act of what I can only call karma. In doing so, it broke. It's stupid but having it near makes me feel loved. I like the weight of it in my pocket.

I turn back to the letter, wondering if I'm even explaining any of this right. How do I address the birth mother who doesn't remember meeting me as an adult?

I write, *The amulet's magic worked. It kept me from*

dying on several occasions—vampire attacks, explosions, and, well, other things.

Conrad tried to shoot me, and when that didn't work, he shot Paul. I can't write about what happened to Paul. Seeing his life draining from his gaze...

I gasp for breath as I feel the pain raging through me, trying to leak out of my eyes. I won't let it. I won't cry. Not here in public.

I need that image out of my head. I wish I could claw it out of my brain.

Part of me wishes the amulet would have erased my memory, too. Then I could grieve Conrad as a brother, not a betrayer.

I met Paul at the cemetery. We were both attending different funerals, which probably should have been my first clue that our time together was doomed. Who starts a relationship at a funeral? Well, besides ghouls.

I look up, seeing the retriever run around Paul's legs, almost tripping him. It's good to see him happy. He's a single dad whose cheating, estranged wife just passed away. The internet was all over the fact Nancy had been giving a guy head in a car at the time of her death. People can be such assholes when anonymously making fun of a stranger.

The dog barks. Paul would have gotten the animal for Diana. He loves that five-year-old more than anything, as it should be. It's a joy to hear Diana's laughter as she watches her father play-wrestle the dog. It gives me hope for her future, even though I can't be a part of it.

I'm reminded of the day I met Conrad. I was the same age as Diana now, and I expected a puppy for my birthday, not another brother.

Turns out I had been right. A puppy would have been loyal.

Diana is better off not knowing me. Safer. Being around me almost got her killed on multiple occasions. It did get her father killed. Where would she be if time had not reset? Parentless. Alone. Hunted by monsters. Tormented by nightmares. I'm glad she doesn't remember monsters are real. She is everything I couldn't be at her age. I want to keep her that way—innocent and perfect.

But to do so, I need to stay out of their lives.

I can't be with Paul.

I can't ruin them.

Where did I leave off? I strangle the pen like it might try to escape my hand as I continue to write. The pressure of the ballpoint deepens on the paper.

I know how you tried to protect me as a baby but couldn't when the monsters came. They wanted me as leverage over the Devine empire. You had to give me up, and I forgive you for that. It was right that you gave me to my father and Lady Astrid. They protected me. I don't like it, but it was right.

The reason you don't remember our meeting is because my adopted brother, Conrad, followed me to California. He killed my parents and my half-brother Anthony on my twenty-eighth birthday. He killed other people, too, but that's a long story and I'm not writing a book. He wanted me out of the way so he could inherit the Devine empire for himself. Stupid, really, since there is no way supernaturals will respect a mere mortal in a position of great power. Inherited wealth would have only gotten him so far. Anyway, it wouldn't be long before a vampire brood or shifter clan or warlock coven or necromancers or goblins...

I think she'll get the point. I scratch out part of the sentence.

...supernaturals burned everything to the ground and danced on all-things-Devine's ashes.

Conrad tried to kill us, too—me and you. When he took the magic amulet from me to harness the power for himself, it backfired and killed him instead. It gave all the deaths that should have been mine to him, but in doing so, it brought me back to the first time I should have died—the fire at my twenty-eighth birthday party. That is why you don't remember any of this. No one else does either. The troll magic set things right, I suppose, in the grand scheme of everything, but it also took away everything I had gained in those erased weeks.

The amulet is now broken. It can't protect me, and I know I'm vulnerable to…

A familiar icy chill crawls over my skin. My body involuntarily stiffens in fear. I can't help it. He's found me.

Fuck. All I can do is wait.

Dogs bark louder, appearing more energized and on edge as they run toward their owners. Animals can sense things humans can't. I imagine they notice the ripple of hate emitting from my brother's vengeful spirit.

"I dare you to send that to her," Conrad whispers in my ear. I can't see him, but I feel him, and I smell the lingering scent of ash and decay that always chokes the air when I'm near his ghost.

They say hindsight is twenty-twenty. For me, I think it's more forty-forty, or sixty-sixty. Is that even a thing? There were so many obvious signs I should have realized about Conrad's true nature, but I had been willfully blind to them all. I gave him leeway because he had the same hard childhood I did. I thought he was misunderstood. Turns out, everyone else was right. I was wrong.

Again, to say life has given me trust issues is an understatement.

I rip the sheet from the notepad, not finishing it. Crinkling the letter tightly in my fist, I feel the frustration boiling inside me. I shove the crumpled ball in my pocket next to the broken amulet. "I'm not sending anything."

"If you contact her, you know what will happen," his voice warns. "I'll finish what I started."

The sun is bright, but I no longer feel it. I don't rise to his baiting, mainly because ignoring him is one of the few defenses I have, and it annoys the fuck out of him.

"Do I need to show you what I'm capable of?" Conrad's body comes into transparent view. His back is to me, and he faces Paul and Diana.

"I know, Conrad," I say in a rush to placate him. "I'm not telling them who I am. I'm just here. It's a park. We're strangers."

This is a time I wish I had magic so I could zap him into eternal rest. Unfortunately, until Conrad, the most experience I had dealing with ghosts was Mr. Farty—aptly named for his smell when we were kids—the residual haunting stinking it up in the country estate's smoking room.

Conrad killed so many people, including our parents, our brother Anthony, his own druggie prostitute birth mother, and my sweet Paul. Fate might have reversed those deeds, but I still feel the pain. I can't watch his ghost torment Paul and Diana.

"We made a deal. You leave them alone, and I don't talk to them," I say. "I kept my word. I have said nothing about you to anyone, and I won't."

That isn't exactly the deal. Conrad allows me to see Paul and Diana because he knows how it tortures me that I can't have a normal life with them. He likes the threat looming over my head. If he kills them, that threat goes away.

It's a fucked up delicate balance.

"If you hurt them, I'll tell everyone what you did," I threaten.

He finally turns to look at me. The hollow pits of his eyes are a demonic black. I wonder if it's a face he puts on to scare me or an actual manifestation of his evil that he can no longer hide.

"Ooh, you'll tattle to mommy and daddy?" He mocks.

"You think Lady Astrid can't find a way to exorcise you?"

"She can try, but not before I tear it all down." He keeps laughing. I hate the sound.

His voice reminds me of all the lies. He'd been my best friend. To know I mean nothing to him...

"Stop," I whisper. "You've got what you want. I'm miserable and alone."

His face appears right before mine, so close we'd be touching if he was corporeal. I hold still. No one else can see him, and I don't want to draw attention to myself by swiping at him like a madwoman. His coldness creeps across my face like a melting ice cube.

"You're not thinking of doing something to your-self, are you?" he asks. "Oh, Tam-tam."

In fact, I have considered it. I'm not proud of it. In those dark, lonely hours of the night, I think of diving from the penthouse gardens onto the street below, screaming, *ego sum avis stultus!*

Sometimes the pain is too much.

But I'd never.

"You die, they die," he warns.

"I hate you," I whisper through my teeth.

"I don't care." Conrad disappears, and the warmth of the sun returns. It takes a moment for it to thaw my face.

I can usually tell when he's close by the chill, but I always feel like he could be watching. It's more than a little creepy. Don't get me started on bath-rooms and getting dressed.

"What up, sis?"

I jolt in fright as Anthony leaps over the back of the bench to sit next to me. He automatically settles with his arm across my shoulders.

"Shit, you scared me." I give him a light punch. "How did you find me?"

Anthony laughs. His lighthearted mannerisms are a stark contrast to Conrad, and I take a moment to adjust. "City hide and seek. You're going to have to do better than a dog park if you want to disappear."

To be honest, I'm emotionally drained, and it takes everything in me to hide my growing depression from him. I feel isolated and alone, but I don't want him to see that.

My half-brother is Conrad's opposite in every way. Born fully into magic, Anthony has never known a mortal day in his life. He inherited power from our father, who hails from formidable Welsh magic, and his mother, Lady Astrid, who supposedly comes from a Nordic line descended from gods. Even though Conrad was older, Anthony has always been the heir apparent to the Devine empire.

I don't mind. I never wanted that headache.

Whereas Conrad brooded, Anthony hides his emotions behind smiles and charm. Conrad had been obsessed with gaining respect through power—both money and magic. Anthony does everything he can to avoid his destined responsibility. Anthony went to a special private school for supernatural children. Conrad taught himself about the supernatural out of the family library—spending endless hours reading the old tomes.

With Anthony always gone, I had logged more childhood hours with Conrad.

The one thing my brothers have in common is they both died in the fire during my twenty-eighth birthday party. Only Conrad's timeline remained. And Anthony was given another chance at life.

Fuck, this is confusing. It's strange having the overlapping timelines in my head. I know this is the *right* one, but...

I glance at Paul, but don't let my gaze linger.

"You have that look again," Anthony says. "I can feel you brooding from across the park. Talk to me. What's swirling around in that brain of yours?"

If only I could tell him. If only anyone knew the truth.

"It reminds me of when we were kids. Whenever I came home from school, I'd see you and Conrad huddled and brooding and whispering secrets like you thought the world was going to end. Something changed in you when he came to live with us. I'm not saying I regret our parents adopting him, but I think you were happier before. I know we were closer before he came. I'm not implying that's anyone's fault. Our parents sent me away to school and trapped you two with tutors." Anthony sighs. "I know I'm not him, but I'm a good listener."

I wish it were that simple. I can't tell him what Conrad did.

"You wouldn't understand." I try to think of Paul's timeline as a dream, or a story I read.

Or a glimpse.

Yes, a glimpse. I miss that feeling of normalcy and belonging I had with him. Sometimes, I wish it hadn't happened because now that love is replaced with an ache for what can't be.

I want to be normal, but I can't. Maybe that means I'm meant to surrender to my supernatural heritage, even though that world considers me defective.

Maybe I don't belong anywhere.

Anthony lets loose a playful sigh and tussles the top of my head before dropping his arm back down around my shoulders. I feel him give me a light hug. He's been more attentive since the fire. I wonder if he's sad about Conrad or if it's become all too real that I have an expiration date and he's going to lose me someday.

Maybe both? It's difficult to tell with Anthony. He's a master at hiding his deeper emotions.

After some thought, he grins. "Ah, you're probably right, little Tammy. I don't understand a lot of things."

"Don't call me Tammy." I jolt him in the ribs, and his whole body jerks before he laughs.

The sadness remains inside me like a permanent scar, but he makes me feel better.

"Seriously, talk to me," Anthony urges. "Conrad's gone. And, you know, I miss him, too. But we're still here. You and me. Maybe I can help if you talk to me. We Devines got to stick together, right?"

"I'm just feeling..." I struggle to find the words.

"Overly mortal. I'm like a puzzle piece that doesn't fit into the family picture."

"Oh." He nods, and I see him struggling to understand what it must be like for me. "Mortal or not, you're a Devine. Your blood is my blood. This is where you belong. With your family. With me. I will not let anything happen to you. I promised you a long time ago that I would find a way to make you immortal."

We were kids. I'm not holding him to a promise he made at the age of seven while feeling guilty about handing me a fireball.

For a fleeting moment, I see his charming smile fade, and I sense his loneliness. Growing up, Conrad and I were often envious of Anthony, believing him to be so lucky. He went on all the adventures and attended supernatural parties while we were confined to the secure corridors of the protected wing of the country estate. As the golden child, he possessed all the inherited magic and charm.

It never occurred to me that he'd feel alone in his crowded rooms.

I look at Paul and think about telling my brother everything.

"How's Louis doing?" I ask instead.

"We're not seeing each other anymore." Anthony's voice is soft.

"Oh?" I lean into him. Louis was a fun guy, and

he made my brother happy. "Is it because of the fire? Did it freak him out?"

Louis died with Anthony in the fire during the other timeline. The dark irony is that they were both in a closet at the time. I'm sure there's a metaphor in there somewhere.

He shakes his head. "He gave me an ultimatum, and it ultimated."

"Have you ever thought about just saying something to the parents?" I ask. "The supernaturals aren't bedroom prudes."

I only half believe what I say. They may not be prudes for sex—*I mean, it's hard to be judgy when half of them eat people, and the other half does gods-know-what with their misspent time*—but magics are definitely elitists when it comes to perception and appearances.

Anthony plasters on an easy smile. I doubt he feels it. "Do you honestly think it would change things? The last thing I want is for them to monitor every interaction. I hate to say it, but they don't care about us, Tamara. They care about the glossy family portraits hanging in the foyer."

"Well, I'm sorry to hear it. I like Louis. He made you smile. But say the word, and he's dead to me."

"Nah, he won't remember you," Anthony gives a small laugh. "I erased his memory of me."

"Anthony!" I shake my head in disapproval.

"C'est la vie." He waves a hand to dismiss the subject. "It is what it is and nothing more."

We sit in a long silence. I lean against his shoulder and watch Paul with his daughter while trying not to be obvious about it.

"Do you believe we're meant to be with one person?" I ask.

Anthony chuckles. "In our family? Sure. It's called an arranged marriage."

"I'm serious." I nudge his ribs with my elbow. "Do you believe there is a single soul mate out there for us?"

Anthony's half hug tightens around my shoulders. "It's a sweet concept, a little naïve and human, but sweet. To answer your question, though, no. I don't think we get one love. One thing I've realized, listening to all the old timers tell their war stories, who we love changes with who we become. We're not the same at sixteen that we are at three hundred. Or in your case, thirty. I think we're meant to have many loves and many heartbreaks."

"I don't know if that makes me feel better or worse."

Anthony's body shakes with a small laugh. "If our father taught us anything, it's we can have hundreds of true loves, but they only last a few months at a time."

"That is so..." I shake my head.

"True?"

"Mean," I correct. "Poor Lady Astrid."

"I don't think anyone has ever felt sorry for our mother. I, for one, would not tell her you pity her."

"Right. Appearances." I nod.

"It's funny that you ask about that now because—"

"Tamara, get back here!" Diana's voice rings out, and I stiffen, instantly sitting up at the sound. I turn toward the child in fear and anticipation. My heart beats to hear my name.

Diana chases her dog.

Anthony laughs. "That dog has your name." He tussles my hair like I'm a pet. "You're such a good little sister. Who's my good little sister?"

I slap his hand away. "You're an asshole."

Diana named her dog after me? I'm not sure what that means. She doesn't recognize me. I've seen her look in my direction.

"That's fair," Anthony agrees.

"Hey, I have a magical question."

"What's that?" He settles back against the bench and stares at our surroundings. I feel his chest lift with a deep breath as he holds it.

I glance at Paul. "Do magically erased memories ever reverse?"

"Like coming out of amnesia?" Anthony shakes his head. "No. It's easier to subtract than replace.

Once you kill something like that, it's dead. Not even the necromancers can bring it back."

I again turn my head to watch Paul, forgetting to look away. "So Louis will remember nothing?"

"Maybe shades of things, like from a dream. Residual thoughts or feelings. He might walk past a bar we went to and recognize the name but not remember how or if he's ever been there. The real concern is that he might run into people he doesn't remember meeting, but they might remember him. You have to stretch the magic out, spreading over connected people like the silken threads of a spiderweb."

That makes sense. The dog's name is residual magic, like the distant echo of a lost dream.

"So you can't undo it." The statement is unnecessary, but I need my heart to hear it. "That hardly seems fair. People should be able to make their own choices without fear of... never mind."

Anthony sighs. "Since you currently think so highly of me, I guess I should tell you why I'm here."

I frown. "Why are you here?"

"Uncle Mortimer is looking to speak to you." Anthony seems torn over whether to be sympathetic or laugh at me. "He's called a family meeting."

I stiffen. The last time I talked to Uncle Mortimer had been during Anthony and my parents' funerals in the other timeline. He'd wanted to set me up with one of his supernatural friends. No, that's sugarcoating it. He wanted to marry me off to a supernatural ancient, then perform magic rites to ensure I became impregnated by said supernatural so that our Devine magical bloodline could carry on.

I'm so happy that didn't happen.

"He gave me a funeral plot for my birthday and is waiting for me to pick it out," I grumble. "I've been avoiding his calls."

What is it he'd said to me when he gave me the gift? *"Since at twenty-eight and mortal, you don't have much time left, Tamara."*

Jerk face.

"He's a class act, that one." Anthony stands and reaches his hand toward me. "I'll say it again, I promised you when we were little I'd never let you die. I intend to keep that promise."

"If you turn me into a zombie, I'm going to be pissed," I tell him as I let him pull me to my feet and guide me away from the bench.

The easiest—*and I use that word with massive air quotes*—path to immortality comes with curses. Vampires and werewolves come to mind.

"Are you sure? I hear necromancers can be real party animals." He holds my hand against his arm, patting my fingers.

"I hear their parties are dead," I quip.

I glance back for one last look at Paul. He's looking in our direction.

"You have good taste. I'll give you that much," Anthony says. "Almost perfect, except for the dad thing. Could you imagine having a kid?"

Yes.

I force a laugh and shake my head. "Never."

Some things are not meant to be.

He walks a little faster, pulling me with him. "Can I help you pick out a mausoleum? We could make it into a clubhouse."

"Are we twelve?"

"The real parties are six feet under the mausoleums," he says. "We can dig a tunnel and tap into the supernatural city underground. A quick drop down a hole and we're clubbing with hot warlocks."

I have no clue what he's talking about. Before I can ask about his joke, he picks up his pace.

"I have a great idea. You distract the parents and make your funeral arrangements to keep Uncle Mortimer happy and distracted. I'll sneak into our father's office to check the company manifests, and then we'll hitch a ride with a shipment to Africa. We'll leave tonight. Let's see how far we can get before they send someone to collect us."

"Africa?" We near the street, and I see a town car slowing as if on cue to give us a ride.

"Sure. I always wanted to check a grootslang off my list."

"List? What list?"

"I have a contest going with some guys from school to see who can encounter the most supernatural creatures. Goblins, trolls, etcetera, are all give-mes, so meeting one of those is worth one point. But a grootslang or ninki nanka? No one has those."

"And this is a game you play?"

"Sure. Hand me your phone." Anthony pulls open the car door.

I hesitate, so he takes my phone from my back pocket and then waits as I slide into the seat.

A car honks behind us as Anthony stands in the doorway, not getting in. I watch my brother look up from my phone to give the upset driver a cocky wave before sliding into the back seat next to me. He slams the door shut. The privacy window separates us from the driver, and Anthony knocks on it to tell the driver to go.

I feel the car move as I watch Anthony play with my phone. He waves his hand over the screen and a blue glow comes from the device.

"Give me your hand," he instructs.

I obey the request.

Anthony presses my palm down on the screen. I feel a sharp jab at the base of my thumb and jerk my hand back. A dot of blood mars my skin, matching a spot on my phone. The blood soaks into the device, and a series of three long beeps sound.

"All set," Anthony says.

He doesn't give me my phone back as he scrolls.

"What's set?" I stare at the bead of blood on my hand.

"Your entry into the game. A simple blood spell is finding everything you've encountered." He reads the phone as he scrolls. "You got all the basics—troll, goblin, vampire, wood sprite, werewolf, succubus, fairy, reptilian, necromancer…" He stops scrolling and frowns. "When did you come across a vengeful spirit? Whose?"

I can't meet his gaze and refuse to answer.

I shrug and turn my attention out the window. Paul and Diana are out of sight, but the ache and loneliness remain.

I just want a normal life.

It's torture. I have to quit seeking them out. I have to let them go.

I have to let myself go.

Normal is not in my deck of cards.

"Seriously, vengeful spirit sightings are rare," Anthony says, completely unaware of how much I hate everything supernatural in this moment. "I don't even have that one."

TWO

Devine Country Estate, Twenty-Two Years Ago...

"But why?" I insist as I lift my hand like I've seen Anthony do a hundred times. I nearly throw my arm off, trying to make the same gestures, but nothing happens.

"I don't know. Maybe you're broken?" Anthony suggests, bouncing a fireball in his hand.

Streaks of light pass over the moonlit field as my brother's friends play fireball tag. I hear them laughing. They normally don't let me play with them because I don't have magic.

But maybe if I try really hard...

Anthony sees one of his friends dart past, and he launches his fireball at the kid's back, barely missing him. Peter leaps into the air and shifts into his wolf form as he disappears into the shadows.

Anthony crouches close to the ground and motions me to do the same.

"Did you have magic when you were my age?" I whisper so as not to reveal our hiding place.

"I've always had it," he says. "The nanny said, as a baby, I used to levitate and float around the room when I slept. They had to lock the windows, so I didn't fly away."

Anthony is seven and has always been wise beyond his years.

My eyes round in wonder at the thought. "Do you think I float when I sleep?"

"I don't know." He gives a shrug. I don't know why he's annoyed with me. I just want to play with them. "I think you have to wake up really fast and see if you're in the air."

I nod. That's good advice. I'll try that tonight.

Peter the werewolf comes running back by, fully shifted and howling.

"Did I tell you I'm getting a puppy for my birthday? And a cake as tall as I am with fairies?"

Anthony grimaces. "Gross. You want to eat fairies?"

"No!" I protest.

"Dammit," Anthony says. "Shh!"

The howling becomes louder, and Peter reappears, charging toward us. My brother becomes serious as he stands from behind our log. He launches fireballs at his friend. I stand next to him and swing my arm with all my might, willing fire to come from my hand. It doesn't.

Anthony misses several times before finally smacking the wolf on the side. Peter yelps. I see trails of smoke coming from his fur.

Anthony laughs and pulls my arm. "Come on, we need to get to a new position."

I don't know what he's talking about, but I'm happy he's letting me come. He leads me through the woods, and I struggle to keep up with him in the dark. Streaks of light show on the tree bark as the others battle it out. He comes to a bush near the field and ducks down.

"Maybe I'll get magic for my birthday. I'll be six," I say. "And then I can be immortal like you, and I can go to school with you."

He scrunches up his nose. "Stay quiet, Tam-tam."

I mimic his movements, crouching and cupping my empty hand at the ready.

He sees me and gives a soft laugh. "Do you want to try?"

I nod, eager.

He looks around at the field before manifesting a fireball. "Okay, hold out your hand. I'm going to give you the magic and you throw it as hard as you can when you see Peter dart past. He's the target tonight.

Try not to let him see where the fireball came from, or he'll get us, and we'll lose."

Excitement makes me jittery, and my legs jerk as I bounce in anticipation.

"Ready?" Anthony holds the fireball.

I nod and whisper, "Yeah."

He places a hand under mine and holds me steady as he brings the fireball close. He drops it down onto my fingers.

Fire bursts over my fingers, and I scream at the terrible pain. I shake my hand, but it only makes it worse. I start to run.

"Tamara!" Anthony shouts after me.

I keep screaming.

Suddenly, a dark shadow sweeps in from above, and I'm wrapped in cold arms. The fire goes out against the creature's chest. I feel my body moving as my feet are lifted from the ground.

"Tamara!" Anthony calls out. "Tamara, where did you go?"

I'm crying and can't stop.

We land on the ground on a forest path. When I look up, I see my grandfather's vampire friend. "Easy, child, what's happened?"

His voice is calm, almost soothing. I know to be careful. Vampires can take over your brain and make you do things. Anthony told me.

"What did you do?" he asks.

"I tried to... cast... off... magic... my hand... but..." I sob as I try to explain.

He takes my hand in his as he studies it before pressing his fist against my palm. The cold feels good against the burn and lessens the sting.

"Ar-are you going to eat me, Constantine?" I ask him, sniffling through tears. "I don't want to be a snack."

He gives me a strange look. I see the moonlight hitting his fangs and cry harder.

"Tamara!" Anthony screams in panic.

"Anthony," I yell back. "Help! The vampire is going to eat me!"

"Hey, stop that," the vampire orders, with an awkward pat on my shoulder. "I'm not going to eat you. You're going to be all right. Your grandfather can fix your hand good as new."

I wish he could fix the missing magic in my hand.

"But why aren't you going to eat me? Is it because I'm broken and taste bad?" I sniffle.

The vampire is scary. Mainly, I think it's his fangs. And because Anthony told me that vampires liked to drink people, and I need to stay away from them because I'm people. He also said that I would be a tiny snack to a vampire because I'm so small. Like an appetizer.

But Constantine's eyes don't look mean. They're not kind or anything like that, but they're not all angry red, as I've seen in some of the comic books that my brother showed me.

"Do you want me to eat you, little castoff?" he asks with a small smile. I don't know that I've ever seen him smile.

I violently shake my head no.

"Good, because I do not eat my friends," he answers.

"Are we friends, Constantine?" I ask in surprise. I didn't know I had a vampire friend.

"Sure. And you should call me Costin. That's what my friends call me." He stands, keeping his icy hand in mind.

"Tamara!" Anthony is closer now.

"Young Anthony," Costin says to get his attention. "I'm taking your sister back to the house to have her hand looked at."

"Tamara, are you all right?" Anthony asks, hurrying to me.

"Costin put me out," I say, using my vampire friend's name.

"I'll take her to the house. We don't need you," Anthony tells the vampire as he lifts me into his arms and starts jogging through the trees toward the estate.

"Be more careful," Costin orders behind me.

Anthony ignores him. I cling to my brother, holding tight. I hear him whisper, "I'm sorry Tam-tam. I'm sorry. We're going to be in so much trouble."

My hand hurts, but I don't want to get my brother in trouble. He slows as we come to the estate. The great windows are all lit as if to cast light on the yard outside. I see figures moving around.

"I'm okay," I lie. "We don't have to tell them."

"Let me see." He holds my hand to the light and tries touching the burn.

I flinch and struggle to keep back the tears.

"No, you're hurt. We have to tell them. Don't worry. I'll take all the blame," he says. "I should have never let you hold the magic. It could have killed you."

I cry harder. "I don't want to be killed."

"Hey, look at me." He takes my face in his hands. "I don't know why you can't do magic, but I swear to you, here and now. I'm going to find a way to make you immortal like me. You're not going to die. Okay?"

I nod, believing him. My brother would never lie to me.

He begins walking me inside to face the elders.

"I promise, you're going to live forever with me,"

he swears. "Besides, you're all right for a little sister. We Devines got to stick together."

Anthony is so smart. I nod my head and swipe at my nose. "Yeah, we got to stick together."

CHAPTER

THREE

The last thing I want is to have a conversation with Uncle Mortimer about my future accommodations. I don't know what is supposed to happen when we die, but I hope it is nothingness. I don't want to be an angry ghost haunting people like Conrad. Spending an eternity watching what I can't have sounds like the thirteenth level of Hell.

Actually, it sounds like my current life.

Not that I know the actual levels of Hell, but I'm pretty sure Dante's Divine Comedy got them wrong. If I remember the literature correctly, to paraphrase, he thought disloyalty to your appointed master was the worst sin, more so than violence.

I think of all the violence and death I've witnessed. I think of Paul's eyes draining of life as he stopped breathing in my arms.

Yeah. Dante got that wrong.

My mind is eager to continue the philosophical debate over what constitutes the worst kind of living hell. I could rant for a century about the idea that it's worse to disobey your appointed master than being the one who's subjugated. Ask any abused wife or victim of assault in a power dynamic which sin is worse.

If I'm thinking about this, I'm not thinking of other things.

I stare at my reflection in the library mirror, the dark room wrapping me like a shroud. The tinted glass of the floor-to-ceiling penthouse windows mutes the glow of city lights, and forms one wall. I like being fifty stories high in a city full of people. The streets are so crowded that it feels like up is the only way to escape. Sometimes, I imagine the lights from other buildings are stars, and I'm drifting through the universe untouchable.

I close my eyes and think of Paul's face, the gentle warmth of his smile, the way he made me feel safe. That feeling is beginning to fade, and I do everything I can to hold on to it. Unfortunately, it's being replaced by the sharp dread of imminent danger. Conrad's hauntings are taking a toll.

I have come to this room to hide from my family. It's tucked into a quiet corner. Something about the dark wood paneling on the walls and rows of old leather-bound books on the custom-built book-shelves sets it apart. Some shelves are so high a ladder is needed to reach them. Brass sconces would give ambient light if I bothered to turn them on. A dormant fireplace anchors the wood with ornate marble.

It's a room of reflection and intellect. So many secrets fill the volumes, ones I can't read because I don't speak the ancient languages. No one thought it necessary to teach me.

I hate to admit it, but the room reminds me of Conrad—the Conrad I thought I knew before he betrayed me and tried to kill everyone I care about. He might be bad, but that doesn't mean I don't miss the brother I thought I knew. Even now, I can hear the distant echo of his voice telling me about a spell he'd read about. I imagine I'll see him if I turn around, limbs draped over the arms of a tufted leather chair with an old tome braced on his stomach. Conrad had taught himself how to read the books. I should have insisted he teach me as well.

I wonder why I never tried. I wasn't lazy or stupid. I think maybe I was scared—of failure, of my limitations, of proving everyone right. My whole life, I've been told I'm delicate like a butterfly and monsters trample butterflies. I hid in that cocoon my family gave me, believing it to be safe. If I didn't think about it, if I went along with their plans, everything would be all right.

Then I met Paul and Diana.

I don't move, not even blinking as I meet my eyes reflected back at me. My vision wavers and blurs, distorting me like I'm staring into a funhouse mirror. I want it to pull me into the reversed world where I can be with Paul.

But Paul can't save me from Conrad or the supernatural. It's not fair to wish that he could. He's human, and I know better than anyone what being mortal means. Even the fantasies of shared normality are filling me with guilt. I need to forget him and move on. This isn't a romance novel. It's reality.

The fact that my features are shadowed feels like a blessing. I don't want to see how tired I look. Even the slinky red dress I found laid out on my bed when I got home, and a layer of makeup can't hide my exhaustion.

Lady Astrid picking out my clothes is nothing new, but the dress indicates that more than Uncle Mortimer might be coming over. The scarlet V-neck chiffon clings to my hips before flaring at the skirt. The spaghetti straps leave my arms exposed, and I feel a chill from the air conditioning. I lift the toe of my shoe and twist the high heel into the rug. They pinch my feet, but I'll trip on the floor-length skirt if I take them off.

This outfit is not what I would've picked out for myself. It reminds me of my childhood. I'm Astrid's living doll, and to her, appearances are everything.

Suddenly, my senses prickle with intense awareness, and I stiffen.

"In all my centuries, I have never seen a beautiful woman so angry with her reflection," a man whispers. The softness of his voice doesn't hide the danger in it.

I inhale sharply. The surprised sound is more audible than I would like. I didn't hear anyone join me in the library. I'm not even sure how he got in here. Still, I don't make sudden movements.

"Hello, castoff."

I let go of my breath, recognizing that mocking, bored tone. The vampire scares me, but I don't think he'd attack while I'm in my parents' home. Closing my eyes, I acknowledge, "Hello, Costin."

The vampire gets off on calling me a little castoff. There is no world in which that's a compliment.

My disposition continues to sour. What is the bloodsucker doing here? I'm not in the mood to deal with him.

Lord Constantine, master vampire and pretentious asshole. I'm unsure how he'd feel about my title for him, but it's true. He's been lurking around my family's shadows since before I was born. I remember seeing him at my parents' parties, hoping he wouldn't notice me peeking out from my hiding place. His eyes always seemed to find me, though.

I should be nicer to him, but there is just something about his predatory nature that puts me on edge. He was never inappropriate with me when I was a child, and he's never threatened me directly, at least not in any way that would hold up in front of a supernatural tribunal. But he looks at me strangely, like the only thing keeping him from devouring me is my family name. Even now, there is an intensity in him. I used to think he didn't like me, maybe even hated me. But then I realized he didn't think I was important enough to hate.

I'm human. Food.

The fact I'm untouchable is the only thing that would make me interesting to an elitist creature like him. He can't kill me, but he can be annoyed by my existence.

Then why has he been invading my thoughts recently? He keeps appearing at the edge of my nightmares, watching me. I can hardly blame him for my brain's fucked up dreams.

When he doesn't move, I can't stop myself from glancing in his direction. There is something about him that makes me both uncomfortable and inexplicably drawn to him. I assume that's his vampiric nature. Everything about him is made to lure humans into his death trap of an embrace.

He is the Venus flytrap, and I'm the fly.

My gaze goes to his parted lips, to where I'll find sharp fangs. They're hard to see in the shadows, but my mind can easily fill in the darkness. I use it as a reminder of his threatening nature. Feigning bravery, I turn my attention back to the mirror.

I don't see my reflection. Instead, flashes from my erased timeline fill my memories. Costin had died in my birthday fire. I had tried to save his life and put him out, but he'd turned to ash beneath me. The tactile sensation of his death fills my hands, a pressure triggered by memory. Later, his sister Elizabeth had led a brood of vampires to attack me. If not for my amulet, they would have killed me. The memory locks my legs into place and makes it hard to breathe. I remember the feeling of them surrounding me behind a dark gas station in the middle of nowhere.

I reach for my neck, but the amulet's protection is no longer there.

Vampires. There is a reason they hold a high throne in the horror echelon.

I drag in a breath, forcing myself not to panic. That moment no longer exists.

Of course, Costin won't remember any of that. Why would he? No one else does.

He's not speaking. Or moving.

It's creepy.

I turn toward him, not making direct eye contact. Vampires can mesmerize, and it's one of those fears I've carried since childhood. I don't want my will to be taken away from me. Most kids worry about an invisible boogeyman under their bed. I met the boogeyman and all his supernatural friends. My parents invited them over.

I ignore every instinct inside of me to scream and run.

I stare at Costin's chest. Power radiates from him. Not some visual aura, but a magnetic energy I can feel. It hangs thick in the air, demanding attention. It's not magic, not like the members of my family wield. It's more primal and primitive. I imagine it to be death trying to suck the life from everything around him like a black hole making its own gravity. At his core, Costin is a predator. He needs to drink blood to live. This isn't a monster I want to be alone with.

I need to remember that. He's not my friend.

My gaze follows his long black hair upward before darting back to his chest. His face is cast in shadows, but the windows outline his body to reveal his shape. He looks exactly the same as when I was five—a monstrous sculpture built of nightmares and bloodlust. It's unnerving, but I'm used to it. My parents don't look like they age either. It's strange to think that in twenty years, I'll look older than they do.

The difference between when I was a kid and now is that now I appreciate Costin's handsomeness. I would *never* admit it out loud. Most women I know like to fantasize about bad boys, and vampires tick those tough, naughty boxes. However, admitting someone was attractive in the abstract is one thing. Pursuing a vampire, in reality, is quite another.

I mean, he's hundreds of years old, eats people, and is a supernatural chauvinist. I can't get past any of that.

He is the exact opposite of the safety and mortality that Paul represents.

He tilts his head. The subtle movement breaks my thoughts, and I realize I've been staring at the elaborate stitching on his waistcoat.

Did I mention he often dresses like he's about to strut an 1800s catwalk?

I watch his chest lift as he takes in a deep breath.

What is he doing here?

"Did you come here to stare at me, or did you need something?" The rude words come out before I think to stop them.

I'm grouchy and on edge. Maybe I shouldn't have skipped dinner.

"You're bleeding," he says in a way that makes me think he's looking for a snack. "It's distracting."

I frown and look at my palm to where the dot of blood has dried. I instantly ball my hand into a fist to hide it behind my back.

He steps closer and smirks. A chill runs down my spine. The scent of him—dark and earthy—tickles my nose. He looks clean, but I can imagine him sleeping inside a coffin deep within the earth. His eyes, sharp and unreadable, bore into me, as if daring me to move, to flinch, but I hold my ground. A soft glow enters his gaze. I watch from my peripheral as he gives a meaningful glance downward.

"Oh." I gasp with surprise as I realize his meaning before instantly grimacing. "Ew. I'm not discussing my period with you."

He arches a brow. This conversation is clearly more uncomfortable for me than it is for him.

Before I realize he's even moving, he's suddenly closer, invading my personal space with ease. I glance up. It's a mistake. I find his eyes peering deeply into mine. The way the inner light swims in his gaze mesmerizes me.

Fuck.

I can't look away. He's pulling me in.

"You're tense," he says like he's telling a secret. "I wonder why that is."

"Maybe because you're standing too close," I

answer defensively. It takes everything in me to resist his pull.

"Maybe." Cold fingers wrap around my wrist and lift my limp arm. I feel him rub his fist against my palm in a strange caress. The action feels vaguely familiar, but I can't place it. His fingers slide against me as if he's going to lead me in a waltz.

I want to pull away but can't.

He draws my arm to the side before gliding it between us. He holds it up and turns me so the dim light reveals a cut on my forearm. A small trail of blood mars my skin as if the drop had already dried. I realize that is the blood he was referring to.

I don't remember cutting myself. I never even felt it.

His eyes move from mine, and I feel a rush of air enter my lungs as if he's released a hold over my chest. It pants out of me, loud in the library's stillness.

My heart hammers in fear. Danger radiates from him. This moment feels intimate. I want to be repulsed, but I'm not.

Cool lips brush the wound. A gentle kiss before the hard bite? It feels like a warning, and I'm helpless to stop what's coming. I shiver at the touch, and the sensation floods my entire body with awareness.

I feel myself drawn to the death in him. He could

take the decision out of my hands. I can let go... just... let go.

I think of Conrad's fate.

I think of Paul and Diana.

My pain doesn't matter.

"Stop," I whisper.

To my surprise, he releases me. I rub the spot he licked against my waist, trying to erase the feel of his mouth. The soft brush of the dress material does the exact opposite. It makes the sensation worse.

His expression is unreadable, and he gives nothing away. I hate that about him.

This is me brewing for an argument. I'm in a rotten mood, so maybe that's why I can't shut up, even though it would be prudent.

"This is a bad habit of yours. That's the last time, Costin. I'm not on a tasting menu."

He has the audacity to chuckle at the statement like I'm some cute little kid throwing a tantrum. "Are you sure? You always seem to bleed around me. It feels like an invitation. I think there is a part of you that enjoys feeding me."

Is he serious?

Is he... flirting?

"Not on purpose." I grind my heel into the carpet. I wonder if my shoe could double as a stake. Maybe then he'd respect me.

He places his hand over his heart like he can read my mind.

"When I was a kid injured on the driveway? You think that was an invitation?" I demand.

"You were such a sweet, giving child." His look seems to add, *what happened?*

"Right. Giving," I drawl sarcastically. "As a twelve-year-old, I thought, 'Hey, I wonder if my parent's guests are hungry,' and so I jumped off a balcony and broke my arm hoping you'd like your snack. I guess you did because you were ready to eat me until my grandfather stopped you."

I want to turn from him, but I'm too wary to let him out of my eyeline, so I focus on his chin. It's not just his looks—that perfect face or the way his presence commands the night around him. He makes me feel on edge. My pulse quickens for reasons I don't want to admit to myself. There is a pull between us, something dangerous and irresistible, and I hate that I want to explore it.

His mouth twitches up at the corner. It's a brief gesture, but I see it. I amuse him. "There was no jumping. You yelled something about being a bird, and then Conrad pushed you off the balcony. If you need to feel anger about that night, I am not your target."

Glancing around the room, I wonder where my brother's ghost is hiding. I don't feel Conrad with us, but that means nothing. I don't want to stir his spirit by talking shit on him.

Costin keeps his attention steady. I wish he'd turn his intensity away. "I know human brains are limited, but do you not remember?"

Limited?

Asshole.

Did he come here just to insult me?

"I remember everything. I remember your blood-stained fingers in the moonlight as I lay helpless on cobblestones." I put my hands on my hips. "I remember the look on your face."

"Waste not, want not."

"So gentlemanly of you to help a kid out." Sarcasm drips from my tone. My hands clench into tight fists. "Licking me while I'm dying on the ground."

"Hardly dying. It was only a broken bone." He counters. "You humans are always so dramatic."

I've irritated him. Good.

"Humans are dramatic?" I can't help the unamused laugh that escapes me. "Seriously? Supernaturals are the biggest drama queens in the—"

"I came to your aid. George sent me away before I could do more. And I did not *lick* you. I do not lick children. You were dazed, and I tasted your blood for poisons. When I came to the hospital, George said it was handled."

Was he at the hospital after I broke my arm? I try to remember.

"What more would you have me do?" he asks. "Throw young Conrad off the balcony to avenge your fall? Though I wouldn't have minded, seeing as your brother was—"

"Okay, okay." I hold up my hands to stop him. I don't need Conrad pissed off—any more than he already is. "Just go away. My parents are in the formal living room. I'm sure they're expecting you."

He doesn't leave.

I dare a glance at his face and ask in exasperation, "What do you want? Seriously, Costin, I'm kind of dealing with a lot at the moment and I don't need whatever this interaction is. Can you just go away and leave me alone? Please."

He doesn't go. Instead, he scolds, "You think you're the only one struggling with what you've lost. But we all have ghosts, Tamara."

Ghosts? Does he know about Conrad?

I look around the room for my brother, not seeing him. But the threat of him lingers around me. It takes me a moment to realize the vampire speaks metaphorically and not of my dead brother.

My heart is racing from the rawness in his tone. It's not exactly what he said, but it's how he said it— like someone who understands loss all too well. His expression shifts before I can press him further about it, and he becomes distant again. I wonder if he regrets revealing as much as he has. It's the tiniest of cracks in his otherwise powerful demeanor, but he's shown it to me, and he can't take that back.

The knowledge that he is more than just a monster, something that I technically already know, makes me more vulnerable to him. I don't want to sympathize with the vampire. And yet here I am.

"You're..." He tilts his head. "You're scared of me."

"No," I deny. It's not convincing.

I don't think it's possible, but I feel like he leans closer. "You don't trust me."

I cross my arms over my chest in a protective gesture, if only to keep him from closing the distance completely. "Should I?"

He smirks. "Probably not. But you're not backing away."

I try to deflect the challenge in his gaze by saying, "Maybe I enjoy playing with fire."

What the fuck? Did I just flirt with the vampire?

"Careful," his voice drops in warning. "I'm not the kind of fire you can control."

The words send a shiver through me, and I refuse to back away. I don't want him to know the effect that he has on me. I remind myself that control is an illusion, and I'm not sure how much longer I can hold on to mine.

"This forcefulness in you is new. You're irritated with me," he reasons. "I spoke ill of your brother, and his death is recent. I am sure he had... qualities."

It's not exactly an apology.

I want him to leave. "My parents—"

"I didn't come for your parents."

"Then... Anthony?" I gesture toward the library door. "He's probably with my parents."

Or in my father's office, looking for shipping schedules to get us out of the country. Initially, I thought the idea was crazy, but the more I think about it, the more onboard I am with the plan. Leaving holds great appeal.

"I came here for you." His hand lifts toward me.

I jerk back, taking a step to avoid making contact. "Uh, why?"

"I gave you time to grieve, but it's time."

"Time for what?"

"The prophecy."

Is this some kind of strange vampire come on line? Why is he looking at me like I know what that means?

"George's prophecy," he insists.

A memory tickles the back of my mind of Costin and my grandfather, but the complete form of it eludes me.

The paranormals are always going on about spells and prophecies and magical duty. None of it has anything to do with me. I'm in their world, but I don't matter to it.

"I'm not interested." I want less supernatural in my life.

I want to be normal.

I want Paul.

I don't want a sexy blood-driven vampire.

What's that stupid quote? Methinks the lady doth protest too much?

"You mean now is not a good time?"

"No. I'm not interested. Ever."

He visibly stiffens. "It does not matter if you are interested. That is not how destiny works."

I think of all the things the supernatural world has taken from me. I wish I never knew it existed. I wish I were never born a Devine. "I'm mortal. I'm not special. But that does not make me an idiot. I'm not part of some grand prophecy. I don't know what game you're playing, but I grew up around this bullshit, and I'm clean out of shovels. Go away, Costin. I'm tired."

"George didn't tell you?" He crosses his arms and lowers his chin toward his chest to give me what I assume is supposed to be an imposing look. "This isn't a game. Far from it. You're needed."

I automatically reach to touch the amulet around my neck, but it's never there. I remember its broken pieces in the pouch now tucked away in my room.

There are many things my grandfather didn't tell me before his death. The last secret I tried to uncover led me to my birth mother, who I lost alongside Paul and Diana. Now Conrad is haunting me, and it's all I can do to keep it together.

I'm not going on another magical adventure.

I wish everyone would just leave me alone.

The need to scream fills my chest and burns my throat. I suppress it.

He reaches inside his jacket and pulls out a small leather-bound book from his inner pocket. He tries to hand it to me.

I shake my head and take another step toward the door. If he's not going to leave, I will. "I don't want it. I'm not pulling a sword out of some stone to become king or stopping the world from ending or giving birth to the destroyer of the universe or whatever scheme has been cooked up by bored elders at a dinner party. At best, this is a prank. At worst, the prank kills someone I care about. So, thank you for the offer to be the butt of your joke, but I'm going to have to decline."

I turn to make my hasty exit and instantly crash into Costin's chest. He passed by me without me seeing him move. Before I can stumble away, he has me gripped by the arms. His fingers dig into my flesh. He lifts me off the floor like I'm no heavier than a throw pillow and lets my feet dangle. Leaning close, his swirling eyes demand attention. I want to kick him to free myself, but I can't force my legs to move.

"Do you think this is what I want to be doing? Do you think I want to be here?" There is a gravelly darkness to his voice that I haven't heard before. It strikes fear into me, and all I can do is shake my head in denial. "You don't like me. Fine. I'm not a fan of partnering with humans. A promise is a promise. Prophecy is destiny. I owe a debt, and I will repay it, and you will do your part."

I hang, helpless.

"Do you understand?" he enunciates.

I nod.

"Good. We'll continue this later."

He lowers me to the ground. The chill of his hands remains on my arms when he lets go. My heart pounds. I wonder if he can hear it. Every piece of me focuses on him. I open my mouth to speak, but he stops me.

"Mortimer," Costin states.

I frown. Not following his meaning.

Costin steps aside and reveals my uncle approaching behind him.

"Constantine." Uncle Mortimer's voice sounds jovial, but I recognize the forced tone he puts on for guests. His skin has a sickly pallor, and there are darkened half-circles under his eyes. Still, he is immaculately dressed in an Italian suit. The cut is a little more modern than I'm used to seeing him in. "I didn't know you were expected."

"I'm not. I came to speak with Tamara." Costin stands beside me. His arm brushes mine.

Mortimer looks surprised, but it's nothing compared to what I feel when Costin takes my hand in his. His cool fingers wrap around mine and hold tight. What's more surprising is that it sends a shiver up my arm and is not entirely unpleasant. I try to jerk away, not wanting to feel the sensation. The only explanation for it is that Costin is planting subconscious thoughts that are not my own.

Fucking vampires.

Devine Country Estate, Sixteen Years Ago...

Pain makes it difficult to breathe, but that doesn't stop me from trying to grunt for help. After twelve years on this Earth, I know what monsters are capable of, and I do not want to be caught helpless and broken in the middle of the night, lying in the driveway like a rag doll.

And yet, here I am.

I hear the stomp of demonic horses as the animals pull against their tethers. They smell my blood, and it stirs them. I imagine it reminds them of home, of the tortures of the netherworld.

Music comes from inside my family's country house, muffled by stone and glass. It's the sound-track of my life—music from a party I'm not invited to attend. I see flashes of magical light, like warning shots from another universe.

I never asked for this life or to be born mortal and weak. I can't fight monsters. I'm just a girl.

I don't want to die.

The smell of my blood will awaken the worst in my parents' friends. There is one rule I must always follow—don't leave the protected wing of the house when the supernaturals are visiting. This driveway is not protected.

I look up the side of the estate to the upper balcony from where I fell. One of Anthony's friends sold Conrad flying dust, but it didn't work. I dropped like a stone.

Conrad was supposed to jump with me, but he's gone. He's left me alone to fend for myself.

I draw a ragged breath, trying to control the fear.

Who will find me first?

"Hello there, little castoff." A shadow falls over me as the vampire Constantine leans to block the view of the empty balcony. He told me he likes to be called Costin.

Why do women think these pasty monsters are beautiful? I see it all the time in books and movies and on the internet. They're drawn to the idea of darkness and power, of immortality, but I don't think the reality would live up to the fantasies.

Vampires are manipulative, savage killers. There is nothing beautiful about that.

Costin's long black hair is caught up by a breeze, the color a stark contrast to his pale skin. He towers over me, looking down like I'm roadkill littering the lawn. I'm not naïve. I know his eyes swirl with bloodlust. My bleeding has drawn him out for a snack. Dim light catches his fangs, and I can't look away from them.

I try to draw a deep breath. It hurts. I can't move. I don't stand a chance against him and the hell his mouth offers.

Costin's movements are a blur as he comes to kneel beside me. The chill of his fingers moves along the nape of my neck, scraping me with his fingernails. I wait for him to cut me. He doesn't.

The vampire pulls his hand away, and I see my blood staining his fingers. His gaze shifts to his hand, and his eyes continue to swirl. He pulls the fingers into his mouth and makes a strange noise. His eyes close.

"So fresh and innocent," he whispers.

I can't stop shaking as tears stream down my temples. Everything hurts. I can't move, can't fight. He's going to kill me. I just know it. Any second now.

Fear rushes through my veins, petrifying me. I start to shake. I manage to mouth a plea. "Please."

I don't expect anything I say will stop him.

"Constantine," my grandfather George's stern voice warns. Relief floods me as he comes to my rescue.

The vampire tenses at the command. His eyes continue to swirl with bloodlust. I'm not sure what he'll do.

"Step away from her," George insists. I strain my neck to look at him. He's wearing one of his vintage suits. The man radiates a debonair calm, and his familiar presence is comforting. He's one of the most powerful magics I know. And he loves me unconditionally. He might be the only one in my life who does. "She's protected."

Costin hisses and swipes his arms forward before his body becomes a blur. He disappears from the drive, leaving us alone.

My grandfather is instantly beside me as he checks my legs for injury. "What hurts?"

I moan as I cradle my arm.

"Your arm looks broken." He feels along my neck before touching my scalp. "Your head is bleeding. How did this happen?"

I don't want to tell on my brother, but I can't help glancing up at the balcony. Conrad hasn't returned.

He frowns and follows my gaze upward. "Why, little dove?"

I don't want to tell, but there is something in the

caring sound of his voice that forces me to answer. I try to hold back my sob. "They said we could fly."

The demonic horse dances in agitation to the sound of my pain.

"Who?" George asks.

I shake my head and decline to answer. I press my lips together as if that might keep the words inside. There is no way I'm willingly ratting out Anthony or his supernatural friends.

My grandfather makes a slight noise as if coming to a decision. He lifts his hand and faces his palm toward me. "We need to get you to the hospital. I'm going to petrify you so you can't feel it."

I want to make him stop. The idea of being magically petrified into darkness terrifies me. But before I can utter a word, I feel the sting of his powers washing over me. Darkness closes in.

"It's fine. The others think I'm feeding. What is so important you needed to see me tonight?"

Costin's voice cuts through the dark fog in my brain, almost like a dream.

"You tasted my granddaughter," Grandfather George says.

"You called me away for this? I would not hurt her. You know better. I respect our friendship too much, George. Other than food, I have little use for humans, let alone a child."

I try to open my eyes, but my lids refuse to move.

"Then it is unfortunate for you that your fate is now bound to hers."

Muffled sounds block the conversation, and I start to drift back into the haze.

"...will protect her," my grandfather is saying.

"All right, let's get this cast on, Miss, uh..." A woman's voice trails off, and I feel someone tapping my cheek. "Miss Devine?"

"She was restless." My grandfather sounds closer like he's standing next to me. "They gave her a sedative. You may put on the cast."

I'm too weak to follow what's happening.

"Don't wake up," my grandfather whispers, his breath tickling my ear. The dream slips away.

FIVE

"Another time, Tamara." Costin gives a polite bow of his head. My name sounds strange when he says it. Normally, he's mocking me as a castoff. "We will talk again soon."

He releases my hand and is gone from my side by the time I turn to look at him, disappearing into the library's shadows as easily as he arrived. I let go of the breath I didn't realize I was holding. My heart is still beating erratically from his nearness. I hate that he's got to me like this, hate even more than I want him to come back.

"That can't happen," Mortimer states with a dismissive wave of his hand toward where Costin had been standing. My uncle's commanding tone brings me back to the present.

"That's *not* happening," I mumble, utterly confused.

"Though I'm glad to see you are open to a supernatural relationship again," my uncle continues, as if he didn't hear me. "It will make this conversation easier."

I'd rather jump into a pool of hot lava than have a relationship with a vampire. Both would kill me, but at least the lava would have a temperature above freezing. And it wouldn't mock me.

I process Mortimer's comment. "What conversation? I thought you were here to talk about my funeral arrangements."

Crappiest birthday present ever.

"Come, your parents are waiting," he orders.

I don't want to go with him, but I know better than to refuse. Mortimer can make me follow him. I've accepted that I have little control over my life.

I think of Paul's warm hands on my body and begin rubbing off the remaining chill of Costin's touch. I'm not attracted to the vampire. I want Paul.

Why can't I have a normal life?

I leave the library, letting Mortimer set the pace as we cross over the marble floor. The click of my heels sounds abnormally loud in our silence. I watch my uncle's legs move, but his steps are quiet.

Ten thousand square feet of prime real estate, and I don't think the penthouse's décor has changed one bit since my childhood. I remember the statues standing guard over the wide corridors with their judging expressions and the paintings of my parents from bygone eras.

The common areas have an open floor plan. During the day, it's bathed in natural light, but now shadows crawl like they're hiding dirty secrets. The antique furniture is more elegant than comfortable. Nothing here is about comfort. It's about image. It's everything old money is made of—elitist traditions, a fear of change, and a sense of superiority.

There is that saying, *if these walls could talk*. If a spell ever made that true, these walls would scream. I see darkness against the glass doors leading to the wrap-around terrace. Being roughly five hundred feet above the streets, with the fall weather, the outside air tends to be crisp. Still, I'd rather be out there in this slinky dress than heading toward whatever family meeting this has turned out to be.

To the outside eye, this luxury high-rise has everything one could want. Sure, I can soak in a tub with skyline views and walk on heated marble floors, but I would trade it all for a bungalow with Paul. Is it wrong that I envy people who have to think about things like mortgages and utility bills? I feel like they have an innate understanding of life that I never will. I tried living on my own, by my own income. It didn't work out too well.

I hate how my childhood has trained me to live in this world. It gave me all the expectations and manners, but it could not give me the magic. I'm a mimic. A fake. I have all the dangers of being a Devine without the ability to protect myself.

"Constantine is an ambitious choice." Mortimer clearly isn't letting his mind wander. "How far has the courtship progressed?"

Courtship?

Gross.

I often find when people ask me questions in this family, they aren't really expecting me to answer. I'm a placeholder for their own thoughts. So I keep my mouth shut.

"Clearly, you're feeding him. You look pale and tired. More than normal."

Gee. Thanks?

He's one to talk. He looks like he's on death's door. I'd be worried if he weren't immortal.

Come to think of it, maybe I should worry. Immortality is a misnomer. Immortals can die under the right circumstances. My uncle might be an elitist prick, but he's still family. The polite thing would be to ask him about his health.

"We won't tell your mother about the feedings," Mortimer continues. "She wouldn't approve. You're smart to keep the bite marks hidden."

I want to tell him he's stupid and doesn't know

what he is talking about. I don't. That would make me an idiot.

"I wish you would have sought my counsel before taking up with him. I understand you might feel a little rebellious after Conrad's passing. Death has that effect on some. I myself have enjoyed a tryst or two with the darker side. But vampiric alliances are not for the faint of heart. Constantine is powerful, to be sure, and he is an ambitious choice for a mortal, even one with your connections, but there are protocols in place for good reason." Mortimer stops walking, forcing me to do the same. "He's not the forever kind, Tamara. He won't marry you, at least not for any reason you would want."

He turns to me. His brow furrows in thought. After a few seconds, his expression softens as if he's forcing himself to look caring. It's not convincing.

"I understand that, at twenty-eight and mortal, you feel the pressure of time. Your life will be over soon." His hand lifts to my hair, and he awkwardly pats me like some family pet. "The idea of immortality must be a great temptation, but... vampirism?"

"Grandfather liked him." I don't know what makes me defend Costin. It's not like I care. I don't want to be turned into a vampire, and I don't want to be someone's portable feeder blood bag.

"My father had a soft spot for..." Mortimer holds up his hands. I see the faint swirl of blue magic wrapping his pinkie finger before dissipating. "He would not have wanted a vampire to join the family, especially not one as powerful and feared as Constantine. Alliances need to be carefully planned. The joining of the most powerful magical family and a master vampire who rules all of North America will not make the other vampire broods happy. I know it's difficult for you to understand, but there is a delicate balance to the supernatural world that must be maintained. Wars have broken out over less. I have seen great empires fall. This is not just about you. I'm sure you're aware of Constantine's sister. We do not want Elizabeth to take over if the vampires rebel. And we don't want the European vampires thinking we're part of some vampiric uprising."

I should tell him I'm not dating Costin, but his arrogance is irritating, so I decide to let him fret over it.

I meet his gaze. "My relationship with Costin is my business."

It's not a lie. There just isn't much of a relationship.

His eyes narrow, as if answering my silent challenge. All softness leaves his expression. "Everything you do is family business. There is an order to things, whether or not you like it." He taps his finger against his palm to emphasize his meaning. Tiny bursts of magic light up with each contact. "The family must be preserved and protected."

All this talk about my love life and family business is worrisome. There is more to his visit than picking out my burial arrangements. I have a feeling I'm not going to like where this evening is heading.

"Anthony is expected to carry on the bloodline." Mortimer tries to bury his frustration, but I can hear it leaking from his tone. "He's young. He has time to find someone."

Ironically, Anthony is older than me.

And my brother isn't exactly on the procreation track.

"You're innocent. It's not your fault you're mortal. You can't help it," he continues.

I brace myself for the patronizing speech I feel coming.

"You don't understand the real world. You never had to. Your parents babied you because of your mortality. It's time to grow up. Rival factions will try to use you as a pawn, as a way to worm themselves into our family. Mortality makes you vulnerable, and there are those who would take advantage." He awkwardly pats me again. "You must trust your elders. We will guide you. We know what is best for you and for the family."

I want to leave, but there is nowhere to run. I won't make it to the elevator before he stops me. I hate being petrified by magic—not knowing what happens when I'm unaware.

Maybe I can escape with Anthony on a shipping container to Africa? That idea sounds better and better.

"Whatever happened with you and Jasper Blackwood?" Mortimer studies me expectantly.

When have I ever, in the history of my existence, made my uncle think I wanted to discuss my love life with him? Jasper was my last boyfriend, well, not counting alternate-timeline Paul.

"The Blackwoods are a solid family from an old line of magic," Mortimer insists.

"Jasper cheated on me." That fact might embarrass some, but I see it as his weakness, not mine. "He was only with me because he wanted to be close to the family. He kept asking about shipping schedules and wanted to know how much family money I could access. If you're looking for worms circling the family apple, there's one."

My father's fortune is tied to his shipping company. He specializes in moving things that can't travel by other means—enchanted objects, vampire coffins, fairy rings, trolls. Those are the shipping containers I know about. I'm sure there are many things I don't know.

"So, no chance of you two...?" He lets his words dangle like I'm going to suddenly change my mind and want to take Jasper back. "I suppose that makes the choice easier."

"What choice?"

"Your parents are waiting for us." Mortimer resumes walking, forcing me to go after him.

"What choice?" I call after him, hurrying to follow.

"All will be revealed." He moves faster.

First, my brother's ghost tormented me in the park. Then Mr. Vampire tried to sign me up for some prophecy. Now Mortimer is poking his nose into my love life. This day has really taken a turn for the worse.

My parents are waiting for us in the living room. The light is on in the kitchen behind them, but I don't see anyone else here. The room catches my eye for a moment. I was wrong in my musings earlier. The kitchen appliances have changed since my childhood, a requirement of the family chef.

Davis and Astrid Devine have been married for a long time. I see glimpses of affection between them, but they're fleeting moments, almost as if it's an old habit rather than rooted in passion. On the surface, the family shines like a glossy portrait of perfection. I wonder at what point in their long lives Lady Astrid decided her lifestyle was worth more than a faithful husband. I'm living proof of his affair with my birth mother. I wouldn't blame Astrid for leaving him, but then I don't blame him for finding comfort else-where. Astrid will never be accused of being a warm person.

The crystal chandelier above our heads holds my mother's attention. I see Astrid's eyes move as if she's tracing each shard for defects. She is perched on the edge of the couch with a martini glass balanced between her fingers. A speared olive swirls in circles.

My father stares out the window at the terrace. Or maybe it's at his reflection in the glass. I can't be sure. Magic snakes lazily through the curved fingers of one hand like he's playing an air piano. An empty whiskey glass is on the floor by his foot.

Is there a better example of what immortality looks like?

Most people imagine living forever as a great gift of time. I see it as boring decades that drift aimlessly into eternity. Immortals aren't lucky. They're living fossils who lose the ability to be anything but the shell of themselves.

That thought is a little harsh.

Fuck, I'm irritable.

"Ah, Tam-tam," my father says when he sees my reflection. The magic dissipates from his fingers as he turns to look at me. "You look lovely tonight."

"That dress is all wrong," Astrid says at the same

time. "I told them the scarlet was too orange. You need crimson."

I automatically glance down at the criticism. One comment from Astrid can always make me feel so small.

"Good fairy seamstresses are becoming a rarity," Astrid mumbles. "It will have to be redone. Luckily, there is time before the charity ball."

"Drink, Mortimer?" Davis lifts his empty glass before producing a bottle hidden beside his chair.

"No. This isn't a social call." Mortimer takes a seat close to my father before turning his full attention toward me.

"Drink?" My father gestures toward me with his bottle.

I shake my head in denial. I've given up alcohol since my birthday fire. Not that any of them have noticed.

"Have a seat, Tamara," Astrid motions to the empty spot next to her on the couch.

I obey, mimicking my mother's pose by perching on the edge and crossing my ankles.

"You look like you've just crawled out of a werewolf den after a full moon Mardi Gras." Davis eyes his brother. "What is so urgent you need to see us?"

"Since the birthday fire, I've been flooded with strange dreams," Mortimer says. "I know the pieces are important, but the full picture has eluded me."

"You've forced a vision?" Davis inches forward.

Mortimer nods.

"That's tricky work," Davis muses to himself.

By tricky, my father means dangerous.

"I felt I had no choice," Mortimer says.

"Enough mystery. This isn't an Agatha Christie novel, and you're not Miss Marple," Astrid grumbles, using her martini glass to enunciate her demand, "Out with it."

"I've seen death that should not be there," Mortimer states. "Time has an overlap like it's been folded and twisted in all the wrong ways."

I stiffen and hold my breath. Does he know about the other timeline? And what is this about more death? I don't want more death in my life.

"Who?" Astrid's expression shows no fear, but she is more alert.

"You," Mortimer directs a nod at Astrid, "Davis and Anthony."

No. Not again.

A wave of panic fills me and centers in my chest. I start to speak but am cut off.

"Anthony should be here." My father doesn't say it, but I know he thinks there isn't any way I could help during a crisis.

"No. Tamara should be here," Mortimer says. "There is nothing for Anthony to do at the moment. No need to worry him."

"As far as I can ascertain, Tamara lives." Mortimer refuses to look at me. "Every divination I performed in the last year has changed. I think the birthday fire was meant for the three of you, but it got Conrad instead. That seems to be where the ripple in the timeline starts. I honestly don't know what has caused this shift in destiny, but we must act to disrupt this timeline. Clearly, Tamara is not under threat for being magical, but she is a Devine. If anything were to happen to the three of you, she would inherit everything. I don't know who is planning an attack, but it's ingenious."

A sense of overwhelm fills me. I fight the memories of their previous deaths, of standing outside the Devine mausoleum with Mortimer, watching as pallbearers carried three coffins inside. I remember thinking the gothic entryway reminded me of a giant evil beast consuming my family like a meal.

"It's up to you now, Tamara," Mortimer had said to me in that alternate life. He might not remember the conversation, but I do. *"The bloodline must be preserved and protected above all else. You're too innocent to know it, but rival factions within our world will try to use you as a pawn because of who you are and the position you now control. Everyone is watching. Your mortality makes you vulnerable. There are those who would take advantage. But I don't want you to worry. I'll take care of everything. You might be the last of my*

brother's line, but we can fix that. You will be expected to carry on the legacy by marrying a person of great magic. I'll have to find the right spells, of course, but I'm sure we can have you pregnant with an heir within a year."

I blink rapidly to get the images of the past that didn't happen out of my head.

"The visions keep coming, each one worse than the last," Mortimer mutters, his hand brushing nervously over the edges of his suit jacket. He paces the length of the room while he speaks. "Shadowy figures... power beyond our reach... it's all closing in around the family. I've seen this very building collapse."

I frown, hating the creeping sensation of dread that settles in my stomach. Mortimer always had a cryptic streak to him, mumbling about some unseen threats, but this time, there's a nervous edge to his voice that cannot be ignored. There's a genuine fear beneath his showmanship. I can see that my parents notice it as well.

"You want me to marry." It's the only answer that makes sense. Of course, he'd come back around to this crap-filled idea when faced with the same situation as before.

Mortimer clears his throat in surprise that I guessed his plan. "Well, actually, yes."

"No." The word slips out of me before I can stop it. I was repulsed the first time I heard his idea of turning me into a supernatural broodmare. I don't want to hear it again.

Here's the truth about predictions—especially forced predictions—they're more like high probabilities. They don't come organically from the universe.

"Are you sure?" my father asks.

"Yes," Mortimer answers.

"No," I repeat at the same time.

"An alliance with the right family will offer all of us protection." Mortimer disregards my protest.

"Don't leave everything to me," I put forth. "Make a new will. Leave it to Mortimer. I won't protest."

I don't want control over any of it, anyway. I want to find a way out of the family drama, not dig deeper into it.

"You know I would handle the Devine holdings in your absence if I could, but that was never my path." Mortimer rejects my idea. "I would, of course, counsel the children if the need arose."

It says a lot that Mortimer isn't eager to take over the family business. He knows the burden of it. I think he might also suspect he doesn't carry the same respect as my father in the supernatural world. I'm sure there is a lot of history there that they think I'm too mortal and too young to know about.

"It is my belief," Mortimer continues, "that even though Tamara is mortal due to unknown—"

"She knows," Astrid interrupts. "I told her."

"—that even though Tamara inherited her mortality," Mortimer easily amends, "she still has Devine blood. With the right spells, she could carry a supernatural child as long as she marries a person of great magic."

I don't bother to explain that babies do not require marriage.

Or that I have no plans to get pregnant. Ever. Why would I bring a baby into my world?

He doesn't bother to needlessly explain that an arranged marriage in this family doesn't necessarily require my consent. If I'm not careful, I'll find myself magically petrified and dragged down the aisle.

I look at my hands in my lap. My gaze moves to the small cut Costin had licked earlier, and I turn my arm to hide it from my view. Goosebumps rise over my flesh, and I visibly shiver. I don't want that vampire in my thoughts.

"I should tell you something…" I take a deep breath. I think Mortimer is worried about past residual from the amulet's magic. The premonitions he's having are from the erased timeline. All this worry is probably for nothing.

I feel a chill work over my back and stiffen as the smell of Conrad's spirit wafts past. I glance around to find him standing near the kitchen. The light comes through his transparent body. No one else turns to look.

Conrad shakes his head once and draws a line across his neck with his thumb in warning. Black ooze begins to bleed out of his eyes, dripping down his face. It's become one of his favorite go-to threats: talk and die.

"Yes?" Astrid prompts.

I force my gaze away from Conrad, refusing to finish the sentence.

"She's dating Constantine," Mortimer answers for me, even though that is not what I was going to say.

"No, I—" I start to protest.

My father chuckles. I can't tell if he thinks it's impossible or just ridiculous. He gives a slight lift of his glass before taking a drink.

Astrid arches a brow. "A vampire? You can't be serious, Tamara."

"I'm not," I say. "It's not. We're—"

"No denials. Your secret is out," Mortimer answers. I wonder what happened to his plan not to say anything. "I have explained to Tamara that a relationship with Constantine cannot happen."

"We do not want the European vampires visiting," Astrid agrees. "Savage lot. And that Elizabeth..."

Astrid takes a drink.

"Do we know where the threat to our family comes from?" Davis asks. "Any clues?"

"It's magical, so I suspect the Blackwoods or the Freemonts. Not that I can prove either case." Mortimer takes a deep breath. "I also strongly feel Tamara should marry into one of those two families. Both are powerful and either alliance will be advantageous for us. Either the alliance will stop a takeover, or the alliance will make the other party think twice about trying a takeover."

"Both have shown interest in Tamara," Astrid agrees.

Jasper Blackwood or Chester Freemont. The former is my cheating ex that I want absolutely nothing to do with. The latter and I had a series of botched dates arranged by my parents. He actually talked about how many mistresses his father kept like it was a benchmark he needed to surpass.

I won't voice my thoughts on a husband taking mistresses to my parents. There is no kind way to point that out to Astrid when it reflects her life.

I don't want her life.

I don't want *this* life.

Please, universe, make my life normal.

I don't think the universe hears me. Or cares.

"Freemont," Astrid sounds like she's coming to a decision. "They're more respectable."

"Blackwoods have better connections," my father counters.

"Better for what? Shipping routes?" Astrid shakes her head. "Freemonts have that property in France."

"True." Davis nods at his wife's logic. "And there was that unfortunate issue with their shipping container. That could put this issue to bed once and for all."

"The Freemonts' magic is powerful, stronger than most. This could be the only way to secure the family's future. The Devine name will be torn apart if we don't act now. Of that, I am sure," Mortimer says.

Astrid nods.

I stare at them, feeling the weight of their words settle on my shoulders. They can't be serious. This is not just about Chester, even though I can't stand the man. This is about locking me into a life I have fought so hard to avoid. The legacy. The family. The endless politics. And for what? Power? Protection? I try not to care about any of that. I care about getting out and being normal. I care about living a life where I am not someone else's pawn.

But can I turn my back on my family? Does what I want matter?

If what Mortimer says is true, and the visions are real, do I have the right to refuse? The thought makes my chest tighten, anger bubbling beneath the surface. It's not just Chester I hate—it's the idea of being forced into a future I never wanted.

"I..." I glance toward the kitchen. Conrad is still there, staring at me. I can't force the words out. "You really think Chester is the answer?"

My tone is more disrespectful than I intended. The name alone makes my skin crawl.

"You don't understand," Mortimer states, his voice strained. He paces behind the couch and leans to grip the back. I watch his knuckles turn white. "We're walking a tightrope, Tamara. We'll lose everything if the Freemonts or the Blackwoods turn against us. They have resources we can't match, and if they side with our enemies, we won't survive what's coming."

I stare at him, taken aback by the genuine fear in his voice. Mortimer has always been so calculating and in control. I don't think I've ever seen him scared.

I try to think of a solution that isn't marriage. "But Chester—"

"Is our only option," he interrupts. "I'm not asking you to like it. I'm telling you that you have a duty to save your family."

I try again. "Maybe we should see if your premonitions change—"

"He's the only answer," Mortimer interrupts, his

eyes flashing with frustration. "My visions don't lie. If we do not solidify an alliance, we won't survive what's coming."

I want to point out that he just admitted his visions changed.

"I know you think we're being unreasonable," Astrid says, her voice cool as ever as she adjusts her diamond bracelet. "But this isn't about what you want, Tamara. It's not about what any of us want really. This is about the survival of our family, of our legacy."

My father stares into his glass and takes another drink.

I clench my fists at my side. "Please, I beg you. There has to be another way—something that doesn't involve him."

Astrid's gauge flickers toward me, and her lips tighten. "This isn't cruelty. This is survival. We can't afford to let sentimentality or personal feelings get in the way of that. Sometimes, we must do things we don't want because the alternative is far worse. Too much is at stake." Her tone softens, and she adds, "Ours is not a life of Disney fairy tales. We all must make sacrifices."

Her words land like a punch to the gut, and for a second, I wonder if she's speaking from her own experiences.

"But Chester?" I feel like an asshole as the word

escapes me. But my repulsion of him is such a visceral reaction I can't seem to keep it in.

"Would you rather Jasper?" Mortimer asks.

I know firsthand that he's a cheating asshole and a control freak. He never actually hit me, but I saw violent tendencies in him that frightened me. Between the two, at least Chester will ignore me most of the time.

I shake my head in denial.

"Tamara, the Freemonts hold more power than you realize," Astrid says. "I know you don't fully understand the inner workings of the magical world."

I can't help but think that's their fault, not mine. They're the ones who decided I needed to be sheltered from such things because of my mortality.

"Their reach extends into the highest levels of the magical councils," she continues. "They control key alliances we can't afford to lose, and if we're tied to them through marriage, no one will dare make a move against us. Including them, if indeed they are the threat we are facing."

Bile rises in my throat. History and logic tell me not to keep pushing, but this might be my only chance to protest the decision. What is it with today and fate? First, Costin and his prophecy nonsense. And now Uncle Mortimer with his premonition. Part of me wishes I could break the amulet all over again to erase this timeline and start a fresh one.

"Do you really think Chester's family is going to protect us out of the kindness of their hearts? Maybe this gives them exactly what they want," I say.

"Kindness has nothing to do with it," Astrid says. I can tell by the coldness in her gaze that I have pushed too hard and too far. "The Freemonts are pragmatic, and they understand the value of strategic partnerships. If we offer them what they need, they'll give us the protection we require. It's simple math. Power for power. Alliance for an alliance."

I can tell by her tone that she believes this marriage to be a political necessity, and that my resistance could have real consequences for the family. If I continue to protest, it would be like saying I don't care if they all die.

But I do care. I can't live through that again.

Everything inside me turns cold. I have no choice. I have to do what they ask. I want to cry, scream, run myself right off the side of the building to fall to the sidewalk so I don't have to face it.

This isn't fair. This can't be my life. I beg the fates to make it go away. What did I do to deserve this fresh hell?

"Are we decided?" Mortimer asks.

My parents nod even as I'm shaking my head. I

see Conrad grinning, the dark expression mocking me. Of course, he's enjoying this. He knows how I feel about Chester. His spirit slowly fades from view.

"I'll make the necessary approaches." Mortimer stands.

"Get some sleep first," Astrid instructs. "You need to be at full power."

Mortimer nods at her advice.

My father stands and helps him to his feet. "I'll walk you out."

I turn to Astrid next to me on the couch as we are left alone. "I don't love Chester. I don't even like him. Please, you can't ask me to do this."

"These arrangements are never about love or like." Astrid's expression holds a touch of pity. It's slight, but it's there.

"Is that why you married? You were told to?"

She takes a drink, finishing her martini before setting the glass on the floor next to the couch. She studies the rings on her hand. "Who knows? It was so long ago. I'm sure there were many reasons."

I want to say something comforting to her. Blood or not, she's been my mother my entire life. Things may be complicated, but that fact is not. I might not always like her, but I do love her.

"I'm…" I don't know how to say what I'm feeling. We don't talk about feelings. "I'm sorry."

She arches a questioning brow.

"It couldn't have been easy for you," I clarify. "Having me around."

Her expression changes, and her brow furrows. "Life is not meant to be easy. It is meant to be lived."

It's not what I want to hear from the woman, but then, it is what I expected her to say. I want to ask if she loves me, if she ever did. I want to ask if any part of her feels connected to me. I might resent her and her coldness sometimes, but I feel that invisible thread of family—even if it's worn and scraggly.

To my surprise, she touches my hand gently. It's a rare moment of contact.

"I regret the way you found out about your birth." Astrid releases my hand. To the outside world, it might not look like much, but to me, knowing my mother, the contact is equivalent to a hug. "That color isn't right for you. Go change and leave the dress on the bed."

CHAPTER
SIX

Twenty-Eighth Birthday Fire, Manhattan, Three Months Ago...

"Tamara."

My head is fuzzy. I can still smell Conrad's flesh burning. Fear has me locked in the horrible moment.

"Tamara."

One second, I'm standing in my birth mother's living room in California, and the next, I'm on a sidewalk in New York, choked by the acrid smell of smoke and ash from a burning building. I stare at the hand that had been stained with Paul's blood. I can't believe Conrad shot him. My vision blurs and I'm forced to blink. Instead of red, it's now smeared with black soot.

What's happening?

"Tamara!"

I turn toward Lady Astrid. She's patting my face, saying, "You're all right. Don't move from this spot. I'm having them bring the car around."

"Paul?" I try to speak, but my throat is raw.

Time feels accelerated for everyone except me. People rush around, trying to manage the fire while I remain completely still. I hear crackling voices on a radio giving out commands.

Lights from emergency vehicles illuminate the scene, but they pale compared to the orange glow emanating from the windows of the old stone building. Smoke pours out of the broken windows of the banquet hall, drawing my eyes toward the night sky. Familiar embers flicker against the darkness like dying butterflies, and their ashes gently fall to the ground like a fine snow covering everything.

This isn't right. I've been here before. It's my birthday party.

This is not what happened. I was dragged out by a fireman and taken to a hospital.

Confused, I look over the crowd. I see Louis jogging backward down the sidewalk as he watches the building burn. Anthony stands near the paramedics, watching his secret boyfriend. Lady Astrid is ordering people about. My father is talking to a group of powerful supernatural men. They were all dead.

They're not. They survived. Relief floods me.

Is this a second chance?

Has time reset to make things right?

Was it all a nightmare?

My head is dazed. Am I still high? I remember smoking with Anthony and Louis in our little side party inside a janitor's closet. What the hell did Anthony lace that pot with?

Where's Conrad?

I instinctively reach for my necklace, seeking the reassurance of the amulet's presence. My fingers comb through the hollow of my collarbone, but it isn't there. I slide my hand against my chest, looking for it, but I don't find it loose in my clothing.

A glint of green on the sidewalk by my feet catches my attention. The red stone has changed color and is now shattered into pieces.

Conrad stole the amulet from me, thinking he could steal its protective power before he killed me. His plan didn't work, and I watched him die instead.

I find it hard to concentrate as I kneel on the ground to lift one of the shards. The broken edge cuts my finger, and I drop it with a tiny yelp of surprise. I stare at the dot of blood, confused.

A figure appears next to me, and cool fingers wrap around my wrist. The temperature shocks me back to awareness.

"Hello, castoff," Costin says, his voice soft.

I hate that nickname.

I inhale sharply and belatedly try to jerk my hand away. The vampire keeps a firm grip, refusing to release me.

He focuses intently on my blood, breathing deeply as he brings the bloody digit between his lips for a taste. His kiss is warmer than I thought it would be. To my surprise, he makes a small sound of pleasure. It's a bold move, considering anyone can see us.

I'm not sure how to react.

An inner light swirls within the depths of his gaze, and I worry he's trying to mesmerize me. I try to look away but can't. My finger slides out of his mouth, wet from his tongue, and he lets go. Blood-lust churns in him, and I can see he wants more.

"You can't…" I start to panic, but his words stop me.

"You saved me." The vampire licks his lips, showing me the tips of his fangs. "Now I can always find you."

Before I have a chance to reply, he vanishes. My hand lingers in the air, still in the position he left it, with my damp finger pointing skyward.

What was that?

The chaos of the moment recaptures my attention. Emergency workers talk over their radios about survivors and deaths. I try to listen through the drugged fog, trying to calm the nausea bubbling in my stomach.

My mother appears next to me. "You broke your necklace."

Her words prompt me to gather the pieces, careful not to cut myself in case Costin takes it as another invitation to dine.

"It's Conrad." Anthony appears stricken. "That body they found. It's Conrad."

I don't know how to feel. They stare at me on the ground, clutching my broken necklace. I feel moisture trailing down my cheeks as I reach to make sure Anthony is really there.

I'm not crazy. The wizard sealed him inside the tomb. They were all dead.

Everything feels like it's happening to someone else.

"Anthony," Astrid orders, "get her off the ground. We need to get her to the car. People are staring. This is a private family matter."

Anthony loops his forearm around my back and pulls me to my feet. I lean against him for support.

"You're alive," I tell him.

"What the hell happened in there?" Anthony asks, guiding me toward a limo. His eyes are as glazed as I feel.

A driver opens the car door, and I'm urged inside.

I collapse onto the seat, clutching the broken amulet like a lifeline to sanity. The door slams shut.

"Hand me the yellow vial, then go find your father," Astrid says. "Tell him we're going to leave without him if he doesn't hurry."

Anthony leaves. Astrid appears next to me, stroking back my hair. "Sit up. Drink this."

She forces me to drink the potion before I can form a coherent thought. The small grip I have on reality fades like the last swig of too much alcohol before passing out.

"That's it. It will calm you down," Astrid soothes. Normally, her voice is so cold. The warmth in it now lulls me to close my eyes. "Just rest. Let the potion take all your pain away."

SEVEN

Fuck today.

Anthony lies sprawled on my bed, a pillow jammed over his face, while I change my clothes. He's been lying there ever since he marched into my bedroom with a growl of frustration and nothing else.

I'm only too happy to get out of the dress. The thin material makes me feel too exposed and on display. I replace it with jeans and a baggy T-shirt. The obscure band logo flipping off the world on the front feels like a mini rebellion. Out of habit, I take the amulet. The pouch feels uncharacteristically cold, and I rub at the shards inside. A creepy sensation tries to travel up my arm, like an army of spiders parading toward my armpit. I instantly shove the pouch into my pocket and rub the sensation away.

We're alone in the room. Even though it's not, I can imagine that this place feels like a sanctuary to my brother. No one will come looking for us in here. At least they won't come looking for me and accidentally find him. They've already dictated what they require me to do.

"You all right under there?" I inquire.

He grumbles incoherently against the pillow. The weight of his frustrations is almost palpable.

"Why so glum?" I cross over to look down at him. "I take it you overheard the big news that Mortimer and the parents want me to get married?"

He lifts the pillow slightly, his eyes narrowed. "You mean the part where they're selling you off to Chester 'The Slimeball' Freemont? Yeah, I heard."

I roll my eyes and sit next to him on the bed. He pulls the pillow fully from his face and tosses it aside.

"I mean, out of all the people they could choose —Chester? Were they drunk?" He gives a teasing half-smile that doesn't fully reach his eyes. "Or do they just hate me?"

"Yes. Because clearly my marriage to Chester will deeply affect you." I chuckle at his attempt to lighten the mood, but there's a heaviness that lingers beneath his sarcasm.

"I guess, technically, they gave me a choice of

either Jasper or Chester." Saying it out loud doesn't make me feel better.

"You know, my buddy Peter thinks you're cute, and he owes me several favors. We can fly up to Las Vegas, find an Elvis drive-thru, and get you hitched. Then you can't get married because you'll already be taken."

"Isn't Peter a werewolf?" I scrunch up my nose at the idea.

"You like dogs." Anthony grins.

"As pets."

Anthony's grin widens. "Peter will let you pet him. He likes to be told what to do. He's a good boy."

I refuse to laugh at his joke, even though it's funny. "Thanks for the offer, but I'm going to have to pass."

My resistance only adds to his temporary amusement.

Anthony pushes himself up to sit beside me. He grins, but the smile still doesn't quite reach his eyes. I know he's frustrated for both of us.

"Everything with the elders is about tradition, legacy, status. We're all pawns in some twisted chess game of life. It's never about what we want." There's something more in his voice now, an edge of bitterness that makes me look closer at him. He avoids my gaze as he stares down at his hands.

"Have they been pressuring you, too?" I know

that they'll expect him to marry eventually. And it will not be to the person he chooses.

"Always and forever." He shrugs, trying to brush it off with his usual easygoing charm. "But you know me. Always dodging expectations. As long as I'm smiling and playing the role of the dutiful son, they don't look too closely at what I'm doing."

Our parents might not look closely at him, but I do. Beneath the humor, I can feel his discomfort—the weight of what is eternally left unsaid. Anthony has always been the special one, the one who fits in. But I know that's just what he lets people see. Since Conrad's death, the more time I spend with Anthony, the more I realize how much I assumed about him that isn't true. His life is not easy. He's a hostage of this family's expectations, just like me.

I reached to pat his knee briefly. "What are you going to do when they dictate it's time for you to marry and have kids?"

Anthony falters for a fraction of a second and his expression falls. He quickly recovers and gives a slight shrug. "I guess I'll deal with it when the time comes."

The nonchalance in his voice is forced. He avoids my gaze again, and I suddenly feel the weight of his secrets pressing down on him.

"Anthony, if you ever want to talk—"

He cuts me off with a tight laugh and runs his hands through his hair, messing the locks.

I refuse to let him deflect. This is too important, and I need to say it. Considering my future staring down at me, I need him to know that he has my unwavering support. "You shouldn't have to live like this, pretending and hiding. I'm your sister. And I love you no matter what."

"You know it's not that simple, Tam-tam. I will say it again. It's all about appearances and keeping the family going." Anthony adjusts himself on the bed, moving to lean against the headboard. He stares at the distant wall. Even though he can't fix my problems, his presence is comforting. I wish I knew what to say to him to make things better. I wish I knew what to say to myself.

"Let's run away. Let's go to Africa," I suggest. "Tonight. Just like you said. Let's disappear where they will never find us."

He turns his head to look at me. "The only shipment heading in that direction is a family of goblins. We don't want to hitch a ride with that smelly mess."

My heart sinks a little. "It doesn't have to be Africa. Let's just leave."

Honestly, I'd be happy going to Antarctica right now. Anywhere but here.

Costin's face flashes in my mind. For a moment, I

feel the intensity of his gaze, as if he's standing right before me. I hate that I keep thinking about him, about the secrets he dangles in front of me. Why him? Why now? He was cut off before he could tell me about the prophecy, about the future waiting for me. I can't help but wonder if his prophecy and Mortimer's premonitions are the same thing. What are the odds that they both came on the same day—my family's expectations, the growing danger, the prophecy?

I'd be lying if I said my preoccupation with the master vampire is just the prophecy. There's something else there, too. Something dark and dangerous, something I don't want to admit that I'm drawn to. I can't even afford to fantasize about the vampire. That's a treacherous path I do not want to travel.

Besides, the odds are Costin is not attracted to me; rather, he's just fucking with me because he's bored, and he can.

Anthony moves down on the bed to sit beside me and nudges me with his elbow, pulling me out of my thoughts.

"Stressing about it will not make it go away."

I force a smile, but my mind is still racing.

"Hey, you want to see something fucked up?" Anthony asks, and before I can answer, he adds, "Yes, you do."

He rolls off the bed, grabs my hand, and pulls me behind him.

"Seriously, I think you should consider Peter. It's a good option." He hooks his arm through mine and forces me to walk with him out of the bedroom.

"One quick bite, and I'll be howling at the moon in no time," I joke. "Immortality, baby!"

He drops his hold, only to drape his arm over my shoulders instead. "Please marry Peter. For me. The look on our mother's face when you... bring him to family dinner..."

He starts laughing and can't finish. I can't help it. I try to hold back, but a small snort escapes me. The unladylike sound only makes my brother laugh harder.

Anthony stops. "In here."

We're outside of Conrad's room. I feel my insides clench.

"Anthony," I shake my head to stop him, "no."

He reaches for the doorknob, not listening to my weak protest.

I must have been inside Conrad's suite a million times, but I don't want to make it a million and one. I expect Conrad's ghost to be waiting as I watch the door open. Instead, the room is exactly as the servants would have left it.

The air is stifling, as if we're stepping into a

tomb. Maybe it's my imagination, but the musty smell is familiar.

"We shouldn't be in here," I whisper.

Time has stopped in the room. Conrad's bed is made, and everything is in its place. The curtains are drawn as if to protect a shrine to his life. Little treasures line an antique dresser. I don't think they're magical beyond the meaning they carried for Conrad.

I feel guilty thinking about it, but I can't help but wonder why Astrid kept the room as he left it. There was no love lost between Conrad and his adoptive parents. The only conclusion I can come up with is that she is resistant to change.

"Over here," Anthony says, opening Conrad's closet and stepping inside. I hear something sliding.

Still, I hesitate.

Light flashes from inside the closet.

"Tam, come here!" Anthony calls.

I step across the large rug, letting it pad my steps to keep me quiet. I wait for the chill that means Conrad is watching, but it doesn't come.

The walk-in closet is crammed with clothes and has the lingering scent of cologne. My hands begin to shake as memories flood me. He wore the green jacket to an art gallery event and stole a tray of bacon-wrapped shrimp for us because I'd missed dinner. The yellow shirt was from when he refused to hold a cab for me and left me alone on the sidewalk. Then there is the suit and long coat jacket that reminds me of the style favored by vampires. It's laid out as if waiting. He wore that suit in the other timeline to our family's funeral.

Seeing it here, now, waiting to be worn, I am struck with just how much detail Conrad planned his takeover of the Devine empire.

I don't want to be in here.

"What do you make of this?" Anthony stands at the back of the closet in front of the flashing lights.

I go to see what he's found. A secret compartment in the wall is pushed aside to show several security monitors.

"Who are these people?" Anthony insists.

The first monitor is the Turnblads' kitchen in Kansas City. They were Conrad's foster family before our parents adopted him. I've never been inside their home but recognize Larry in his barbeque apron. I met alternate-timeline Larry seconds before his house exploded. Toys litter the otherwise clean home as a couple of small blurs run under the odd angle of the camera. If I had to guess, the camera is hidden inside a smoke detector or something. No one appears to know it's there.

The second monitor is a hallway in an apartment complex, watching for people to come up the stairwell. I can just make out the number 204 on the apartment door. I've been there too.

The third monitor is the dirty junkie's den inside apartment 204. A half-naked woman is stretched out on an old couch, smoke curling from a cigarette. Graying brown hair is pulled into a scraggly ponytail. Her t-shirt rides up her waist, but she doesn't seem to care. Liquor bottles and food wrappers dirty the already matted carpet. Lamplight shines from an exposed bulb, spreading over the couch like a spotlight. A bare-assed man comes into view and heads toward the couch. The smoking woman lying there is indifferent to his approach as he climbs on top of her.

"This is like the worst porn cam ever." Anthony grimaces, even as he watches the dirty man's ass begin to pump. "I knew our brother had issues, but this is just..."

I know that woman. It's Conrad's birth mother, a junkie prostitute. Conrad sent me to her apartment in an attempt to kill us both. She'd abandoned him as a kid outside a gas station to score some meth.

Even so, why would he want to watch the woman in such degrading positions?

"Turn it off," I tell Anthony. "We should just..."

I wave my hand, wishing I could erase the images.

"What do you think Conrad was doing with this stuff?" Anthony asks.

"How did you find it?" I counter.

"I saw Uncle Mortimer's little family meeting in the living room and decided to hide out until it was over. When I ducked in here, I saw the monitor light coming from the closet. This compartment wasn't closed all the way."

"No good can come of this." I yank a cable behind one of the monitors, shutting off the Turnblads. "Whatever he was doing, Conrad is dead. No one else needs to find this." I pull the cable out of the second monitor and go for the third of the prostitute.

"Yeah." Anthony reaches for it at the same time, and we both end up jerking the cable out together. The sex show stops.

I feel a chill and rub my arms. "Can we get out of here now?"

"One second." A blue light surges from Anthony's fingers and travels into the cable before disappearing. He repeats the magical act with the remaining two. "That will sever the connection, making it untraceable back to us. This weird perversion is a scandal the family doesn't need."

Anthony closes the hidden compartment.

I wait for my brother to leave the room with me, afraid of running into Conrad. He's not going to like that we canceled his shows.

"I sometimes feel like he's still hanging around," Anthony says. "I hope I'm wrong. Most spirits are without power. They're trapped in loops, reliving the same thing over and over. It's no way to exist. I wouldn't wish that on anyone."

"What about the spirits who have power?" I ask.

"Active hauntings? They're rare, fueled by intense rage or emotion. Those are so much worse. Conrad was moody and weird, but I don't think he was angry enough to become vengeful."

Yeah, I wouldn't be so sure.

I think it, but I don't say it.

"You really miss him, don't you?" Anthony nods as if answering his own question.

I miss a lie.

I don't say that either.

"Enough sadness. We need a distraction." Anthony hooks my arm. A playfulness comes over him. "I want to know what's going on between you and Costin. He's not my normal type, but I have to hand it to you, he's definitely handsome."

"Nothing," I protest. "He was just here giving his..."

"Giving his...?" Anthony grins. "His all? His best? His full effort?"

"Condolences," I lie. I want the teasing to stop.

Anthony reaches into his back pocket and pulls out a piece of folded parchment. "Is that what the cool kids are calling sex in the grave these days? Seriously, a vampire boyfriend? Well done, you little freaky freak."

"Me with a vampire doesn't make sense. Don't you think he's a little old for me?"

Anthony laughs. "You're an adult. Who cares if he's ancient? He's hot. But, hey, since you're all into fangs now, I'll say again my buddy Peter is always ready for a—"

"What are you going on about?" I grimace at the idea.

He hands me the note. "I found this love note on your pillow."

"And you took it?" I snatch it from him to see what it says.

"*Midnight. Marcheur de Nuit Mausoleum. Catacomb entrance. Costin.*"

"Somebody's got a sexy date in a dirty place," Anthony continues. "I wholeheartedly approve, by the way."

I grimace.

He does a little dance, slapping an imaginary ass as he sings, "Costin's gonna take my sister down to funky town."

"I don't even know what this means." I crumple the letter.

Anthony is clearly entertained. "It means we're going out tonight to party like supernaturals at the end of the world, little sister. Time for an adventure into the darkness, aka the supernatural city beneath New York."

"*Marcheur*... why does that sound familiar?" The name tickles my memory.

"*Marcheur de Nuit*. The nightwalker crypt in lower Manhattan. You remember. Our parents made us pay our respects at that ghoul ceremony."

"Oh, gross." I shake my head and cover my nose. The memory of that smell is as potent as the day it happened.

Ghouls live underground and dig their way into graves, desecrating them to eat the flesh of the unembalmed. During the ceremony, they did it from above. It was some important magic dude's dying wish. That is one supernatural event I wish they would have banned me from.

"Have fun with that," I say. "Tell Costin sorry I'm never going anywhere with him, let alone into the catacombs to play inside the supernatural realm."

There is no way I will meet a vampire in an underground graveyard filled with ghouls in the middle of the night.

No. Fucking. Way.

EIGHT

"I hate you," I mutter to my brother as he forces me to walk next to him down a dark cobblestone path toward the *Marcheur de Nuit Mausoleum*.

Yes. It's by force. He put a spell on my shoes.

"You love me," he denies. As Anthony and I approach, I notice a low stone wall with iron posts towering above us, separating us from the lush grass on the other side. The iron posts are not just for decoration; they're meant to contain any ghouls or other supernatural beings within the enclosed area. No one wants them out adventuring in the city. With a wave of his hand, Anthony conjures a shimmering magic that envelops the fence before physically pulling me through the solid brick to the other side. "And you need me."

"Debatable."

Old-fashioned lamp posts with flickering gas flames line the edges of the enclosed graveyard. Cloudy glass attracts white moths, which flutter around the lamplights like ethereal spirits. I recall a tutor who likened these nocturnal creatures to butterflies of the night, drawing a fascinating parallel between their activities and those of their diurnal counterparts.

"I'm a delicate butterfly in a world of fiery dragons."

Grandfather George had taught me that saying when I was little, his warning to be careful in a dangerous world. The insects remind me of my birth mother. She has a butterfly tattoo on her chest and thinks of me as her little butterfly because of a butterfly mobile she put over my crib when I was a baby. Not that she remembers telling me that.

Anthony threads his arm through mine, forcing me to walk beside him. "Would you, honestly, rather be in the penthouse of broken dreams waiting for Uncle Mortimer to bring over your future husband, Chester, to negotiate betrothal agreements and breeding obligations? Or would you rather hide out with your amazingly awesome brother, partying until dawn in the supernatural underground?"

Are those my only two choices?

Tourists can freak themselves out in the catacombs beneath the Basilica of St. Patrick's Old Cathedral in lower Manhattan for a forty-dollar ticket. Although these catacombs are in the same part of the city, this is not the same thing. There is no discernable way in or out of the yard, even though you can peek through the iron bars. The only way through is with magic.

I've seen the outside of the nightwalker mausoleum, but I've never been inside. It's the secret entrance to the catacombs underneath. And I'd put the word secret in air quotes since there are a lot of supernaturals who know about it.

Anthony and I make an interesting pair. I'm in my fuck off T-shirt and sneakers. He looks ready for a VIP table at the hottest nightclub. No one will ever accuse Anthony of being out of style. The sequined pinstripe black velvet shirt feels a little showy for a graveyard party, but what do I know?

"Hey." Anthony stops and cups my face, forcing me to look at him. "If you really don't want to be here, Tam, I'll take you home. I just thought we could both use a little forgetting. I promise I won't let anyone hurt you down there. The ghouls won't bother the living."

He doesn't need to say more. I see it. He feels alone, like me.

Anthony acts protective. As much as I love his company, I can't help but feel he's clinging to me because he needs me to comfort him, not the other way around.

Conrad and I spent our childhoods sticking beside each other—two mortal children against the supernatural world. Only after Conrad's death did I begin to see that maybe Anthony could have used membership in our little club. As the favored child, Anthony received all the parental attention and had all the cool friends. It never occurred to me that he might need my support. All the constant attention came with its own set of problems for him.

I'm not sure which is worse—being forgotten or never being left alone.

Like most of his serious moments, this one is fleeting. Anthony lets go of me and shoves his hand into his jacket pocket, only to pull out a joint.

"Never use breeding obligation in a sentence again." I visibly shiver. "The thought of Chester's clammy hands…"

I dramatically gag to prove my point.

"Fair enough." Anthony laughs and snaps his fingers, producing a small flame that he uses to light the tip. Taking a long drag, he offers it to me.

I shake my head. The last time I smoked one of his party joints was my birthday. I don't know what it's laced with, but that is one club-drug-magic-carpet-ride to passing out on a public restroom floor I don't want to have again.

Cemeteries shouldn't bother me. When you grow up around the supernatural, things like mausoleums and the undead are commonplace. But now, the afterlife has a new meaning. I expect Conrad's spirit to appear from behind every crooked tombstone and weather-beaten statue. It keeps my stomach knotted and my heart pounding a little too hard. If his revenge is to preoccupy my thoughts and keep me in fear, he's succeeding.

Blurs pass by like flighted creatures, moving in the same direction we are walking. They draw my attention to a large angel with spread wings standing guard over the graves. Even in the moonlight, the stone looks weathered and stained, and I see a chunk missing from her hand. Time has not been kind to her.

My hand goes to my neck only to be reminded that my amulet is broken and in my pocket. I'm not protected by magic.

The smell of marijuana comes from my brother. I think about reaching out to take it from him. Maybe oblivion is better than fear.

"You brought protection?" Costin's voice stops me. I didn't hear him approach.

Anthony's arm automatically slides over my shoulders before I can turn to face the vampire behind us. "My sister better not need protection."

"All beautiful women need protection. This is a cruel world we live in." Costin appears next to me.

Beautiful? The compliment takes me by surprise.

A small part of me might find pleasure in the word, but my logical brain knows better. Costin needs me for his prophecy quest, and he's buttering me up.

"And perhaps it is most cruel to those who deserve it the least." Costin's voice is low, almost like he's flirting.

What the hell?

He looks at me expectantly. I turn to find Anthony craning his neck to study me.

"Monsters like squishing delicate things." It's the only thing I can think to add to their conversation.

"Indeed," Costin states.

"Here's to delicate things." Anthony holds up his joint and gestures it like he's clicking a glass for a toast. Bringing it to his lips, he mumbles, "And here's to fighting monsters."

He takes a long draw.

"Anthony, may I escort your sister?" Costin lifts his arm for me to take.

I lean away, pressing into my brother's side.

Anthony's arm tightens in a half hug. "I think that would be up to my sister."

My first instinct is to say no, but something stops me.

Costin asked for this meeting. He probably just wants to finish stating his case. I doubt he will give up until I at least listen to his proposal. I look toward the mausoleum. The gothic structure waits like a demon's mouth offering hell. I don't want to go into the land of ghouls and monsters. Out here in the open is better.

I can't believe I'm doing this.

"Sure. I'll be fine, Anthony." I squeeze my brother's hand before sliding him from my shoulders. "Costin and I need to have a quick conversation. You go on and have fun. I'll see you at home later."

Anthony studies me for a moment. "Text me if you come down, and I'll find you. Don't wander alone."

The request is strange. No one ever asks me to check in. If they want to find me, they can.

"Sure." I nod.

"Constantine." Anthony gives a parting nod. His tone and look could be translated as a warning.

"Anthony." Costin nods back.

My brother walks backward several steps, keeping his gaze steady on the vampire. When he finally turns, I want to call him back to my side. I watch a trail of smoke follow him into the shadows.

"You surprise me," Costin admits when Anthony is out of earshot.

"Oh?" I keep my eyes on my brother's back for as long as I can see him. He disappears into the mausoleum.

Chilled fingers touch the side of my neck, and I shiver at the contact.

"I don't know many humans who would willingly walk into a boneyard to meet a vampire in the middle of the night." I watch him in my peripheral, not meeting his eyes.

"If that's true, then why invite me into your lair?" I point out. "Why not just come back to the house?"

"Lair? Hardly." He chuckles. "Your house is crowded tonight. I thought we'd have more privacy here, on neutral ground."

This place hardly feels neutral.

If anything happens to me, Anthony knows I'm with the vampire. I'm safe.

Why don't I feel safe?

The light scratch of his nails moves over my pulse as if contemplating my artery. I tense.

"I owe you an apology." Costin pulls his fingers away from my neck.

"Okay?" I hug my arms across my stomach.

"I should not have lost my temper with you earlier. I thought George would have explained things better to you, but it is clear you don't know, and I have taken you by surprise."

I have to admit, his new approach doesn't bring me much comfort. Apologizing doesn't feel natural on the vampire. I can't help but wonder if this is some type of manipulation.

Did I mention I have trust issues?

"Thank you for the apology, but my mind hasn't changed. I want nothing to do with supernatural prophecies." I think of the last paranormal adventure I went on. Vampires chased me across the country, a fairy waitress had a temper tantrum, and Conrad killed the man I love. "They won't make sense to you, but I have my reasons. I'm mortal. I accept that. I can't change the world. Now I'll kindly, and with the most respect possible, ask you to leave me be."

"No."

No. Just like that.

"I don't want to do your stupid prophecy." My voice sounds loud in the quiet cemetery, and I take a calming breath. "Find someone else."

"The way you speak to me." Costin comes to stand in front of me and lifts his hand to nudge my chin with his bent knuckle. He forces my face upward to meet his. I stare over his shoulder. "And you won't do me the courtesy of looking me in the eye when you do it."

"I don't like it when you mesmerize me." I glance at his face and back to the side.

"When have I mesmerized you?"

That doesn't make sense. I couldn't resist him when he held my arm in the library. I wonder if he's attempting a joke. It's so hard to tell sometimes with his kind.

I feel like he's daring me. Lifting my gaze to stare at his eyes, I hold my breath and wait to be taken over.

He gives a slow smile. "There you go."

I keep very still, aware of his nearness. The dark silence of the cemetery surrounds us. Even the normal sounds of the city seem at rest here. The moment feels intimate. He looks at my mouth, his expression unexpectedly soft, and I wonder if he's going to try to kiss me.

"Take a breath," he orders, his voice smooth and unbothered.

I do. I try to step away but can't.

"Are you doing it now?" I whisper, unable to move.

He gives a small shake of his head. The vampire can deny it all he wants, but I feel the truth.

"I don't believe you." I want to run. Why in the world didn't I go underground with my brother? Hanging in the supernatural realm with him sounds so much better than being alone with a seductive vampire hellbent on making me do some kind of quest. "My legs don't work."

"Then that is your issue, not mine." His tone darkens, and he sounds exasperated. His bent finger extends beneath my chin, and his sharp nail brushes my neck like a warning. His presence pulls at me like gravity.

I feel a vibration against my hip, and at first, I think it's him. I instantly touch the spot to push him away but realize it seems to be coming from the broken amulet.

"Shall we go?" He motions toward the mausoleum.

As I'm about to respond, I hear a faint rustling in the shadows. My heart skips a beat, and I find myself moving closer to Costin out of instinct. "What was that?"

His mouth opens, but before Costin can answer, something bursts from the shadows, leaping onto a nearby tombstone. The small, goblin-like creature has glowing red eyes and sharp teeth, and it screeches incoherently at me. Before I can react, it lunges at me. Its gnarled claws swipe toward my face. I scream and stumble backward. My hands lift to shield me from the attack, but the creature is too fast. It lands on my arm, teeth bared as it tries to bite my throat.

Suddenly, there's a blur of motion. Costin is in front of me, moving faster than my mind can process. With a swift, almost lazy motion, he grabs the creature by the throat and holds it in the air like an angry doll. The thing screeches, thrashing about as its claws cut into Costin's flesh, but the vampire doesn't even blink.

"This one's harmless," he says, his voice eerily calm. "Just misguided."

Misguided?

Misguided!

I touch my neck and face, searching for wounds.

"She's protected." Costin tightens his grip, and the goblin whimpers before falling limp. He tosses it aside, and the creature scrambles back into the shadows, disappearing as quickly as it came.

I stare after it, my heart hammering violently in my chest.

Costin's eyes sparkle with a sinister and predatory gleam, hinting at the danger lurking within. The full threat of the moment barely registers before he says, "You're welcome."

I exhale, realizing I've been holding my breath. "I didn't... I didn't need your help."

He arches a brow and drawls sarcastically. "Of course not. I find screaming and flailing to be an effective means of protection."

I hug my arms around my body and ignore him as I search our surroundings for other threats. My self-defense instructor would be so disappointed in me.

"He'll tell the others. You have nothing to worry about." He sounds confident as he dismisses my fears, but strands of threatening red still swim in his eyes.

I feel butterflies fluttering in my stomach at the look. I hate that I feel this way. I'm drawn to him, even though I know I shouldn't be.

"Are you done with your accusations? Are you ready to listen?" He picks up the conversation as if the goblin attack didn't happen.

I nod. I don't want to, but the reaction is out of lingering fear.

Costin strikes me as the type who is not used to being contradicted.

"I'm listening," I whisper, wishing I sounded braver.

He reaches into his jacket and pulls out a small leather-bound book. He holds it between us.

I don't want it. I feel like if I touch the book, bad things will happen. No part of me wants another supernatural escapade.

Why can't my life be normal?

I don't want this.

I don't want to be here.

Tears threaten. It takes everything in me to hold them at bay.

"Take the book." Costin gives it a little shake. He looks at me like I'm a puzzle he's trying to solve.

I hate that part of me wants him to solve it.

I hesitate. Not because of the mausoleum or the goblin, not because of the prophecy. But because of him. The closer I get to Costin, the harder it is to remind myself why I need to stay away.

Defying him seems like a mistake, so I finally reach to take it. Nothing happens when my fingers touch the book, and I feel a captured breath release from my body. I turn it over in my hands to examine the plain leather cover. It looks old and smells musty, like wilting paper in the unused section of a public library.

I feel his eyes on me as I flip the cover open and look at the yellowed parchment inside. I squint, trying to see in the dark. The penmanship is old with an artistic flair, and I read, "*Wyrd bið ful aræd.*"

I struggle to sound out the words as I say aloud, "Word biofuel a road?" before shutting it. "Who wrote this? Medieval monks? I don't speak Old English."

I try to give it back to him. He refuses to take it.

His motions blur. I feel cold wrapping my wrist before my hand is jerked forward. Before I can process what is happening, I feel a sharp bite clamp into my palm. I yelp in surprise, and he lets go.

"What the fuck, Costin?" I demand, slamming my fist into his chest before backing away from him. "I told you I'm not a snack."

My blood stains his lips, and he slowly licks it. The gesture is wholly sexual, and I hate that I notice.

"Blood magic," he says.

"Annoyed human," I retort, balling my bleeding hand into a fist.

"Blood lock." He glances down at the book.

"I hate riddles. Can't you just get to the point, Beowulf? What is it you want from me? I don't have the time or inclination to get a doctorate in medieval literature."

He takes the book from me and opens it. "Hold out your hand."

I frown but obey.

"The other hand." He nods to where I'm bleeding.

I lift my bleeding palm. He places the book under it and catches a drop of my blood. The page shimmers with magic, and I watch the words transform so I can understand them. I squint to make them out. The phrase I read before changes, and I make out, "Fate cannot be changed."

"Hm," Costin looks at the page. "That is the translation you see? Interesting."

"Why? What do you see?"

"Roughly, fate is wholly inexorable," he answers. Whatever that means.

"Okay, fine, fate is fate," I dismiss, putting my fist down by my side to drip blood onto the grass. The wound throbs, but I try to ignore it. "So what? That's it? That's the great and important message?"

You can't change shit. That's the message my

grandfather sent from beyond the grave through a vampire to tell me? I'm helpless to change the past. I can't have Paul or the normal life he represents. All I have is whatever this reality is.

Costin turns the page to where more Old English words await.

"Don't tell me I have to bleed on every page." I frown, shaking my head. "This is gross. Just give me the condensed version."

I don't want to stand in the dark, trying to decipher an old crappy story that's going to fuck up my life.

"You should read it for yourself," he insists. The vampire waits like he expects me to do it right now.

"I know it's been a really long time since you were mortal, but this," I point at the moon hiding behind the clouds, "is not great reading light."

He studies my face and then nods.

"Of course, I forget human frailties." He closes the book and hands it to me. "Be careful with it. It cannot fall into the wrong hands. Don't show it to anyone, not even your family."

"Sure." I nod, tucking it under my arm.

He glances around the tombstones. The cemetery is empty except for the two of us—well, that is, if you don't count those resting beneath us. Heck, if you don't count those partying beneath us.

I wish Anthony would come back. I don't like being here. When Costin leaves, I'll be alone.

I don't know which is worse, hanging with a master vampire or being abandoned by one in a graveyard frequented by ghouls and other creepers.

He starts to turn, and I'm afraid he's leaving.

I purposefully soften my expression and let a note of vulnerability lift my tone to keep him from going. "Won't you tell me what this is about? Please, Costin. I promise I'll read it later, but don't keep me in suspense."

It works. His entire demeanor toward me relaxes.

Code switching for the win. Even undead, it would seem men are easy to manipulate. They all want to believe we're damsels in distress—helpless and in need of their eternal protection.

The idea gives me a sense of power, even if it is short-lived.

"George should have told you this. Soon after you broke your arm and he first gave you the amulet, he came to me. He had done a deal with trolls for the amulet you wore for protection. He should have known better. Troll magic is powerful, but it comes with..." He gestures his hand as if looking for the right words. "Side effects."

"Like resetting time?" My mind is instantly brought to the alternate timeline, to my birth mother and Diana and Paul. Sweet human Paul.

"So you do know. It happened?"

"I lived it." My hands are shaking, and I have to force myself to breathe. I reach into my pocket and take out the pouch with the broken amulet pieces. I hear the shards clinking against each other. They no longer vibrate, and I wonder if I just imagined it.

Finally, I have found someone who understands the depth of my experiences. It's astonishing that it turns out to be him. As I look at his face, I sense an indescribable shift within me. There's an unspoken connection that binds us together, palpable yet invisible.

What is happening to me?

"Do you remember anything from it?" I ask.

In that other timeline, he burned to death on my birthday. There is nothing for him to remember beyond the fire and his death.

"Those memories are yours alone." Costin appears to come closer, but I don't see him move. "Was it the fire? Was that the event? When I found you with the amulet on the sidewalk? Your blood tasted heavily of magical residue that night. It stung my tongue it was so thick."

"That's where time restarted." I don't speak of the weeks I lived through before the reset.

"What changed?"

I look around the cemetery, wondering if Conrad

is nearby. I don't want him to hear us, and I don't know how much to tell Costin.

"It doesn't matter."

"Tell me."

I don't want him to force me to speak the truth, so I say a condensed version. "Someone tried to steal the amulet magic for themselves, and it broke. Time reversed. Here I am."

"Someone?" he muses.

I silently beg him not to dig too deeply. "Like I said, it doesn't matter."

We remain silent. A chill lingers in the air. Shadows from clouds and moonlight slither over the tombstones. He appears unaffected. Perhaps he's simply accustomed to the night.

I wonder what it would be like to be condemned to darkness, to have to hide half of every day because sunlight equals death. To spend century after century walking the earth, dining on the same meal —human blood.

I love a good New York slice, but I wouldn't want to eat pizza every night for an eternity. The thought makes my stomach grumble.

"What are you thinking just now?" He stares at me so intently, like I'm the only thing that exists.

"I'm craving pizza," I answer. It feels kind of like a slight because he can't have any. "I guess you don't know what that's like."

"People taste like what they eat." His eyes dip over me. "Would you like me to escort you to a pizzeria?"

Of course, he took my comment like it was some bizarre offer to feed him.

I instantly shake my head and lift the book. "I want you to tell me what this is all about."

"Very well." He nods, but I sense his disappointment. "George had a premonition that led him to the prophecy."

That makes sense. My grandfather was skilled at premonitions, even more so than Uncle Mortimer.

I'm not going to think about Uncle Mortimer right now. One problem at a time.

"He mentioned that if the amulet ever broke, it meant you had saved my life, and I would owe you a life debt. He made me promise to keep you safe. It was only after gifting you the necklace that George discovered the prophecy linked to the amulet, but by then, it was too late. You had already put it on. He entrusted me with that book for safekeeping, cautioning that we must act when the moment arrives."

"What do you need me to do?" I inquire, hoping it's something easy, like tossing the pieces into a river or chanting an eerie incantation.

It won't be. It never is.

"Do you know the story of how the trolls build

their mountains to hide away from the world?" he asks.

I shake my head in denial, even though it sounds vaguely familiar.

"It was in the time before time long before magic was tamed and before man overtook the planet like a plague. They built their homes over an ancient power, an evil so great it consumed everything. It's that magic they tapped into when they made their little trinkets for the gods." He nods at the pouch I'm holding with the book. "The amulet did more than protect you. It kept something asleep, but now that it is broken, that ancient evil has been poked awake. The amulet must be mended, and the evil needs to be stopped."

Fuck me. Ancient evil?

"Mended? What, like with super glue?" I don't expect that to be the solution, but a girl can hope.

"This is not the time for jokes. This evil will consume all of us. Humans, vampires, trolls, ghouls, everything. It will bring us to the time that was before. Into chaos and pain. Humans are lucky. They will die quickly. We immortal will face an eternity of anguish."

"Who's joking?" No part of me finds this funny. "I'm very serious. Do I look like a lapidarist? I don't know how to mend magical jewels."

"It was my desire to take you down into the catacombs tonight so we could figure this out," he says. "There is a troll who—"

"How much time do we have?"

"We should act soon. I've felt a shift in the paranormal realms, a stirring. Can you not feel it in the air?" He lifts his arms to the side.

I glance around the graveyard. He keeps thinking I know something I don't. I shake my head. The only thing I feel right now is a hint of period cramps, carb cravings, and a deep fear of an ancient evil taking over the world.

You know. The usual.

"I wanted to allow you time to mourn your brother. I thought you would approach me before now. I've been waiting. Since George didn't share this with you before his death, I realize now that I should have contacted you first."

I never imagined it would turn out like this, but this reset I'm experiencing might end up worse than the previous timeline. I could end up losing everyone all over again.

The weight of the broken amulet feels heavy against my hand. What happens when I fix it? Does time start over? Will Paul and Diana remember me?

Will Paul die all over again?

What happens if I do nothing? All humans die, and Anthony and my parents suffer for an eternity.

"I don't have a choice, do I?" It's a rhetorical

question. I pull the book and the amulet close to my chest. "I should go home and read this."

"Of course." He nods once. "We can meet again tomorrow."

Everything about him is stiff and formal, from his posture to his gestures. It's not just the vampirism. He was born into the aristocracy—and not the modern-day kind. We have class differences today, but not like his era. Costin is from a time when feudal lords ruled with armies and lived in castles. They took what they wanted openly, and no one denied them.

I see those traits in him in the way he looks at me, his jaw slightly lifted, and his eyes pointed downward. He has a domineering quality to him. The swirl in his gaze hints at his blood hunger.

I'm drawn closer. There is a deepness inside of him, a dark vortex of loneliness. I feel it radiating into me. Centuries reside there, time ticking by in an endless procession. The graves fall away, as do the shadows surrounding us. The ground trembles softly against my feet like the ground releases a shaky breath.

I've known him my entire life, and yet I feel as if this is the first time I really see him. Dark lashes and smooth skin, pale from living in moonlight. His lips are stained red from tasting my blood. I've always told myself that vampires smell like ash and death, and some do, but not him. He smells of nature like the wind blew through him and left behind traces of evergreen and flowers. I feel that wind now, tickling my back and traveling over my skin.

I'm drawn into that vortex, wanting to warm it, wanting to crawl inside to bring the sun into his darkness. But he can't have the sun.

There is an ache that fills me, stopping just short of pain. The need is too strong to resist. My entire body vibrates and heats. I hear my heart beating louder and faster. I lean forward, and my eyelids feel heavy.

Someone whispers in my ear, but I can't decipher what they're saying.

Costin's face is the only thing I see. His skin seems to shimmer and blur, and he's so beautiful. I want to touch him.

No. I *need* to touch him.

"Costin," I whisper, feeling my grip on the book and amulet loosening so I can reach for him. My eyes fixate on his mouth, to the hint of parted fangs.

"That is what being mesmerized feels like," he answers.

Instantly, the fog goes away, and I'm left disorientated. The sounds of traffic blare into the silence, and I stumble on pitted concrete.

The cemetery is gone, replaced by a dank alley. The smell of nature instantly becomes the unmistakable stench of garbage wafting out of a nearby dumpster. I can no longer feel the vortex inside of Costin's chest, but the ache that came with it still lingers. The vibrations and heat leave me with an intense sexual arousal. The knowledge of it repulses me.

Correction. The knowledge of it should repulse me. To my everlasting shame, it does not.

"Where are we?" I demand, not recognizing the location.

His eyes are swirling with red. I can't tell if it's hunger or excitement. "A block from your home. I thought it best to at least escort you this far. You never know what kind of monsters you'll run into in the middle of the night. A lone human should take precautions."

I'm not sure what annoys me more. His advice or the superior way he says it. Between the two of us, I think I'm more equipped to know the danger of being a human in this world. It's the one lesson I have been told since I was old enough to understand that there really are monsters that like to crawl under your bed and hide in your closet.

"Go home, little castoff. Read the book. I will meet you back at the mausoleum at dusk."

And with that, he leaves, disappearing from the

alley as if he had never been there. I collapse against a brick wall. Now that I'm alone, I allow myself to gasp for breath. What the fuck was that?

I have never taken ecstasy but imagine this is what it would feel like. My nerves are hyper-aware, sending ripples through my body with every brush against my skin. My temperature is out of whack and too high. My hormones are crashing inside of me. I want to grab the closest man and kiss him.

No. Another correction. I want to call Costin back to finish what he started inside of me.

However, I have to give him credit for one thing. He was telling the truth. If this is what being mesmerized by a vampire feels like, he did not enthrall me before now.

I forced myself to push away from the wall and stumble toward the sound of traffic. Lights flash, letting me know that I'm heading in the right direction. I come out by a busy city street, instantly recognizing where I am. I tightly grip the book and amulet, tuck my head down, and hasten home.

I don't make eye contact with those on the street. I'm afraid if they look at me, they'll see my heightened state. No matter how hard I try, I can't walk in a straight line. My knees are weak, and I stumble as if I'm drunk.

If the expression on the doorman's face is any

indication, I look like I'm drunk, too. He's unable to hide the smirk when he sees me.

The man waits for me to approach. He looks uncomfortable and fidgety in his well-fitted navy uniform, crisp white shirt, and tie. A brass name badge and white gloves complete the ensemble.

"Miss Devine," he greets. I know he's told me before, but I can't place his name at the moment, and I can't focus my eyes long enough to read what's on his nametag. He holds the door open, and he stands inappropriately close when I move past. If I'm not mistaken, he inhales deeply, as if trying to smell my hair. I do my best to ignore it. Normally, the doormen are overly professional with polished manners. This one has a coarseness to him. He's not going to last long in this building.

Thankfully, the ecstasy effect is wearing off. The last thing I need is to get caught making out with the doorman in front of my parents' penthouse.

Keeping my head down, I rush to the elevator. My sneakers on marble sound abnormally loud, drawing attention. As the doors close, I press into a corner and stare at my distorted reflection on the shiny gold wall. My heart begins to slow, and I concentrate on regaining control of my senses. The elevator moves, and I watch the numbers count upward. Tension fills me in those seconds between each floor as I hope no one stops my ascent.

I don't want my parents or the staff to see me frazzled. I can't even think of the words I would use to explain my heightened state. Only now is it beginning to dawn on me that somehow I moved from lower Manhattan to here without memory of the trip. What had been seconds of blissful haze in my mind had to equal a minimum of twenty minutes in reality.

Unless we teleported.

Or Costin carried me with his supernatural speed.

Did he carry me? I don't remember him carrying me.

Movement along the corner of my eye startles me, and I try to chase the reflection along the doors. It's nothing. I'm still alone in the elevator.

I resist sliding down the metal wall to curl into the elevator floor. Holding my breath, I watch the doors finally open, and the foyer comes into view. I don't wait as I stumble toward my bedroom. I try to keep my footsteps quiet by running on the balls of my feet to keep my heels from thumping. I rush inside and shut the door behind me as softly as I can.

I push my back into the wooden barrier just as I pressed against the brick in the alley. Now that I'm alone, I visualize Costin standing in front of me. I try to capture that feeling of when I was under his enthrall. My body tries to make my mind follow the seductions, but my brain insists on figuring out how he moved me from the graveyard to the alley without me being aware.

There is no answer. All I remember is him—his shimmering face, that deep ache, and the smell of...

Pizza?

I frown, coming out of my thoughts as I cross the room to turn on a lamp. A pizza box sits on the end of my bed. I spin around, looking for Costin, but he's not there. I put the book and amulet pouch down and slowly open the box, feeling the heat of the food from within. Pineapple, green peppers, and ham? That's an interesting choice. Though, I suppose it's more the thought that counts. He probably stole someone's order and dropped it off in the time it took me to ride the elevator up.

My phone dings and I give a little jolt of surprise at the noise. I fumble to pull it out of my back pocket.

It's a text from Anthony. *"Come down. Let's find trouble."*

"No. Home. Have fun," I answer before tossing the phone on the bed next to my homework for the night.

I see his answer light up the screen notification, *"Boo. Boring."*

If he only knew. My life is suddenly anything but boring.

I grab a piece of pizza and begin picking off the green peppers to drop them into the box. When I bite into the slice, I can still taste the residual flavor. I wonder what made him get it for me. The gesture seems almost... sweet.

Blood smears my palm where he bit me, but it's no longer bleeding. I stop to study my hand and wonder why I don't feel as repulsed as I should.

My attention goes to the book. I'd be lying if I didn't admit I am terrified. Everything in me wants to throw it into a fireplace and forget it exists. I have enough problems with my brother's ghost haunting me, and now Mortimer's plan to marry me to a magical idiot. The idea of ancient evil coming for us is almost too much to bear.

I'm just a mortal. How am I supposed to save the world?

"Grandfather?" I whisper, wishing it was his ghost lurking in my shadows. "Why didn't you warn me about this? I don't think I can do it."

Maybe he planned to at the right moment but died before he could.

He doesn't answer. I don't expect him to.

I remember how, when I was growing up, reading books of magic had been strictly forbidden. Now, as I sit in my room, I can't shake the feeling that I'm doing something wrong. I reach for a pocket knife from my nightstand and pull the box of pizza next to me on the bed.

"Why did it have to be a blood lock?" I mutter, lifting the knife tip to my finger. With a heavy sigh, I resign myself to a long night of translating a prophecy that I want no part of, feeling the weight of my so-called destiny pressing down on me.

NINE

Here's something I now know for a fact. Prophecies written by old wizards locked in towers with too much time on their hands are rambling, slightly incoherent works of crap.

Yeah, I said it.

Well, thought it. I'd never say it out loud. Wizards can be a fun combination of powerful and insane. All that time meddling and poking at the future tends to take its toll.

Anyway, I am now convinced that the only way they could get people to read these great works of, um, "art" was to put a dire consequence at the end of them, so the reader had no choice but to sludge through miles of flowery prose. At least Shakespeare told an entertaining story in his poetic speeches.

This prophecy business is part threat, part badly written instruction manual, and all headache.

"In the moments before the first light kissed rose upon the ashen sky, trolls labored deep inside the belly of," blah, blah, blah, ten highly detailed paragraphs later, *"coaxing stones upward to create the cradle of the mountains,"* more blah, three pages later, *"burrowing the ancient ones deeper into the depths,"* something about titans and magical creatures, skim ahead, *"giving home to goblins and other magic dwellers."*

I want to take the prophecy seriously. I get that it's important, but damn, it made for a long night. Now, as I sit at the bar next to the kitchen, I'm tired and grouchy. Plus, my fingers hurt from cutting them all night.

No part of me wants to save the world.

Heat from the coffee mug warms my hands as I stare into the creamy liquid. I tap my bare toes on the marble floor as they dangle from the stool. At one point in the night, I showered and traded my jeans for blue pajama pants but kept the fuck you t-shirt. It's a small rebellion, but it's mine.

At least my period ended, and the cramps are gone. That's a positive in my sea of negative.

I finally fell asleep around six in the morning, but the four hours before Astrid had a housekeeper wake me were fitful and filled with nightmares. The kitchen is empty except for me and the current personal chef placing a bowl of sliced fruit in front of me for breakfast.

"What? No bacon?" I ask, partly because I'd rather have bacon and partly just to see the worry on his face as he tries to tell me Astrid forbids it. Yeah, it's childish, but I've been doing it to the staff since I could talk.

There is no distress as he shakes his head. "I have your dietary restrictions, Miss Devine. It's not on the approved menu. I can make you a bowl of oatmeal or a kale smoothie if you prefer."

I curl my lip at him and reach for a sliced strawberry. "This coffee better not be decaf, or I'm going on a rampage."

Seriously, a girl can only take so much.

He leans toward me and winks. "Of course not. I'm not a complete monster. Want me to sneak you an espresso shot?"

"You're all right, uh…" I look at his uniform for a name. It would have been on the staff memo Astrid left in my room, but I rarely read them. She goes through a lot of changeovers in the penthouse.

He points at his chest, "Howard."

"You're all right, Howard," I say, pointing into my cup for that shot.

Howard sets to work at the espresso machine. He's a lanky man in his forties with inky black hair vainly clinging to the top of his balding head. I notice calluses and scars on his hands. There are peeks of full-sleeve tattoos on his arms from beneath his uniform. I watch him return with the shot to dump it into my coffee.

"Bless you, sir," I mutter instantly, sipping the stronger liquid.

"So, are you nervous?" Howard asks conversationally as he makes a show of wiping down the clean counter.

I blink, confused. How does he know about the prophecy? "I'm sorry?"

"The wedding."

I choke a little on my coffee and clear my throat.

"Lady Astrid mentioned you're getting officially engaged tonight." He looks at his smartwatch. "I promise the menu will be worthy of such an event. I'm expecting a delivery of fresh shellfish in the next hour. It's being flown in. How about I sneak a little bacon into the recipe for the bride-to-be? Don't worry. We'll still make sure you fit into your wedding dress."

I resist the urge to answer. Nothing I say will be appropriate. I hide my expression in my coffee mug and force out a strange sound that's supposed to double as a response.

"Don't be worried. Tonight is for celebrating," he chuckles. "Cold feet are for the wedding day."

"Thanks for the coffee." I push up from my stool

and take the mug with me. Trying to say something polite, I add, "I have so much planning to... yeah."

I hurry from the kitchen as fast as I can. Nowhere in this house feels safe, but my bedroom is the best option. I don't make it very far.

"Hold it right there," Astrid orders. The snap of her fingers follows her voice as she beckons me to her.

Years of childhood training kick in, and I instantly obey. I turn toward the foyer, where Astrid stands by the front door, holding a blue silk gown draped over her arm. As always, she looks immaculate, with perfect hair and makeup. Her dress is the height of New York fashion. Just once, I want to see her with a ponytail and pajama pants, eating ice cream out of a tub.

She crosses to me and holds the dress material against my face.

"This color is much better suited." Astrid drapes the gown over my arm, careful to miss my coffee mug. "Is that decaf?"

I nod and lie, "Uh-huh."

"Good. I don't want you all hyperactive and fidgety tonight." Her expression is all business. "You will wear this gown. We'll have to figure out another dress for the charity ball. The Freemonts will be here at six to sign the betrothal agreement. It's with the lawyers right now. I just came from there. After it is signed, an elder from the wizard council will seal it."

"That was fast." I feel like a deer in someone's gunsight as the start of my horrible future is laid out for me. I hold the soft silk over my arm to keep it from dragging on the floor.

"No reason to put a decision off once it is made," Astrid answers.

I'm deciding not to marry Chester. And I'm definitely okay not putting that decision off.

"What's wrong with your hand?" She eyes the puncture wounds. The skin is a little bruised and discolored. "Vampire?"

I don't answer.

"Never mind. I'll give you something to heal that before tonight. The Freemonts will never know."

"Thanks."

"Your affair with Costin stops now. We can't have anyone finding out about that."

I don't bother denying the affair. None of them seem to believe me, anyway.

"After a few years of marriage, people will lose interest, and you can discretely take up with him again," she says. "Nod that you understand."

I nod.

"Have you seen Anthony? He wasn't in his room this morning. I want to make sure he puts in an appearance tonight. It's important that the family shows solidarity." She looks at me expectantly.

I shake my head in denial. "I haven't seen him this morning. I believe he went out with friends last night."

"Very well. About tonight… Before signing, you will be expected to formally apologize for that unfortunate business with their lost shipping container," she continues. "Keep it short and don't get emotional. It's a formality."

I worked for a short time as a shipping clerk for my father's company. I miskeyed an entry, and a secret shipment was lost somewhere in the Atlantic. I have no clue what was in there, but it was enough to get me instantly fired. I had no idea it belonged to the Freemonts.

"What are you going to say?" Astrid asks.

"Um." I frown. "I formally apologize?"

"Good." She nods. "Hopefully, this marriage will end that discussion once and for all. Between us, I wouldn't be surprised if that is the cause of this whole threat against our family."

Gee, thanks, Mom.

"If you ask me, they're being ridiculous about the whole thing. We have the merfolk and every other sea creature searching the ocean bottom for it. What more do they want?" She waves her hand as if she can erase the whole unpleasant incident. "Mabel

Freemont is a drama junkie who hasn't seen a fainting couch she didn't want to land on. Between us, she's always been jealous of me because she wanted to marry your father. Instead, she wound up with Francis Freemont, who has the face of a puffer fish."

I snort, trying to hold back a laugh. "I never understood how that man got a stable of mistresses."

The second I say it, I regret it. I don't want my mother to think I'm criticizing her life.

Astrid takes a deep breath and then gives a wry smile. "Love potions and a yearly membership to the aquarium. His latest mistress has the mouth of a trout. I wouldn't be surprised if she's a fish shifter."

This time, I can't hold my laughter back. Partly, I'm shocked that she said it to me, but mostly, it's the fact she's laughing too. The sound is very rare in our conversations.

I have to wonder what is causing this shift in her demeanor toward me. Does she see me as an equal now that I'm marrying into her same circumstance? Only I need to believe she loves my father in her way. I don't love Chester. I don't even like him. The sound of his voice makes my skin crawl.

I'm not stupid enough to ask.

My laughter fades, and her expression returns to the reserved façade I'm used to seeing.

Astrid studies me for a long moment and I wait for her criticisms. Finally, she says, "I'm proud of you, Tamara, doing this for your family."

Proud of me.

The words strike me hard in the chest. Astrid may be reserved, and I might complain about her, but she's said nice things to me over the years. This is different. All I ever wanted was for her to be proud of me as a daughter. Even after I found out she wasn't my birth mother, I still seek her approval. Now I have it, and all I have to do is give up my future.

I've spent my whole life trying to earn her approval. Even now, part of me still craves it. Maybe if I go along with the family's plans—marry Chester, secure the alliance—she'll finally look at me like I'm not a disappointment. Maybe she'll finally see me as something more than just the mortal lovechild she got stuck with raising.

It's a foolish dream. No matter what I do, I'll never be enough for her. I'll never be her true daughter.

"Thank you," I whisper, unable to say anything else.

She lightly touches my cheek. "And you'll do something about your hair? The curls are escaping captivity again."

It's not a question, but I nod that I understand.

I can't stop staring at her face, knowing that soon her expression will turn to disappointment. What she's asking of me is too much. I can't condemn myself to a life married to Chester.

"I appreciate everything you've done for me," I tell her.

"I need to speak to the chef to finalize the menu," she answers, turning her back to me. Whatever sweet moment that passed between us is over.

I watch her walk away, wondering what my future will hold. I pray it won't be an arranged marriage. Out of all my fates facing me, that one feels like the worst. At least with an ancient evil, it will be a fast end. The idea of spending the rest of my short, mortal life looking down the dining table at Chester, letting him touch me, thankful that he has his mistresses so I don't have to spend time with him, putting all my attention into appearances... that's the real definition of hell.

I head toward my room with renewed purpose. The amulet changed my future once. Maybe it can do it again.

When I enter my bedroom, I find a maid has left the curtains open to let the daylight in. The bed has been made with a fresh comforter and sheets, and my dirty clothes have been picked up off the floor. The pizza box has also disappeared.

I set my coffee on the nightstand before laying

the gown across the bottom of the bed to keep it from wrinkling. I then hurry to change out of my pajama pants into a pair of jeans. I shrug out of the t-shirt, discarding it on the floor only to replace it with another. This one has the word "*love*" written across the chest in cursive. It does not fit my mood as well as the finger flipping off everybody, but it's clean and was on top of the pile.

I drop a pair of sneakers next to the bed before kneeling on the carpet to dig the book out from behind my dresser where I hid it. I can't help but think it's pathetic that I'm twenty-eight years old and going to run away from home.

Then again, I know there are some who would argue that it's a little pathetic that I'm twenty-eight and still living in my parents' home.

Those people can kiss my ass.

The air in the room feels still, too still. I hear a soft scrape. The heavy feeling in the pit of my stomach tells me I didn't imagine the sound. My attention goes across the room to a framed photograph on my nightstand. It's of me and Conrad during happier times. A maid must have taken it out of my dresser drawer and put it back. The picture appears to move on its own, the motion so slight I almost miss it.

A chill works up my spine, causing the hairs on

the back of my neck to stand on end. I freeze, stuck with my arm between the wall and the dresser.

"Congratulations are in order." Conrad's voice is loud. His energy is up. That's not a great sign.

I release my hold on the book, leaving it where it is as I withdraw my arm. Touching my earlobe, I ask, "Have you seen my diamond earrings?"

"One of the maids probably stole them," he answers.

I push up from the floor. He's standing by the bed, staring at the blue silk gown. His form is more solid than usual. I can barely see through him.

"Lady Chester Freemont," he mocks. There was a dark, gravelly quality to his voice. He doesn't sound like he did when he was alive.

"I think the word you're looking for is Mrs."

"Ah, come on, don't sell yourself short. As Lady Astrid Junior, I think you deserve the same made-up title of aristocracy." He turns toward me, the black pits of his eyes reminding me of the darkness inside of him.

"Let me guess, you're here to tell me I better not marry into a family so powerful." Finally, there is one thing we would agree on.

"No," he says to my surprise. "I want you to marry him. I want to watch you squirm when he comes into the room. I want you to squeeze out his ugly babies. Every time he touches you, I want you to know that you are trapped in a loveless sham and can never have Paul. And I'm going to be there as your constant companion, watching you grow old and wither."

"What happened to you to make you so twisted?" I'm not trying to be an asshole. I really want to know. "I loved—"

"I loved you, Conrad. I loved you, Conrad," he mocks my voice. "I considered you a brother, Conrad."

"You're not funny."

"Please," he gives a wave of his hand, "spare me your emotional bullshit."

"It's not bullshit," I defend weakly. "I would have done anything for you."

"Apparently not," he laughed. "Otherwise, you would have died in the fire like you were supposed to."

If he had not been born human, I might wonder if he was the ancient evil that I am meant to stop. But to classify Conrad as evil... I can't do it. Even now. Even after everything. There is a part of me that wants to make excuses for him, that doesn't want to see what he truly is even as it stares back at me from those lifeless eyes.

Conrad is not evil. He's broken, and he's done evil things.

I am making excuses for him again, just like

when he was alive. Deep down, I know better. I've seen the darkness in his eyes, the cruelty that lingers behind his smile. I have to tell myself that he wasn't always this way—that there was a time when we were just two kids trying to survive in a world we didn't belong to.

Somewhere along the way, everything distorted inside of him, and now I see nothing left of the brother I used to love.

And yet, a piece of me still hopes. I want to believe that I can save him, that there's still something good inside him. I take a deep, calming breath. I know better. The last time I made excuses for him, Paul died. I have seen what he's capable of. He's dangerous. And I can't afford to forget that.

"You're thinking of running, aren't you?" He glances down at my sneakers and smiles before gliding closer to me.

I take an involuntary step back. My fear gives him pleasure.

He comes close. I can feel the chill radiating off his spirit. "Sorry, little bird. This is one cage you can't escape."

I watch in horror as he vanishes from sight. The sound of the lock on my bedroom door clicks loudly. I rush to the door, frantically twisting and shaking the doorknob, but it refuses to budge. I am trapped inside.

Conrad's laughter reverberates through the room, reminiscent of the lively music from the parties we were never allowed to attend as children. My heart races with anxiety. This can't be happening. I can't be here. I need to get out.

I desperately knock on the door, hoping someone will come to my aid and open it. I scream for help, but no one answers. Realizing that I'm trapped, I let go of the door and back away. The sulfuric smell of Conrad's ghost lingers in the room, leaving me at a loss for what to do.

My mind races. I look around the bedroom, turning in circles as I try to formulate a plan. Seeing the picture, I grab it from the nightstand and throw it in the trash can in my bathroom. I don't want Conrad staring at me.

I don't know what to do. I'm just a human. I'm not special. Isn't that what they've been telling me since the day I was born?

I want a normal life with Paul. But that's never going to happen. My life is too dangerous for normal. Not for the first time I tell myself that I need to forget him. They're better without me. Besides, I really only knew him for a week. Am I really going to let myself pine away over the love I had for one week? My brain and my heart have two very different answers to that question. Logic needs to win. I need to let him go.

The family elders expect me to marry Chester. It would be the path of least resistance. It would make a powerful alliance for the family. Astrid would be happy. I would finally have her respect. It would keep them safe from the threat of Mortimer's premonition. But I can't do it.

I wish my grandfather was here. He would know what I need to do. He would never let them marry me off to the Freemont family.

Then there's Costin and the prophecy.

Costin is dangerous. I feel it every time the vampire is near me. I can't get the look in his eyes out of my mind. There is a darkness in him, ancient and untouchable. He's a predator that's been stalking the shadows of this world for centuries.

My grandfather trusted him, but why? Why place the weight of this prophecy in the hands of a vampire?

Costin acts like he's just a guide sent to protect me and see the prophecy through, but he knows more than he's letting on. I'm not sure I want to find out what that is.

But the scariest part is, despite all my fears, I want to trust him. I want to let him in, to believe that he can keep me safe.

What is wrong with me? I'm a hot mess.

What was my grandfather thinking when he neglected to tell me about his alliance with a master vampire on my behalf? If the prophecy is true and an ancient evil is rising from the depths of the earth to consume us all, then my other problems don't matter. If this ancient evil is real, and if it succeeds, everyone will be dead or tortured. It won't just harm the people I love—it will bring suffering to the entire world.

Considering the potential consequences, there is no question as to which path I need to take. I need to confront this threat, even when that path is uncertain and filled with danger. I grapple with the weight of this responsibility, and I find myself questioning my place in this crazy world.

Grandfather George is the only person who ever really loved me unconditionally. Despite my aversion to vampires, I trust my grandfather. And he trusted Costin. He put the book of prophecies in the hands of a vampire over those of our family. He told Costin about the magical curse attached to the amulet, but no one else.

It looks like I'm going deeper into the supernatural realm. It is a place I don't belong. But then, I really don't belong in the mortal world either.

"Conrad?" I say to the empty room. "Are you there?"

He doesn't answer. The scent of his spirit is beginning to lighten. Although I can't be one hundred percent sure, I think he's gone for now.

I wait for a few minutes, listening to my surroundings before carefully retrieving the book. Someone will come to let me out of the room eventually. All I need to do is wait.

Piling the pillows along my headboard, I make a comfortable nest to read. I flip open the book and see the words, *"Fate cannot be changed."*

I turn past the flowery, very detailed troll history lesson—it's literally like the first two-thirds of the book—to the meat of the prophecy. No matter how many times I went over the words last night, I couldn't find any actionable clues. Most of it is vague statements and dire warnings. I can only imagine what it would sound like if the blood lock didn't translate it into something I can supposedly understand. Sure, the words make sense, but for fuck's sake, wizards.

My book report would read: *I have to fix a magic stone somehow, or everyone dies horribly.*

Here's me trying again. Maybe daylight will make it easier to understand.

"A mortal born with immortality lost..."

Okay, I'm relatively sure that means me, the mortal in an immortal family.

"...upon the shattering of the troll magic, the countdown commences, and swift action becomes imperative within four full cycles of the lunar moon."

Let's forget for a second that "lunar moon" is

redundant. I had to look this one up on my phone, but a moon cycle is roughly equal to a month, or a little less. It's been over three months since Conrad broke the amulet. That means the clock is ticking. Costin wasn't being dramatic when he said we needed to get going on this.

"When the destined soul beholds these words, omens shall guide their way to the realm of prosperity."

I look around the bedroom, not seeing any magical signs. Unless the locked door is one? It's telling me don't do it.

"Maybe I'm not the chosen one," I mutter, turning the page.

"...embracing a power long laid dormant..."

I don't have any dormant powers. I've never had them. That's the one true fact of my life. Now, suddenly, this book is telling me I need to embrace my supernatural heritage?

Or is it telling me to embrace the evil power that's been dormant?

Or is it telling me the wizard who wrote this is an asshole?

I vote asshole.

It's impossible to stay positive considering everything that's going on.

Oh, and here's my favorite bit. Feel the sarcasm leaking from my eyeballs.

"In the depths of shadows, foes masquerade as

friends. Their hidden truths poised to unfurl and rend. Tough decisions must be embraced, or a world unmade lest dire fates befall, and all efforts begin to fade."

What. The. Fuck.

Don't trust Costin? My grandfather did. He basically sent him to be my life-debted adventure buddy. That means something. Unless this is a test.

Don't trust Uncle Mortimer? Done.

Don't trust my future—*gag*—husband? Never have.

Or is it referring to Conrad's betrayal? Is it something that already happened that kick-started these events?

I don't want to be doing this. None of this.

"Behold the shattered fragments in need of mending, where the restless wickedness yearns to be unchained but shall instead be forever tamed."

Fix amulet. Got it.

Maybe that's my dormant power? The amulet's protection. If I fix that, maybe I fix everything.

But do I really want to go through this again? What happens if time is reset? What if I'm not enough? The thought of falling deeper into the supernatural world—into that scary realm beneath the mausoleum—makes my stomach churn. I can only imagine what is down there, and it terrifies me.

Costin wants me to follow him, to trust him. But how can I trust someone who's part of this prophecy

I never wanted? A master vampire at that. Humans shouldn't trust vampires, that's kindergarten stuff.

And yet, what choice do I have?

I try not to let myself think about Paul. Even if I get the opportunity to pursue that life, I don't think I should. This prophecy business proves that. I need to let him go. Maybe everyone else is right, and I need to lean into the supernatural protection that my family can offer. Maybe it's time to grow up and embrace my responsibilities. I can only hope that does not mean marrying Chester.

The last page is an illustration. It's difficult to tell, but I think it depicts people dying in a river of lava coming from a volcano. This is the one page I didn't drop blood on to translate. I search the details for clues, but don't see any. I'm not sure it will do any good, and I'm not exactly sure I want to see what it has to say, but I scratch at the scab covering one of the puncture wounds from Costin's bite.

Taking a deep breath, I glance nervously around the room, looking for Conrad. I don't see him. Squeezing a little blood out of my hand, I tap it against the page.

Nothing happens.

The smear of my blood soaks into the page. I stare at the lava river, not seeing any changes. There don't appear to be any answers hidden within the drawing.

I hear a click on my door, and it creaks open to reveal a sliver of freedom.

"Oh, thank goodness." I hop up from the bed and grab my sneakers, phone, and the prophecy book. Clutching them to my chest, I rush to escape the bedroom.

I don't know who opened the door, and I don't care. All I know is I can't be here tonight to sign a betrothal agreement.

Conrad is not waiting for me in the hallway.

The penthouse feels stifling, all marble and glass

reflecting the luxury of my family's world. The chandeliers overhead glitter, casting a soft light over the spotless surfaces. Yet all I can see are the invisible cracks underneath—the secrets, the manipulations, the expectations. This is the life they want me to live, trapped in a cage of wealth and power. But none of it matters—not Mortimer's premonitions or my engagement to Chester—not with what's coming.

I clutch the prophecy book tighter, feeling its weight in my hands, and for a moment, I wonder if this could be all just a bad dream. The thick windows silence the sound of the city below. Not for the first time, I think we're living in a bubble, disconnected and lifted from the chaos outside.

But I know that bubble is about to burst.

I feel the floor tremble beneath my feet and instantly reach for the wall to steady myself. It is a strange sensation, but it stops as quickly as it begins. I continue to make my way toward the elevators. I stay close to the wall and keep my head down so as not to draw attention. I hear sounds from the kitchen and assume that Howard is preparing for tonight's party.

I call up the elevator and use the time waiting to tug on my sneakers. The elevator dings its arrival, and I flinch at the noise. The second the door opens, I slip inside.

"Whose there?" I hear my father's voice as the doors shut.

I press against the corner so he doesn't see me.

I shove my phone into my back pocket and lift my shirt to tuck the book into my waistband. It's not comfortable, but I let my T-shirt hide it from view.

I watch the numbers count down from the penthouse. I'll figure out a place to hide out until dusk, when I can meet Costin by the mausoleum.

Errrrrrrch.

A loud groan sounds overhead, and the elevator jerks. I grab onto the handrail, gripping tight as I stare at the lighted numbers. I'm only halfway down.

Err. Err. Errrrch. Screech.

The metal box vibrates and shudders, only to lurch several times. It tosses me around as I lose my footing. My hands shake as I try to hold on. The numbers tick down slowly. I think everyone, at one point or another, has imagined what it would be like to have the cables in an elevator snap. It seems like it would be a pretty common fear. I never actually thought that fear would become real.

The screeches turn to grinds as if the metal is scraping against metal. The shaking stops, and I feel like I'm moving faster. The numbers tick by one after the other, blinking at a speed that cannot be safe.

"Help!" I yell, the sound coming out more like a scream than a word.

My body suddenly becomes light, as if I'm in free fall. My stomach does little flips, and my heart beats so hard I feel like I might throw it up. I scream as the elevator barrels down toward the lobby. I close my eyes tight as I approach the final countdown. Suddenly, gravity returns, and I fall to my knees, still gripping the rail. I feel tears on my face, and I can't move. I can't force my eyes to open.

The sudden ding of the elevator startles me, and I gasp as the doors slide open. Relief washes over me for a brief moment, but it quickly dissipates as I'm met with the dissonance of terrifying sounds.

The blaring of car horns from the street blends with the screams of people running past the lobby window. As if that weren't alarming enough, deafening explosions momentarily drown out the chaos, and plumes of dust fill the air, adding to the sense of panic and fear.

"Get down! Get down!" The doorman runs inside, covered in dust, before diving behind the front desk.

Despite the sense of impending danger, I sprint toward the front door, compelled to see what's happening for myself. Pressing my face and hands against the glass, I feel the thick security door quiver. Suddenly, another deafening boom reverberates through the air, accompanied by a cloud of dust. The piercing sound of more screams stampede past.

The scene is chaotic. Dust swirls in the air as I struggle to make sense of the commotion. A woman frantically runs toward me, clutching a small dog in her arms. Without hesitation, I push open the heavy door, allowing her to seek refuge inside.

As she hurries past me, I catch a glimpse of terror in her eye. The air is filled with piercing screams and the distant sound of sirens, disorienting me further. Instinctively, I cover my nose and mouth with my sleeve, attempting to protect myself from the swirling dust and debris.

Suddenly, an unseen force yanks me outward, pulling me from the relative safety of the building and onto the frenzied sidewalk. The disharmony of screams and shouts grows louder, seeming to emanate from all directions. Confused and struggling to regain my footing, I attempt to understand the unfolding events.

Another deafening boom echoes through the city streets, sending shockwaves over the ground. I stand frozen, watching in horror as a nearby building crumbles into a pile of rubble. My breath catches in my throat as I brace for the suffocating plume of dust rolling toward me, but to my surprise, it doesn't engulf me.

Panic seizes the crowd as people scatter in all directions, desperate to escape the attack. I find myself swept along with the frantic throng, my heart pounding in my chest as I try to make sense of the unfolding mayhem. Everything is chaos. No one seems to have answers.

All at once, the daylight changes, taking on a mesmerizing orange hue. It casts a warm glow as it encases the dusty air. Suddenly, a strange rumble fills the air, and the sound of rubber tires pop in rapid succession. The screams behind me grow fainter, swallowed by the unsettling noise. The orange glow intensifies, bathing the scene in an otherworldly hellscape that compels me to stop running and turn to face the source of the phenomenon.

A river of scorching lava snakes its way through the streets, swallowing everything in its path. The acrid stench of burn fills the air as billows of black smoke blackout the heavens, obscuring the once-bright sun. All we have now is the orange glow of death coming for us.

As I frantically attempt to flee, a sudden impact sends me crashing to the ground. I gasp for breath as a heavy foot forcefully presses into my stomach, and then a sharp blow to my ribs follows as panicked figures trample past in a frenzied attempt to escape.

Before I can make it to my feet, the lava reaches me. I don't expect to survive. I push up from the ground just as it rolls against my legs. I automatically scream in fright, waiting for the feel of my body melting just as it consumes those around me. The prophecy book slips out of my waistband, and I watch it sizzle into oblivion.

The pain doesn't come. I feel the pressure of the lava against my legs, but it doesn't burn. I turn to look around. An eerie silence replaces the panic, and I realize I'm the only one left standing. An alarm blares in the distance, but it's way too late to warn anybody.

The deafening roar of falling buildings reverberates through the city. The air is heavy with a suffocating mix of dust and ash, obscuring everything in a murky shroud. I desperately spin in circles, seeking an escape from the lava, but there is no refuge to be found in this desolate landscape.

A loud rumble sounds behind me, and I turn in time to see my home crashing to the ground. Chunks of concrete rain down, splashing into the infernal landscape the street has become.

Tears stream down my face as I come to a chilling realization. My parents are in that building. They may be immortal, but that does not mean they can't be killed. There is no way they would have survived the fall.

I took too long to heed the prophecy, allowing

doubt to cloud my judgment and ignoring fate. Now, I am faced with the grave consequences of my inaction.

How am I still alive?

I don't understand how I survive when everyone else is dead. Is this a punishment? Is the universe holding me responsible for my inaction? The lava swirls around me, consuming everything else in its path, but I remain untouched, a spectator to the end of the world.

I can't help but wonder, why me? Why am I the one who has to fix this?

Can it even be fixed?

I want out of the lava. I see it rushing around a large chunk of the building, and I hurry to climb onto the debris. Sharp edges cut my hands, but I don't care.

The air grows thick with ash, choking the sky. Every breath feels like it should be my last. I taste the ash against my tongue, but I somehow keep breathing. The actual terror isn't the destruction but the emptiness that comes after. The horrible silence. The screams, the panic... all of it is gone.

The buildings continue to collapse around me like sandcastles under a rising tide of molten lava. I watch as glass windows explode, showering the streets with glittering shards, while the once-proud city skyline crumbles into ash. I am alone in a world on fire, the last witness to everything I've ever known turning to dust.

Why won't it kill me, too?

Why didn't I go with Costin when he asked me to?

The heat is unbearable, but what's worse is the hard knot in my chest where my heart should be. I watch as smoke rises from the destruction. I can't bury the knowledge that this is my fault. I let this happen. I failed. I didn't listen to the warnings, and now there's no one left to save.

I remain trapped on the rubble, hearing more buildings fall in the distance. The sounds seem to stretch on forever.

This can't be it.

Why am I alive?

I search for signs of life, but there are none.

"Help!" I yell. "Is anyone there?"

How do I stop this? How can I make it right?

The amulet reversed time once before, maybe...

I fumble to feel my pockets. In my haste, I forgot the amulet upstairs. I look at the destroyed building. I'll never find it now.

My fingers bump the phone in my back pocket, and I grab it. The screen is flickering and I'm not getting any signal.

I set the useless object down on my concrete

island and pull my knees to my chest. I close my eyes and lean my head down, willing it all to go away. I don't know how long I sit there. More crashes puncture the silence. I can't begin to comprehend the full depth of my loss. Everyone I care about is gone.

This is how the world ends, and it's all my fault.

ELEVEN

"Stand up straight," Astrid orders in a hushed breath. Her annoyance is clear, but I don't understand how she got there.

I gasp, opening my eyes and lifting my head.

The apocalyptic landscape is gone, replaced by the undamaged penthouse foyer. Confused, I look around the home. How did I get back up here?

I'm standing upright next to my mother. I instantly try to hug her, relieved that she's alive. Astrid blocks my arms and knocks them away. I see magic surge defensively on her fingertips before she catches herself. I caught her by surprise.

"I told you that dash of potion in your coffee would make you feel better. No need to sit in anxiety all day when magic can make it all better." Astrid keeps her voice low. She pats my hair, and it reminds me of the seconds before I passed out in the limo after my birthday fire. "Now compose yourself. The Freemonts are waiting."

The weight of the apocalyptic vision still clings to me, like the vestiges of a world that no longer exists. I can still feel the heat of the burning city, the suffocating silence of a world that crumbled under my failure. But here I am, back in this gilded cage, about to be forced into a marriage I never wanted.

How can she not see it? How can she be blind to what's coming? It felt so real.

If I do nothing, that is the future that awaits us. I think of the burning city, the ash raining down like some twisted mockery of snowflakes, and I know—if I run from this, there will be nothing left to save.

I want to scream at her, to make her understand the stakes, but the words stick in my throat. She doesn't know about the prophecy. All she and the rest of the elders care about is power and alliances and Mortimer's premonitions. Chester Freemont is just another piece on their chessboard, and I'm the sacrificial pawn.

I can't be here. Costin was right. I have to act. I have to go with him and face my fate. But how can I do that when I'm trapped, suffocating under the family elders' expectations?

"I chose well. That gown is perfect on you," Astrid says.

Gown? I follow her gaze downward. Who cares about gowns?

I'm in the blue silk dress and high heels. The material hugs my curves, the flowing fabric cool against my skin. The glint of diamonds around my wrist catches my attention as they glisten in the soft light, casting tiny sparkles of light onto the nearby wall. The puncture wounds on my hand are healed. Something weighs down my head, and as I reach up to touch my hair, my fingers bump against cold, smooth stones.

Am I wearing a tiara?

"How did I get—?" I don't remember her giving me a potion to drink. In fact, she never touched my coffee.

"Are you sure you don't know where your brother has gone off to?" Astrid talks over me. "We can't find him. He should be here."

I could answer that I last saw him at the *Marcheur de Nuit Mausoleum*, but I'm not ratting him out. There is no point in both of us having to suffer through this evening.

I press my heel firmly into the marble floor and steal a quick glance over my shoulder, assessing my options for a swift escape.

I remember the fear I felt in the falling elevator. I should never have translated the illustration. All it did was scare the crap out of me and cause a time slip that put me squarely where I can't be. Magic clearly explained away whatever state I was in before now by making Astrid believe she gave me a potion.

My mother touches my arm in reassurance. "You have nothing to worry about. The lawyers have seen to everything. Mortimer spoke with the Freemonts. They're on board with the arrangement."

"I don't want to marry him," I tell her, trying to grip her arm in my desperation. "Please don't make me. I find him repulsive."

Astrid removes her hand from me. "Life is rarely about what we want. Focus on why you must."

Mortimer's premonition or my grandfather's prophecy?

I don't want to do either, but maybe I don't have a choice.

A reedy laugh comes from the living room. The sound is unmistakably Chester. It makes my skin crawl, and I recoil.

"Do it for your family," Astrid says. "I can give you something to help with the marital duties. It'll be like you're not even there."

Did she just offer to drug me through my wedding night?

I mean... well, yeah. Not remembering sex with Chester would be the ideal.

Wait, no. I can't even fathom all of that right now.

"Never mind. We can discuss that later. Our guests are waiting." Astrid gestures that I'm to follow her.

I don't want to do this.

As we enter the living room, I steel my nerves and school my expressions. Chester and his parents sit with my father. They glance in my direction, but my appearance is not enough to stop Francis. He's too busy recounting his latest business conquest.

"You must go to the underground market cigar auction in Paris," Francis says to my father, leaning back with a satisfied grin. "I outbid everyone, of course. There was some tech tycoon desperate to get his hands on this box of Cubans. I doubled every one of his bids. You should have seen his face. Worth every penny."

He laughs boisterously, not caring if anyone else in the room joins him.

As they continue to ignore me, I can't help but steal a moment to observe my would-be fiancé, Chester Freemont. He is the embodiment of entitled wealth, and it's easy to see where he gets the attitude. Through no merit of his own and suffering no hardships, Chester made it clear on our dates that he believes the world owes him whatever he wants.

Though he looks like he's in his early 30s, I know him to be older. Such is the way with immortals.

Chester's appearance perfectly aligns with his personality. His hair is meticulously slicked back, so shiny it almost appears greasy. He often dons designer suits that are both wrinkle-free and taste-less, exuding an air of expensive yet questionable fashion sense. His pale complexion resembles that of someone perpetually clammy, and a smug smirk seems to be permanently etched on his face. When he laughs, it's a thin, high-pitched sound that grates on the nerves, echoing unpleasantly through the room. His affected, bored tone slithers through conversations, drawing attention to his unlikable nature and leaving an uncomfortable atmosphere in its wake.

His parents exemplify his attitude. His mother constantly wrinkles her nose as if she's caught a whiff of something unpleasant, while his father dominates conversations, blustering loudly and overpowering anyone else who tries to interject.

"You know, Tamara." Francis finally turns his attention to where I'm waiting. He takes a cigar from his jacket and tips it toward me before placing it in his mouth. "It's important to understand that we Freemonts only settle for the best."

The way he says it, the implication is clear. They're doing me a favor by allowing me to marry into their prestigious family. He produces a second cigar for my father.

Francis's attention causes the others to acknowledge I'm there, as if giving them permission to turn their attention to me.

I can't marry into this family.

I'd rather jump off the balcony.

Only I can't. If I take the easy way out, Conrad will go after Paul.

Fuck, life is unfair!

"Tamara." Chester stands and holds out his arms like he expects me to run into them. "You look lovely."

"Doesn't she," Astrid agrees. "The blue suits her."

Chester is staring at my chest. I don't think he's thinking about the blue. I hunch my shoulders forward to hide my figure. In the slinky material, it does little good.

When I don't cross over to him, he comes toward me. His eyes move over my body as if inspecting a broodmare he's about to purchase. I won't be surprised if he pulls my lips back to check my teeth and lifts my feet off the floor to inspect my hooves.

Even Chester's mannerisms get on my nerves. He's always leaning in too close, like he's trying to dominate the conversation. And that smile of his never quite reaches his eyes, which always appear cold and calculating. His voice oozes smarminess, dripping with fake charm and condescension. Every drawled word is a reminder of his wealth, and he flaunts it so effortlessly that it's obnoxious. It's like he's used to always being treated like the smartest person in the room, but most of his ideas lack substance and seem to rely solely on his family's fortune.

Chester flashes his too-white teeth and reaches to take my hand. His eyes lazily rake over me. His grip tightens as he pulls me closer, once more leaning in just a bit too far to invade my space.

I want to pull away, to wipe the smug look off his face with a solid punch. For a moment, I imagine Costin shaking him like a goblin rag doll before tossing him across the room. The thought makes me smile. Chester mistakes the look as being for him and reaches to run his fingers down my arm suggestively. My skin crawls at the thought of being tied to him, trapped in his nightmare of a family.

My smile instantly becomes a grimace.

"You really should relax, darling," Chester continues, his voice barely a whisper. "Once we're married, you'll see that life can be quite comfortable. You'll have everything you want as long as you behave as I wish."

I lean away from him and resist the urge to slap him. His very touch makes me want to shower in hot acid. He lifts my hand to his mouth and places a kiss against my knuckles. I swear I feel his tongue dart between my fingers. I automatically jerk back.

Gross.

Astrid arches a brow of warning at my reaction.

Chester's mother stands and comes toward me. "We are so happy to welcome you into the family, dear."

Mabel studies me like she's appraising a piece of fine china, not a future daughter-in-law. Her tight smile doesn't quite reach her eyes.

I don't answer. No one seems to notice or care.

Mabel turns to her husband and demands, "Aren't we, Francis?"

"Yes, quite," Francis mumbles.

"You poor thing. You look out of sorts," Mabel continues, her tone clipped. "We understand this must be overwhelming for you, but it's such a wonderful match, don't you think? Our family has been in good standing for centuries, and it's only fitting that we align ourselves with such..." She makes a strange noise like she's being strangled before finishing, "...unique bloodlines."

Unique. The word feels like a hard slap wrapped in false flattery. I can't say I'm shocked. Mabel doesn't see me as part of her world. I'm just an outsider mortal being pulled in for their conve- nience. Her eyes linger on my dress, and I can practically hear her judging it against her own questionable standards.

Francis ignores his wife, not bothering with pleasantries toward me.

I want to scream. I want to run. But all I can do is stand there, smiling through clenched teeth.

"You must forgive me, Tamara, but I must implore you to reconsider one part of the agreement." Mabel grabs both of my hands and squeezes.

I hope she will ask me not to go through with the marriage. I'm only too happy to oblige.

"One grandchild is not enough," she continues. "Please reconsider having six. There will be a financial bonus in it for you. And we need to ensure that the Freemont heir doesn't inherit your, well, you know."

Gross.

"Genetic condition," she whispers.

"Mabel, it's done." Francis saves me from answering. I could almost thank him until he adds, "The lady will want to keep her figure."

I visibly shiver in disgust at the way he says it.

Gross. Gross. Gross.

Where the hell is a grumpy vampire companion when you need one? I picture Costin shaking and throwing all of our guests through the window.

"Here we are." Mortimer appears with a wizard.

I recognize the wizard from supernatural events

at our country estate, but I have never been introduced. Though he looks frail in build, like most of his kind, he has an otherworldly presence. His age is indeterminate, but being ancient seems to be a requirement for wizards; at least, I've never heard of a young one. Long, silvered hair cascades down his robes, which shimmer like stars reflecting off a dark sea. His piercing eyes are an unnerving shade of glowing purple and hold the weight of centuries.

Two servants follow, carrying a podium, which they place in the middle of the room before leaving.

Mortimer unrolls a scroll and sets it down before holding his hand toward the wizard. "Zephronis, if you will be so kind."

Zephronis snaps his fingers, and an elegant quill and ink pot appear on the podium.

I wonder what he knows about the prophecy. Maybe he can decipher it for me.

"Chester," Mortimer commands.

Chester doesn't hesitate as he lifts the quill and signs. When he's finished, he winks at me.

"Tamara." Mortimer looks at me expectantly.

I can't force my legs to move.

"Zephronis is a busy man," my uncle insists.

"I don't..." I try to speak, but everyone is staring at me.

The sun is setting outside the floor-to-ceiling windows, its magenta and orange streaking the sky.

Costin will be waiting for me. I long to see him streaking across the window to come and save me.

I try to buy time. "I haven't read this yet. Shouldn't I—"

Astrid touches my elbow and guides me forward to sign my deal with the devil. "It's taken care of."

The words on the premarital agreement blur as I stare down at them. The ink seems to glisten. Several seals are stamped along the edge. It looks so official.

Mortimer points to a spot next to Chester's signature. Even his handwriting looks pretentious.

"I'm sorry..." I try to say, but the sound doesn't pass my lips.

Suddenly, Zephronis grabs my hand and jerks it toward him. Gnarled fingers hold my wrist firm as he traces a line on my palm. His purple eyes meet mine, and he lets me go just as quickly.

"Go ahead." Mortimer tries to soften his tone, but the order is unmistakable. He lifts the ink pot and quill and sets it down close to the paper to punctuate his meaning. I feel him standing behind me, looking over my shoulder as he blocks any escape I might try to make.

I mouth the word, "Costin," wishing he could hear me.

The wizard leans close, pinning me in on the other side.

Chester comes to stand in front of the podium,

completing the wall and keeping me in my place. He glances down at the premarital contract, barely containing his impatience. His fingers drum against the table as he, yet again, leans too close to me.

"Come on, darling," he drawls, flashing that insufferable smile. "Don't make this harder than it has to be. It's just a piece of paper, after all. Let's get this over with so we can move on to more," he touches my arm, "important things."

His breath is hot against my cheek, and I feel a wave of nausea rise in my throat. His words feel like a trap. The cage is slowly closing around me. I want to scream, but it's all I can do to keep standing.

My hand trembles uncontrollably as I grasp the quill.

Chester places his hand over mine, guiding the quill tip toward the ink. I feel the bile rise in my throat.

"There we go," he whispers. "Good girl."

A droplet of ink splashes onto the podium. I'm overcome with panic. I don't think I can go through with it. I can't marry this man.

A light tap hits my elbow. A surge of magic shoots up my arm, causing my wrist to jerk to the side, accidentally knocking the pot. The spilled ink flows over the document, swiftly obliterating Chester's name in a swirling sea of darkness.

"Dammit," Mortimer swears.

"Oh, Tamara," Astrid sighs.

"I should have known," Francis mutters.

"Now, wait a minute," my father defends. "It's an accident. She's clearly overwhelmed."

"She's nervous about marrying our Chester," Mabel preens. "How adorable."

Chester appears slightly annoyed, but beyond that, I don't think he cares either way. Marriage to me would be an inconvenience to him at most. I have a feeling that the alliance is to get his family off his back so that he can continue to live the life he wants.

"Can it be fixed?" Mortimer asks the wizard as he tries to blot the ink with his sleeve.

"No," Zephronis states. It's the first time I've heard him speak. The deep voice commands attention. "The magic must be pure. Have the documents redrawn. This will have to wait for another night."

Mortimer takes the quill from me with an angry jerk. "I'll call the lawyers."

My arm and hand still tingle, and I realize the wizard must have sent the magic up my arm to make me spill the ink. I look at him questioningly, but don't call him out in front of the family. I want to tell him how grateful I am for his intervention.

"This changes nothing," Astrid says. "We'll still go forward with the wedding plans. We have much to discuss tonight."

Zephronis takes up my hand and touches my palm. The magical buzzing stops as if he's pulling his magic back into his fingers. Calmly, he tells me, "Fate cannot be changed."

That's the beginning of the prophecy.

"That's right," Mortimer agrees, not understanding the message. "As the man said, fate will not be undone, and the joining of these two families is fate. This is but a delay."

Zephronis doesn't correct my uncle's interpretation of his words.

"Maybe it's a sign that we revisit the number of grandchildren," Mabel puts forth. I ignore her. I can't deal with that problem right now.

"I'm agreeable," Chester oozes.

Gag.

I definitely need to ignore him too.

"You know?" I whisper to the wizard.

He pushes my fingers, curling them into a fist before giving me a light tap.

"You've got ink on your gown," Astrid states. "You're excused to return to your room to change your clothes. I'll tell the chef we're ready to dine."

I step back from the podium. Zephronis snaps his fingers. The quill and ink disappear.

My eyes remained fixed on Zephronis. His glowing purple gaze keeps steadily on mine. There's so much I want to ask him, but he shakes his head slightly and turns away. Saying nothing, he shuffles out of the room toward the kitchen.

"Tamara, your gown," Astrid insists.

"Yes." I turn to leave, grateful for the excuse. I don't bother to say anything to anyone else as I hurry toward my room. As I walk, I pull the high heels from my feet, silencing their clicking on the marble. I run the rest of the way barefoot.

TWELVE

As soon as I step into my bedroom, I sag against the door, my body still buzzing with the adrenaline of my near escape. That was too close. A shiver of revulsion ripples down my spine as I think of Chester's face, his greasy smile, his disgusting attempts to control me before our engagement even officially starts.

I escaped this time. But what about next time?

The weight of the unsigned betrothal agreement presses on me like a giant anvil. I won't be a pawn in their elitist games. Marrying Chester? Living my life shackled to that self-righteous, power-hungry family?

Tears threaten. I can't do it.

But could I live with the alternative?

I know which road I'll take if I must choose

between prophecy and premonition. At least with Costin, I have a chance to fight back. To choose my fate.

I jerk the tiara off my head and toss it toward the bed. The bracelet soon follows.

It has to be close to sunset. I waste no time. I slip out of the gown, wriggling and squirming to free myself from its silky trap, before discarding it on the floor.

"You called for me?" Costin's low voice stops me as I reach for a dresser drawer. My breath audibly catches.

I spin around to face him. "Costin. How?"

How did he hear me? I didn't even say his name out loud.

"You called for me." This time, it's a statement, not a question. The seductive sound causes me to shiver.

"*Now I can always find you.*" I vaguely remember him saying that to me once. Is this what he meant? We have some kind of supernatural blood link?

I'm not sure I like that idea.

My room is dark except for lights coming from the outside windows radiating from the city below. If the vampire is here, that means the sun has set, but there are still hints of dusky light in the darkening sky.

The azure hue of his shirt perfectly complements

the shade of my dress. I find it an odd coincidence. He exudes a timeless sophistication that sets him apart. Unlike my brother, he's not following the latest fashion trends, but Costin's choices have a classic allure that withstands the test of time. Adorning his index finger is a substantial ruby ring set in intricately designed silver of the Gothic-style. This is not the first time I've noticed his penchant for wearing antique jewelry. His trousers discreetly reveal polished boots that exude a captivating sheen, adding to the overall aura of refinement and elegance.

Even if I didn't know about his vampiric nature, I would have to admit he draws the eye and commands attention just by standing in the room. Seeing him now, I could easily envision him as the ruler of a grand castle, surveying his domain from a lofty vantage point, looking down upon the common folk who could never aspire to his lofty status.

I dare myself to look into his eyes, even though I know that he's capable of mesmerizing me to his will. His gaze is intense, swirling with an angry red.

"I suppose well wishes are in order," he says. "Chester Freemont is a lucky man."

Is he... mad at me?

If so, he's going to have to stand in line. I'm not on too many favorite persons lists at the moment.

"Oh please," I dismissed with a wave of my hand. "Not you, too."

"Best wishes are not in order?" His expression lightens by a tiny degree. But I see it.

Is he jealous? That doesn't make any sense. I doubt he would even be here talking to me if my grandfather hadn't pressured him into a life debt.

"Chester Freemont isn't worth anyone's well wishes," I say, with a dismissing wave.

Costin's eyes narrow, and I catch the briefest flicker of something dark and possessive. "If that's true, then why are you marrying him?" His voice is smooth, but there's an edge to it, a sharpness that slices through the room.

"Power. Legacy. Survival. That's all anyone seems to care about." I pause, studying him. Is that what this is for him, too? Am I just another piece of the prophecy, another tool in his quest for power?

"And you?" His gaze locks on mine, unblinking. "How do you feel about this Chester? You seem rather... compliant."

He is jealous.

"Can we not talk about this now? We have to get out of here before they come looking for me to rejoin the party." I glance around the room, trying to remember what I was doing. It's unnerving having Costin in my bedroom with me. He makes it hard to concentrate on anything else.

"We?"

"Unless *you* want to stay and marry Chester in my place? I got to tell you that you would be doing me a huge favor if you did."

"I can drop him off the rooftop if you like," the vampire offers.

"Tempting, but that'll make things worse." Not much worse, but worse.

"If you do not wish to marry him, then why are you seeking an engagement with him?" Intensity radiates off him like a palpable invisible force.

"I'm not the one making the arrangements." Why are we talking about this? I don't want to discuss my future with him. It's none of his business who I marry or why.

"If you do not want it, say no. Mortality is no excuse. You are an adult. You should act like one. You do not have to agree." He gives a small shake of his head. "I thought you were made of stronger stuff than that."

I resist telling him to fuck off.

"How do you even know about this?" I demand, crossing over to see his face better in the shadows.

"I pay well to stay informed of what happens in my territory."

Territory. That one word reminds me of just how powerful this master vampire is. He controls all of vampiric North America.

Irritation flows through me. I just want all of this to be over. I can't take much more. "Mortimer had a premonition that somebody is trying to hurt my family. He believes that creating an alliance between us and the Freemonts will negate that danger. I don't know how to tell him that I think he's picking up on the alternate timeline where everyone died at my birthday party, except for Conrad and me. I don't think he'd even believe me if I tried."

"Everyone?" Costin prompts.

"You. My parents. Anthony. Others." I busy myself frantically searching for the book, hoping it wasn't destroyed in the apocalyptic vision. It's not on the bed or nightstand. I feel behind the dresser before crawling across the floor to look under my bed. "Then, after my party, Conrad's birth mother. P-Paul."

I stumble over his name, realizing I shouldn't have spoken about it. The book isn't under the bed, so I sit back and look up where he watches me.

"Who is this Paul?" Costin demands.

"No one. Nobody important. It doesn't matter." I try to step around him, but he blocks my path. "Have you seen the prophecy book?"

"Behind you." He nods toward the corner of the bedroom. "You really should be more careful with that. Anyone could pick it up."

"At least the floor is not lava," I quip, swiping it off the ground.

"You unlocked the image." He nods. "It is a bleak message of what the future will become."

"A warning would have been nice. I thought I was going to die." I take the broken amulet from my nightstand and set it next to the book on the bed. "Now I just need my phone."

"You do not need a phone where we are going tonight," he counters.

"Well, it has my wallet on there, so yes, I do kind of need it." I don't want to point out that I have no intention of leaving the house without some way to communicate with the outside world. Besides, I want to text my brother and make sure he's alright. However, I'm not too worried. I assume he's simply hiding from our mother.

"It is on your dresser," Costin says.

I go to retrieve it. "All right, that's everything. Let's go."

His lip twitches up at the side and his eyes narrow, a wholly seductive gesture. "As much as I appreciate watching you bend and stretch in that outfit, might I suggest something a little more comfortable for the underground? Otherwise, you will have more than Chester to fend off as a suitor."

Only then do I realize that I've been running around in my bra and panties. He interrupted me while I was changing, and I forgot to complete the task. Belatedly, I shield my breasts and stomach with my hands.

The action causes him to laugh. "Yes, good call. We wouldn't want to shock my delicate sensibilities."

I should be angry with him—angry for interrupting my life, for trying to make jokes when my world is falling apart. But instead, all I feel is a strange sense of comfort. His presence, the cool steadiness of it, is a balm against the storm raging in my mind.

"You're distracting me," I murmur, the words coming out softer than I intended.

In a split second, he's next to me.

"I should be the one complaining of distractions. I wasn't running around half-naked." His voice is low, teasing, but there's something else buried there.

Fingers glide along the small of my back, and I shiver. I expect them to be cold, but they're not. He leans his face close to mine. Our cheeks brush, and I feel his breath against my neck. A jolt of sexual awareness courses through me. It centers low in my belly.

I know I should push him away, should tell him this will never happen between us. The prophecy looms over us like a dark cloud. The vision of the world burning is still fresh in my mind. But at this moment, I don't care. I want to forget. I want to experience something that makes me feel alive.

"I have already dined this evening," he whispers against me. "But if you're offering other diversions..."

His breath is warm against my neck. He lets the suggestion hang between us.

Before I can stop myself, I turn to face him. The brush of his smooth cheek moves toward my lips. I stop as our mouths hover mere centimeters apart. I wait for him to kiss me, to make that final move. My breath comes in heavy pants. His fingers skate slowly downward as we stay locked in that otherwise frozen embrace. The tips of his fingers breach the top edge of my silk panties.

What am I doing?

What am I doing?

I can't concentrate. This is insanity.

I wait for his exploration, wanting his hand to dip further down, wanting him to pull me closer. When he doesn't, I say, "Everyone is in the dining room waiting for me to come back. We should leave before they come looking for me."

The words cause my lips to brush against his in a teasingly light caress. I don't know whether it's the stress of everything that's going on in my life, or the intense loneliness I've been feeling for the last several months. But I don't want to be alone. I want to feel something other than fear and regret. His kiss is right there for the taking. All I have to do is press forward.

Never in a million years would I have thought I'd come to this moment with Costin. He represents everything I've always tried to avoid in my life. His kind preys on humans to live. He's about as entwined in the supernatural world as I can get.

There is a monster inside him that terrifies me. He's lived centuries and will go on to live centuries more. I can be nothing more to him than this blip in time. Yet, in this moment, I am not repulsed. Quite the opposite, actually.

Oh, fuck it all.

It's possible that I'm on a fool's mission and will die tonight. Why not steal a moment of meaningless fun before I do? With luck, time will reset, and he won't remember it anyway.

I tell myself what I feel for Costin is carnal attraction, nothing more. It's my body trying to seek comfort through any avenue it can. Plus, he is the only one who knows the truth about the amulet's magic and the prophecy.

His hand moves lower, pushing the panties down my hips. It's almost as if he's testing my response. I close my eyes and wait, not asking him to stop.

He cups my ass and squeezes as he angles me to

fully face him. The panties slither down my legs. The soft cashmere shirt presses against my skin, causing me to shiver. For a moment, I forget everything as I focus fully on how my nerve endings are beginning to tingle with anticipation. Every brush against my flesh is like a jolt of warning.

His lips move against mine, and I feel the tiniest scrape of his fangs pulling out my bottom lip. He doesn't cut me, but I feel the danger in him. My lip springs back, and I wait for him to kiss me. It's torture, those seconds of intense longing. I wonder if he's toying with me or if this is some type of test.

My brain struggles to find a logical reason to pull away from him. But my body doesn't listen. I can't move. If this is magic and he's mesmerizing me to feel this way, I don't care.

I can hear myself drawing in a shaky breath. I'm hungry for his touch. I want him to move his hand around my stomach to find me wet and waiting.

The hand on my back glides upwards, and I feel the clasp of my bra release. He holds my back firmly as if to steady me as his free hand reaches between my breasts to hook my bra and pull it down my arms. I'm left naked and exposed.

Everything about him is so calculating and measured. The more frenzied my need becomes, the more I want him to prove himself the monster I know him to be. I don't know what he's waiting for.

My hands tremble as I pull up his cashmere sweater to expose his waistband. I dare another glance up. He's watching me, waiting. The full length of his arousal lets me know that he's interested, and that this is not a test.

I unbutton his pants, wanting to take the same slow, torturous time he took with me. But the need is too strong, and I end up fumbling in my rush to undress him. I shove my hand down the front of his pants. The monster does not disappoint.

His lips open wide, baring his fangs as if it's an involuntary reaction to my touch. I know he wants to bite me. I think I might let him.

I need this. I need to feel something that isn't doom. And if I'm honest with myself, I need to rebel against all that is expected of me. No one wants me to have the vampire. That only makes me want him more.

I stroke his cock, liking the smooth feel of it against my hand. But it's not enough. The back of his fingers grazed lightly over my nipples, keeping them erect.

What is he waiting for? I think my invitation is pretty obvious.

"Are we going to do this?" I challenge. "What are you waiting for?"

His kiss is sudden, fierce. There's no hesitation, no second-guessing. It's like we're both feeding off each other's desperation. I let the need, the fear, and the urgency of it all take me over.

His fingers skate their way up my breast to my shoulder. He pushes me down, as if wanting me to get on my knees before him. It's not what my body wants. It wants to be filled and taken.

Still, I don't deny him as I get on my knees. His cock is in front of my face, and I take hold of it. I take him into my mouth, sucking lightly. He gives me complete control, not forcing himself deep into my throat. I look up at his body to see his face. His eyes are closed, and he rocks his hips forward as I take him deeper.

I release his length from my mouth. "I need you."

He moves with supernatural speed, swiftly maneuvering behind me. I fall forward on my hands and knees. He presses my back to force my chest lower on the floor. The carpet cushions into my palms and tickles my nipples. My ass is in the air, and I feel him take my hips.

He brings his cock against my opening and thrusts. I gasp with surprise as he fills me. He rides me like a wild animal, pumping so hard that my knees burn against the carpet.

All I can do is hold on as he fucks me. There are no soft, loving gazes or light caresses, only the powerful, primal need. It's almost as if he's punishing me, but I don't care. I want him to. I cry out softly in surprise. Oh fuck, it feels good.

I can feel myself on the brink of climax. I want to come so badly. I need it. I need him to give it to me.

Intense pleasure rockets through me. I quiver and shake. I swear I feel him jerking his release, but he pulls my shoulder upward and brings himself against my back. His mouth clamps against my neck, and the sharp pierce of his fangs only adds a pleasure-pain to my release.

When he lets go, I fall to the floor. I can barely catch my breath. Nothing about this moment makes sense. I can't fathom what I've done and with whom.

"We should go," he says. I hear soft movements behind me, and I roll to the side to see him straightening his clothes. "As you said, the others will come looking for you soon."

It's not exactly champagne, roses, and love songs. But then, I don't expect those things from a vampire. However, a few sweet words of reassurance would be nice.

My muscles are weak, but I force myself to stand. I ignore my discarded clothes on the floor as I pull fresh clothes out of the dresser.

He walks into my ensuite bathroom, and I hear water running. When he returns, he hands me a washcloth. "For your neck."

I disappear into the bathroom, partly to hide from him while I check my neck. Blood smears my throat, and I wipe it off. The bite mark is unmistakable, but it already looks like it's healing. I pull on the jeans and a long-sleeved t-shirt before rejoining him.

His back is to me as he stares out the window. It's almost as if he wants to pretend nothing happened. I put my phone in my back pocket and shove the book into my waistband. When I pick up the amulet pouch, a whisper of cold air snakes around my ankles, sending a chill up my spine. I shake off the unease, but a nagging suspicion remains. I fear that the evil magic behind the amulet is stirring, watching what I'm doing with a hungry impatience.

"Think you can get us out of here without getting caught?" I ask, nervously needing to fill the quiet as I force the amulet into my front pocket.

"As you wish," he mutters.

It's a strange response, and I wonder if he was even listening to my question.

THIRTEEN

I weave on my feet, trying to get my bearings and regain my balance at the same time. My eyes fall on the stone angel with the chipped hand surrounded by the tombstones under her domain outside the nightwalker mausoleum. One second, I was in the bedroom pulling on my sneakers, and the next...

Dammit. Costin did it again. He mesmerized me.

The night air feels thick and oppressive, like the world is holding its breath. My reality shifts back to somewhat normal. I suppose I should be grateful that the vampire got me out of the penthouse unde-tected, but I wish he would have told me before putting me under his spell. After sex, the feeling of being drawn into the vortex of his emotions leaves me feeling vulnerable and connected to him.

I don't want to be connected to a vampire. I want to have used him for sex and rebellion.

Costin is arrogant and condescending. He calls me a castoff for fuck's sake. I'm not even sure I like him.

At least, that's what I'm telling myself. I wait to see if he says anything about what happened in my bedroom. He doesn't and so neither do I.

A strange chirping draws my attention to the shadows. A diminutive, gnarled creature with large ears jerks its head to tear at something it's eating. It stops to peer in my direction with sharp teeth bared. Its round black eyes remain fixed on me as if the creature can vanish from my sight by remaining perfectly still.

"He won't hurt you," Costin assures me.

I slowly look away first, but I continue to listen to its noises.

Costin holds his arm out for me to take. "Shall we?"

I don't accept the offer. Instead, I say, "You mesmerized me again, didn't you?"

"You wanted out of the penthouse. It seemed the most convenient way to travel." There is absolutely no apology in his tone. "Besides, I figured it would be best to come here before you talked yourself out of doing your duty."

"So it was more *convenient*," I repeat.

He arches a brow.

"I think it's time we had a brief discussion about some ground rules for this whole saving the world prophecy business." I put my hands on my hips, hoping that I look authoritative. "Rule number one: absolutely no mesmerizing me without my fore-knowledge or permission. Do I make myself clear?"

"The last time I transported a conscious human, they vomited on me."

"Then I'll pay for your dry cleaning," I quip.

He looks annoyed. "What other rules?"

That was the only one I was thinking of when I started my little speech. Still, I want to delay fate. The fear in my chest is coming out argumentatively. "No vampire tricks. No wordplay or loopholes. You're to do nothing that will take away my freewill to think and move for myself."

He crosses his arms over his chest and waits.

"And no abandoning me underground," I look at the mausoleum. It looks different from the night before. A greenish glow illuminates the edges as a colored spotlight hits it from behind. As if being in the graveyard wasn't scary enough, they needed to add special effects.

I'm keenly aware of where we are. The graveyard feels alive with a kind of dark energy. The weathered tombstones are crooked, as if the earth beneath them has been restless for centuries. Fog rolls through the narrow pathways between the graves, clinging to the ground like it doesn't dare rise any higher. Overhead, the moon hangs low, casting long, eerie shadows stretching toward the mausoleum like ghostly fingers.

Small, flickering orbs of light dart between the gravestones—spirits, maybe, or some other supernatural energy. The air here is thick and presses down on us, weighing heavily on my chest with every breath. Even the statues appear to be watching—the angel with a chipped hand and hollow eyes, gargoyles frozen in time always appearing one blink away from life.

Ahead, the mausoleum looms. I prefer to think of them as mausoleums instead of crypts. Crypt sounds so final. Mausoleum sounds more formal and less intimidating, like a museum. Its gothic spires and ornate carvings stand like a sentinel over the underworld it guards. The greenish glow from behind it pulses faintly and becomes brighter, casting an otherworldly light around the entrance. If the carved spirits in the black stone are any indication, there's no mistaking that many things ancient and dangerous wait beneath.

"Anything else?" he asks.

"And no making fun of me if I get nervous. No stupid human jokes. And you have to stop calling me castoff."

"You're stalling," he states.

He's right. Damn him.

"Fine. I hear your terms," he mutters with a gesture of his hand toward the mausoleum entrance. "May we go?"

I can't shake the feeling that there's something more behind Costin's calm insistence. His eyes—those swirling, ancient eyes—look at me with a depth I can't translate. Am I more than just a pawn in his prophecy?

No. He wouldn't be here if my grandfather hadn't made him promise.

Panic overtakes me. My head churns with rapid thoughts.

I'm a mortal girl tangled up in something far bigger than me. Costin talks about the prophecy like it's inevitable, like I'm destined to be dragged deeper into a world I've fought so hard to stay out of. I don't want to go underground. I don't want to meet monsters or trolls or whatever else lurks in those tunnels.

But it's Costin who scares me the most. Not his power or his vampiric strength. No, it's the way he makes me feel. The way I catch myself wanting to trust him—wanting him to be the one who protects me from all this supernatural chaos. And that's the most dangerous thought of all.

I can't let myself get close to him. At the end of

the day, there is no denying that he's a monster. And worse—his prophecy is unraveling everything I thought I knew about my human life.

I stare at the mausoleum, trying to make myself braver than I am. It's one thing to imagine an abstract story in a book, but another to face the beginning of that tale in person. I can only imagine the dangers that lurk behind those gothic walls, knowing that they're so much more than I can dream up. As a mortal, it will never be safe for me there—let alone a mortal meddling in things I should have no part of.

I touch my pocket where the amulet waits to be repaired. A sense of guilt comes over me when I think of Paul, though I know I have no reason for it. That was a different life, and I'm only torturing myself. I have every right to live mine in the here and now.

I'm selfish. I don't want to die. I'm not a hero. I open my mouth to tell Costin I can't do it.

I think of the rivers of lava. If just reading about the prophecy could feel so real that it sends me to witness the apocalypse, what will going into the mausoleum do?

I look around the murky shadows of the graveyard. The white moths circle the lamps, bumping into the glass while attempting to reach the gas flames inside. I feel a kinship to those poor creatures, bumbling stupidly as I seek entrance into a place I should not go. Just as the illustration foretold, will there be fire waiting to consume me inside the mausoleum?

"Does it have to be this place?" Nothing in the book said to come here. I want an excuse to leave.

"There is a troll who lives here that is friendlier than others." He places his hand on the small of my back, trying to make me walk. "We could travel to Europe, journey long nights across the rocky terrains until we reach the mountain colony. Even if they do grant us an audience, I worry there is not enough time to convince them to assist us. They could just as easily boil you in a stew rather than help."

Why do paranormal creatures enjoy eating humans so much?

The book said I would see a sign.

Well, actually it said something pretentiously asinine like, *"When the destined soul beholds these words, omens shall guide their way to the realm of prosperity."*

Where's my guiding omen? Surely, it's something I'd recognize. I mean, seriously—

Suddenly, the moths leave their posts to swarm upwards, gathering over our heads before traveling toward the mausoleum. Their frantic wings beat wildly as they congregate around the stone entrance. They appear drawn to the unnerving green glow that is now seeping from its cracks. For a moment, I feel like I'm one of them—inexplicably drawn toward something I don't fully understand and can't escape.

"Do you see that?" I whisper, following the moths to get a closer look.

The moths change shape. Their dull and colorless wings reflect the green light and begin shimmering with a hint of magic.

Costin touches my arm to stop me. "What is it?"

The green glow intensifies until I can't look away. I keep walking, drawn to it. The moths continue to grow and change until they are no longer moths. They transformed into butterflies—iridescent, neon-green creatures that don't exist in nature. They flutter around the mausoleum door, their intended destination unmistakable as they bump desperately into the stone just as they bumped into the gas lamps before.

My omen.

"I believe you," I say, all doubt gone. "This is where we need to go."

Costin's touch on my arm keeps me frozen in place. My heart hammers in my chest. Butterflies. They've always been my talisman of sorts.

My grandfather's words echo in my mind, *"The world needs butterflies, Tamara, as much as it needs dragons. Probably more. We all have our place."*

I'm the butterfly, and inside that mausoleum are

the metaphorical dragons. These butterflies aren't delicate or peaceful. They feel like a warning of the danger that awaits below, a danger I must face.

"This is the place," I say.

"What changed your mind?" Costin asks.

"Don't you see them?" I point at the door.

"There is no one there."

I can't take my eyes off the butterflies. The mausoleum looms ahead. I know its black stone facade is old yet appears untouched by time. Clouds move over the moon, darkening the graveyard. The green seeps from the cracks around the door, casting long slivers of light that flicker and dance like specters in the darkness. Every step I take is heavier than the last, and the air is thick with ancient and dangerous magic.

The entrance to the crypt is darker than I remember. I stare at it, moving like the moths toward the flame. The carvings on the door seem to writhe in the strange light, twisting into shapes I can't quite recognize.

I need to get closer.

There's something alive here within the stone, something primordial watching me approach. My heart races until I can't hear anything but the *pound, pound, pound* of its rhythmic thump. Instinct screams at me to turn back.

I can't. Not now.

I reach for the door, and the butterflies scatter around me. Before I touch it, the door creaks open with a groan. The sound sends shivers up my spine. Goosebumps cover my arms. My hand shakes as it falls back to my side.

The door opens on its own, welcoming me in. A few of the butterflies brave past me to go in first. Inside, the green light pulses, inviting and repelling me at the same time. I feel it in my bones—this isn't just a door. It's a threshold. Once I step through, there's no going back.

This is it. The moment everything changes.

Until now, I told myself that I had a choice, that I could somehow escape the destiny laid out for me if I so chose. I'm human, and we have free will, right?

Fate doesn't agree.

The vision from the prophecy's illustration still burns in my mind. So much death and destruction. The city, the people, all gone. Everything I care about is disintegrated and crushed. Costin told me that some of the supernaturals would survive, and their fates would be worse than the humans. And it will be my fault if I do nothing.

Costin said I'm part of this prophecy, but I'm just a mortal girl. What if I'm not enough? What if I fail? The weight of the world is pressing down on me, and I feel like I'm drowning in it. But I can't let fear stop me now. I've seen what happens if I don't act, and I won't let that become reality.

Knowing this is my fate doesn't make this any easier. Every instinct in me screams to run, to hide, to retreat to the safety of my penthouse and pretend none of this is real. If I choose Chester, I can hide inside our magical families. Maybe we'd survive.

Maybe.

But at what cost?

The glowing butterflies are real. This is my future. I have to face it. I have to go underground into the supernatural realm.

I feel Costin move past me through the door, unafraid.

I peek inside before angling my body to step through the opening, careful not to touch the writhing carvings along the doorframe.

The air inside is cold, unnaturally so. My breath comes out in shaky puffs, each one dissipating into the darkness.

I shiver, rubbing my arms. I can't help thinking of my family's crypt, watching as a wizard sealed their corpses into the wall. I shake the image from my mind.

Twelve large metal plaques are affixed to the walls to mark the graves within. Small niches are evenly spaced, and empty flower vases are attached along the outside edges. I listen to the stone to make sure nothing moves inside. An empty coffin platform is in the middle of the room. I don't touch it.

"It's warmer down below." Costin pulls at a sconce, and I hear stone grinding beneath us. He gestures to the corner of the room.

Two butterflies follow his hand, diving into a hole in the floor to reveal a stairwell. Loud thumps sound behind me, and I turn to see the rest of the butterflies hitting the door. They knock it shut behind us with a decisive thud, closing us in.

"Stay behind me." Costin leads me down winding steps.

Shadows flicker at the edge of my vision, stretching between the stone pillars that line the crypt's walls. My pulse quickens, and I fight the urge to run. I can't let this place get to me. This is only the entryway. I can't let the fear take over.

But it's hard. So hard.

I think of my brother down below, and I grab my phone. Anthony hasn't responded to my previous texts checking in. I try again, typing, *"Coming down. With Costin. Where are you?"*

"What are you doing?" Costin asks, his voice tight.

He can be annoyed with me all he wants. "Texting Anthony that we're coming down."

"I will protect you." He sounds defensive.

"Didn't say anything about that. He's my brother, and I promised to tell him when we went underground." I slide the phone back into my pocket.

He says nothing as he leads the way down the stairwell. The green light fades into darkness as we descend, replaced by shadows that twist and curl around us. And then I hear it—the whispers. Faint, barely audible at first, but growing louder with every step.

"Tamara." The voice is familiar, too familiar. *"Tamara."*

"Do you hear that?" I ask Costin, surging forward to press against his back.

"A breeze is whispering against the stone," he says.

"Tamara." It sounds like... Conrad? How can he be here?

I grab hold of Costin's arm and hold tight.

I keep walking, but the whispers follow, circling around me, growing louder, more insistent.

"Tamara."

"Tamara."

"Tamara."

I pull him to a stop, and we wait on the steps. "Someone is saying my name."

He puts his hand over mine and again starts walking. "This place is full of tricks and spells meant to distract you. Ignore them. They are manifestations of your fears."

Each step feels like I'm leaving something behind—my old life, my humanity, my safety. The tomb air becomes thick and oppressive, pressing down to force me inside. The penthouse feels so far away, almost like a different world that I can never return to. I've crossed a threshold. I'm in a supernatural realm, and there's no turning back.

Light appears from below. I lean forward before turning a corner. We reach the bottom. Thick prison bars block the exit.

I lean into the bars and give them a small shake as I try to look beyond at the impenetrable darkness. "How do we get in?"

Costin pulls me against his chest. The sudden full contact of his body takes me by surprise. I lift my face toward his, half expecting him to kiss me.

Instead, his face distorts and blurs. Before I can protest, I feel myself being jolted almost violently off my feet. Everything spins and mushes together, and I become lightheaded, like I've been dropped into a freefall inside a tornado.

As suddenly as it starts, it stops. Costin holds upright as my wobbly knees give out. Nausea churns. I hold my breath as I fight throwing up on the front of his shirt.

"That was traveling two feet," he states.

His look seems to say, *I told you so.*

"You could have warned me." I want to push away, but I'm still trying to regain my composure.

"You're mortal. The only way past the bars is with supernatural help." He lets me go, and I manage to stay upright. "It was faster than another debate. We cannot keep stopping every three steps to discuss what we are doing."

So much for my dictating rules.

"Supernaturals are so dramatic," I mutter.

I become aware of conversations happening around us. The indistinct murmurs create a hectic racket, as I can't pick out any one conversation. Everything is buzzing with energy, thrumming in time with the pulse in my veins. I turn away from Costin and realize for the first time that this place looks nothing like the dark pit I saw through the bars.

The bars acted like some kind of magical filter, shielding the true nature of this realm from the world above. Down here, my skin tingles as though the very air is alive with static electricity, ready to crash over me in waves. It's a familiar sensation, and I wonder if it's a magical residue.

Beneath my fear, there's something else. A spark. A sense of purpose. For so long, I've felt lost, trapped between two worlds, fully human but bound by the rules of the supernatural. Here, in this crypt, I feel something awakening inside me. It quickens my pulse and deepens my breath. I've been hiding from this world for far too long.

The tunnels themselves feel more natural than man-made, as if this place has always been here, hidden beneath the city, waiting. The walls and ceilings are formed of chipped stone, rough in places but worn smooth where centuries of hands have passed. A path polished by endless footsteps leads deeper into the heart of this underground world. Glowing clusters of crystals and gems embedded in the stone provide soft illumination, casting an otherworldly light that dances off the surfaces like fractured rainbows. It's brighter here than I expected, yet shadows cling stubbornly to secret edges. I feel a sense of danger lurking just out of sight.

"Stick close to me," Costin murmurs, his voice vibrating with an undercurrent of warning. "This isn't a place where you want to get lost."

As we move deeper, the narrow tunnels give way to a vast cavern, and my breath catches in my throat. Before me lies a sprawling city that feels like it belongs to another time—medieval yet pulsating with supernatural energy. Towering spikes of stone rise from the ground, connected by intricate bridges and archways that crisscross above us. Stalls line the streets, selling strange, shimmering goods I can't name by every kind of being imaginable. Creatures that would be glamoured and hidden in the human world move freely through the city.

Robed figures flit through the crowd like ghosts, their faces hidden, only their glowing eyes occasionally peeking out from beneath their hoods to glance curiously in my direction. I can't help but overhear snippets of conversations. Most of them are incomprehensible, spoken in languages I don't understand, but a few drift toward me with uncanny clarity.

"...you're kidding. I'm not paying for protection." A werewolf, half-shifted with his claws still extended, is deep in conversation with a delicate fairy whose wings flutter anxiously in the heavy air.

"I swear, he's got a vendetta against anyone who even looks at him wrong," the fairy answers. "Nearly tore off my wing for bumping into him at the market."

If I had to guess by the fairy's lack of clothes, I'd say she was a prostitute.

Then again, that might be a little judgy of me. Fairies aren't exactly my favorite creatures.

I shudder and move closer as Costin walks ahead of me, his steps sure as he navigates the crowd. I can tell he's done this a thousand times. I struggle to keep up, my senses overwhelmed by the sights, sounds, and smells of this place.

I wonder where Anthony might be. Why doesn't he answer my texts?

The hair on the back of my neck stands on end with the sensation of being watched. I can't blame any one creature. Several of them are staring at me.

Another conversation catches my attention—a pair of horned demons haggle with a merchant over what looks like a mason jar filled with a pulsing, glowing ooze.

"...if you can't guarantee it's the real thing, why should I pay full price?" a garbled voice demands. "A bottled soul isn't worth much if it's tainted."

"You can't tell me it's tainted when you can feel its heat," the merchant defends. "That's a pure soul, right from the source. Do you have any idea what it took to get this?"

I tear my gaze away from the jar, bile rising in my throat. A bottled soul? What kind of horrible black marketplace is this?

"You come here often?" I ask Costin. "You clearly know your way around."

Costin glances over his shoulder at me, his expression unreadable, though there's a flicker of amusement in his eyes. "You could say that."

I try to walk beside him, but he keeps angling his body to force me to remain a step behind. "I had no clue this place was... *this*."

"This place has been here longer than you can

imagine. Some parts are older than the city above. Most people live their entire lives without knowing it's just below their feet," he says.

"Lucky them," I mutter under my breath, only kind of joking. My eyes dart toward Costin's back as we pass a particularly imposing shifter, who is staring at me a little too intently. I can't tell what he will become, and I don't want to find out, but his glowing eyes give his ability away. "How often do you come here?"

Costin's eyes flick toward me for a moment, but then he shrugs. "Often enough when duty demands it. Don't be fooled by anyone you meet. They're not your friends. This place will always find new ways to surprise you."

Surprise or terrify?

I hear the subtle tension in his voice. I wonder what he's holding back. Something is making him uneasy.

An apothecary sells wares from one of the stores built into the small caverns along the side. The air is thick with something sweet and metallic, like magical spells seeping through the cracks in the earth. Every now and then, I catch glimpses of things moving in the shadows—creatures with too many eyes, beings made entirely of smoke that twist and curl as they slither between the narrow inlets along the stone walls.

I try not to stare at any one creature for too long. I feel eyes on me. Curious, hungry eyes. Some are watching me from the shadows. Others don't bother to hide their open scrutiny. I can imagine they're thinking I don't belong. On any other day, I would say they were right.

I know full well that in a place like this, I stand out. I pull my arms tighter around myself, wishing I could cast a glamour to disguise my humanity and disappear into the crowd.

We pass by a group of vampires lounging near one of the many inlets, their eyes filling with red as they track my movements. I don't recognize any of them. One stands and sniffs in my direction. I'm a meal they wouldn't think twice of devouring. Costin keeps them at bay with a single, sharp gesture. They don't like the order, but his presence is enough to tell them that I'm off-limits.

Not for long, if they have any say about it.

As we approach a bridge made of twisting stone, I look down into what appears to be a bottomless pit and hesitate to cross. The glow from the crystals doesn't penetrate all the way to the bottom. A crooked figure leads a group of small, jittery beings across. At first glance, she seems like nothing more than an old woman, but as we draw closer, I can see the unnatural sharpness of her movements and the gleam coming from hollows where her eyes should be.

Costin steps several paces onto the bridge before stopping. He frowns as he walks back toward me. "What now?"

I ignore his annoyance as I watch the figure approach from the other side of the bridge. Her form is hunched, wrapped in layers of frayed fabric that drift around her like a tattered, dirty wedding gown. Her pale skin is almost translucent and stretches tightly over her pronounced cheekbones. A tangle of silver hair is pulled back into a severe bun, though wild strands slither around her head as if caught in some invisible current. She moves with unsettling precision, each step deliberate and jerking, her bony fingers gesturing for the small figures trailing behind her to follow.

"Is that a banshee?" I ask Costin, moving close to him as the woman stops on the bridge to wait for the stragglers in her group.

"Witch," he answers. "It's too late now. We'll have to wait for the students to pass."

The children—if they can be called that—are an assortment of supernatural beings. Some have tiny, spiraling horns jutting from their foreheads, others have glowing eyes that flick nervously toward the stone beneath their feet. A few even sport small wings, which flutter anxiously as they move closer to the edge. I see leashes tied around their ankles as they're tethered to classmates. They fill the bridge, blocking passage to all others. They seem apprehensive, casting wary glances down into the chasm below, and I wonder what they've been told to fear.

"Stay close! If you fall in, we're not going after you." The witch schoolmarm's voice slices through the ambient noise, condescending yet laced with a warped sort of affection for her charges.

I see a kid weaving magic through his fingers like I've seen my brother do many times over the years. Is this what school for Anthony was like?

I glance around, looking for my brother, but I still don't see him.

The children shuffle closer together, their collective gaze drifting toward the edge of the bridge. One of the smaller creatures, a boy with curling horns, glances up at the witch nervously, his tiny hands clutching the hem of his jacket. Their murmurs are barely audible over the hum of the city, but their expressions speak volumes.

"We wouldn't want anyone to stray too far from the path, now would we?" The witch's words have a sing-song quality, though there's a menacing lurking beneath the tone. Her back is facing us.

"Is she the one from the fairytale that lures kids with candy before she eats them?" I whisper to Costin.

"You don't want to be overheard making jokes like that down here," he says with a frown of warning.

Who's joking?

The schoolmarm's head rotates on her shoulders even though the rest of her doesn't move. Her razor-thin grin doesn't reach her eyes as she peers at me.

Oh fuck.

I quickly look away. I wait a few minutes before glancing back. Her head again faces forward.

"Who can tell me what lies beneath?" she asks the children.

The answers come in shouted, chaotic waves.

"Nyxorneth," says the horned boy.

"Thal'gorath," shouts a girl struggling to keep her tethered companion from lifting her off the ground.

"Zharog."

"Vorthyx."

"Molgarath," a small cat shifter says, poking the girl next to him with a claw.

She yelps and swats at him. "No. It's Draakmar!"

"Xeltharok!"

"Grav'Zhul!"

"Enough." The witch lifts her hands, and they instantly go silent. "Yes, those are all beings that live deep within the earth. But who is the great creature that sleeps in the pit down there waiting for me to send it naughty children to snack on when it wakes?"

"For fuck's sake, Costin." I exhale in panic. "How many ancient fucking evils are there?"

The witch turns more fully to face me this time and twitches as she steps forward.

"Uh, sorry." I hold up my hands. "Please, continue."

The woman gestures toward the chasm with a bony finger and returns to her students. "We call it Nyxorneth, but it is older than time and has no true name. It's been there for centuries, longer than your families have walked this dirt. But every now and then... someone gets too close. And when they do, they are never heard from again."

She lets the words hang in the air, savoring the rising tension.

I lean into Costin, feeling safer with him next to me. He looks down at my death grip on his arm.

The children stare at her in silence.

The schoolmarm flashes a wicked smile as she turns to stare at me. "The creature of the pit has a gnawing hunger that knows no bounds. It's always waiting for someone foolish enough to look over the edge and—" Suddenly, she snaps her fingers, making the children jump. Her cold cackle echoes across the bridge as the kids join her laughter.

The children scurry along behind her as she

leads them from the bridge. I want to stop her to ask which of the many evils they just mentioned was the one I'm up against. Though, I'm not sure giving it a name will make me feel better.

I glance over at Costin. His expression is tight, but he catches me staring and raises an eyebrow. His posture is tenser than before.

"Can we cross now?" he asks.

"I feel like you're not telling me something." I don't move.

He doesn't answer right away, instead flexing and twisting his arm to force me to let go. His expression sharpens, but not on me—on something behind me.

"I'm keeping you safe. That's what matters." He nods toward the bridge. "We need to keep moving."

I glance at the throng behind us but only see the teacher leading the kids into the crowded marketplace.

I keep to the middle of the bridge as we pass, trying not to look anywhere but at my feet until we're on the other side.

Structures crafted from mud and stone line one side of the walkway. A few of them have windows, and I see wooden furniture inside. The doors to the dwellings are all closed. The foot traffic around us lessens as Costin ducks between two of them.

"The troll lives in there." He points toward a

tunnel's entryway hidden behind one of the homes. "Let me do the talking."

As an independent woman, I should tell him he can't order me around. As a human about to meet a troll in an underground tunnel in the supernatural realm to discuss the nature of evil, I think I can let his tone slide.

"Wait," I stop him.

"What is it?" He sounds annoyed.

"Just give me a second," I insist. "This place is a lot to take in and this is the first moment of privacy we've had since we arrived."

He arches a brow and turns to look at a goblin sprawled on the ground, snoring and hugging an earthen jug. The pointed stick next to him makes me think he's the worst troll tunnel guard ever.

"Costin, please, just..." I'm scared. I don't know what to expect. I've seen trolls before, but I've never held a conversation with one. "Just give me a moment. I need to say something."

"Yes?"

"I never thanked you for the pizza. It was..." I bite my lip. "Nice."

"You needed to talk about pizza?"

"No, I just..." I need to buy time.

He takes a deep breath and lifts a hand to my cheek. "Your heart is beating fast."

"I'm nervous," I say.

"You should try to calm it." His tone lowers seductively, and he steps closer. "It's like a drum calling all vampires within a twenty-mile radius."

I glance back in the direction we came.

"Yes. Those vampires." He strokes my cheek. "They want nothing more than to devour you."

My breath catches and I forget everything but the look on his face.

"They smell your blood." He leans close to my head and breathes me in. "I will not be able to fault them if they can't control themselves. Even I struggle..."

I moan softly as I take hold of his shirt. I pull him to my mouth, offering him a kiss. His fingers curl around the nape of my neck, tipping my head back to better suit him.

I expect an explosion of angry passion like before, but this time, he's gentle. His mouth moves against mine, his tongue slipping past my guard to explore. The sharp tips of his fangs threaten tender flesh but don't injure. I moan, and the kiss becomes almost frantic.

He pulls me tight against him. The full length of his muscled chest molds my softer skin. He's a dangerous man, I know that, but I feel safe with him.

How did we come to this? Just yesterday, I would have denied anything like this could happen. Now, I just want to keep kissing him.

I want time to stop so that I can remain trapped in his vortex. My lungs burn for air, I pull away to draw in a heavy breath. I gaze deeply into his eyes.

He looks away first and tilts his head. "We should keep moving."

"I'm scared," I tell him.

"The wizards would not have written the prophecy if there was not a chance you would survive," he says.

I'm not sure if he thinks that's comforting.

"Do you think I can do it?" I ask. For some reason, the answer is very important to me. I need him to believe in me. I can't help but hear voices from my past telling me that I'm a mere mortal, not special, human. What if they're right?

"You are the only one who can," he answers.

It's not exactly the testimony to my greatness that I want to hear, but I can't fault him for it.

"We should go," he says.

I nod. I still taste his mouth on my lips. My skin aches to continue what we started. I could make love to him right here, hidden behind the mud-brick homes.

One of the green butterflies that followed us inside the mausoleum appears overhead and flies into the tunnel, as if telling me to keep moving. Costin doesn't appear to see it. The magical insect reappears and perches on the tunnel entrance.

Costin looks at me a moment longer before taking my hand to pull me behind him into the tunnel. The drunken goblin doesn't notice our passing.

The tunnel is dark and ominous, as the crystals do not grace the walls to give it light. Firelight coming from within reveals our destination. We turn a few corners before coming to an enormous cavern. A fire burns inside an inlet in the far wall beneath a cauldron. Trinkets and oddities surround oversized furniture made for a giant. Gemmed necklaces hang from the ceiling to create the impression of the night sky.

We're in the lair of the cave troll, but I don't see him.

"Costin?" I stop walking as he tries to go deeper inside. I want to run, but his grip tightens. "I don't think he's home. We should wait outside."

At the sound of my voice, a large rock moves on the ground in the center of the cavern.

"Remember, let me do all the talking," Costin whispers. "No jokes or small talk. Stay quiet."

FOURTEEN

The rock reveals itself to be the crouched figure of the cave troll. His skin has a rough, stone-like texture to it, as if the mottled gray color camouflages him to his surroundings. Cracks and fissures run along its arms and chest, filled with green moss. It only enhances its indestructible appearance.

At our intrusion into his sanctuary, the troll stands. He towers over us. Limbs are long and grotesquely muscled, the sinew beneath the skin rippling with each movement. Massive hands, tipped with jagged, dirt-encrusted nails, hang at its sides, each finger as thick as my wrist. His legs are bowed, succumbing to the immense weight. Wide, bare feet dig into the stone floor as though they've always been part of the earth.

The troll's face is perhaps his most unsettling

feature. Its eyes are deep set, catching the firelight like molten coals. A flat, wide nose spreads across its face, with nostrils that flare with each breath. With each exhale, he emits a low, rumbling sound. Small tusks jut from the bottom jaw, curving upward like broken tree roots.

The troll's gaze sweeps toward us, lingering on me for a moment. I gravitate close to Costin, wanting to hide behind him.

Yep. The vampire can do the talking.

There's something about the troll's eyes. Though it's evidently a creature of brute strength, I can tell it's not mindless. It moves with purpose, its enormous form blocking the firelight when he moves past.

"What brings you to Morvok's domain, Costin and pet?" The troll's low, gravelly voice reverberates over us, and I swear I feel the ground tremble beneath my feet. A grumbly reverberation follows the words, as if he has little cause to use his voice. His mouth is full of uneven, jagged teeth that protrude even when it's closed—shards of broken stone ready to tear through anything in its path.

Honestly. This thing can call me whatever names he wants. I'm not going to protest.

Costin approaches him, his voice taking on a respectful tone. "Greetings, Morvok. We come because we need a necklace repaired."

The troll ambles closer. My instinct is to step back, but Costin holds firm.

Long, stringy hair hangs in greasy clumps from Morvok's head, matted with grime and what looks like the tangled remnants of a long-dead animal.

"Give Morvok." He stretches out his hand.

Costin turns to me. "Give me the necklace."

"Not Costin," Morvok denies. "Pet give Morvok."

The troll's eyes shift toward me.

I pull the pouch out of my pocket and slowly move toward him. I tremble as I stretch my arm as far as it will go to give him the pouch. I catch the faint scent of damp earth and decay, like something that's been buried for far too long. I'm well aware that every step we take forward is pulling me deeper into a world I barely understand.

"M-my name is Tamara." My voice is unsteady as I drag my feet, inching closer. "It's nice to meet you, Morvok."

He grumbles, the sound vibrating the ground beneath me.

The troll holds out his hand, and I drop the pouch into his palm without touching him. He lifts it to his nose and sniffs. Something about what he senses causes him to move. "What trouble did you bring Morvok, Costin? This is an amulet, not a necklace."

I step backward until I bump into Costin. He

places his hand on my shoulder and presses down to keep me there.

Bony ridges protrude from the troll's back when he turns toward the firelight. He tears away the string holding the pouch shut and drops it on the floor before dumping the broken shards onto a worktable.

"Can you repair it?" Costin asks.

"Where did you steal this?" he demands. "This belongs to the gods. You are not a god."

"It was a gift," I say. "My mother and grandfather traded with Norwegian trolls to acquire it."

Morvok turns aggressively toward me. "I don't believe. It broke because it is not yours to have. The three of you need to leave. This stolen magic is not for you."

Three of us? I look behind us. I only count two. Maybe math isn't a troll's strong suit?

"You know what this is." Costin's words aren't a question. "You know we can't take it somewhere else. You know what that stone does."

"It's not right to steal magic and break time." He waves his hand and puts his back toward me. "Leave. You know not what you have done."

"It's mine," I insist. "Someone tried to take it from me, and that is why it is broken. If you're unable to help me, give it back so I can find someone who can."

The troll snorts. He fixes his stare on me. "Yours?"

I don't answer the accusation in his tone.

"You?" he demands. "A fragile girl with nothing more than a glint of light before darkness?"

I stiffen, hating the way he says it like I'm some unlikely hero who doesn't belong. I manage a weak nod.

Costin presses down harder on my shoulder, as if warning me to stop talking.

"It's not stolen. It belongs to me." I try to keep the fear out of my voice. I don't want him to think I'm lying. "According to my grandfather, trolls created the original necklace for an ancient Pagan goddess who was so beautiful that other goddesses envied her, and gods constantly pursued her. The necklace was enchanted to protect her from unwanted advances and the dangers posed by other deities. Later, the necklace was broken up, and I was given this piece. The amulet has protected me many times—from vampire attacks, explosions, and even from being killed in a fire that broke out on my birthday."

"It's broken. You should have taken better care. Now go." He is losing what little patience he has.

"It must be fixed. If you won't do it for us, then tell me who can. If I don't find a way, there's this prophecy and..." I reach to pull the book out of my waistband and hold it up. "Please, Morvok. I've seen what will come to pass if I fail. Lava will run in the streets. Buildings fall. People die."

"Perhaps it is time to wash the earth of humans," the troll says with a dismissive wave. He looks at the ceiling. "They are noisy pests, tearing and stomping and consuming."

I open my mouth to respond, but Costin steps in front of me, his hands resting on his waist. He motions for me to be quiet, but I ignore him.

"It's not just humans," I insist, pushing around Costin. "If we fail to stop this prophecy, everything gets destroyed. Look at the book. See for yourself. Whatever ancient evil that is tied to that magic is waking up. We need to fix the amulet and keep the evil where it is."

Morvok holds out his hand for the book. "Give Morvok."

"Tamara," Costin warns under his breath.

I'm a little braver as I approach the troll this time. I hand him the book. I remind myself that I am Astrid's daughter. Her lessons have not been in vain. I know flattery will get you far with supernaturals. I force a smile. "There's a great story about how trolls built the beautiful mountains."

The book looks tiny in his hands. Morvok sniffs it as he rapidly flips through the pages. The troll's eyes shift toward me, and I can feel the weight of his stare. "You have read this?"

I nod.

"This is your blood?" Morvok asks.

I nod again. I'm not sure how he knows that. The blood drops had soaked into the pages and disappeared. "There was a blood lock."

"You are mortal?" Morvok appears confused.

"Yes," I say. "But my father is Davis Devine."

He grunts, as if the name means nothing to him.

Costin is stiff beside me, but he doesn't answer. I can sense the tension radiating from him, the unspoken challenge hanging in the air. All I want is to get the amulet fixed and get out of here before something more goes wrong.

"Maybe you knew my grandfather, George Devine?" I try to keep smiling. It's difficult while knowing I'm within swinging distance of the troll's rocky arms. "He said to find you when the time comes."

I mean, it's kind of true in a roundabout way.

The troll's gaze shifts to the gemstones hanging above us, then back to me. "Repairing the amulet will cost you. Nothing in this world is free, least of all power."

"I have money," I say. "Name your price."

Can it be possible that this entire ordeal might soon be over?

The troll laughs, the sound causing the entire cavern to shake like the beginning tremors of an earthquake. The gems hanging overhead sway and clink softly together. "Money is not a price. There is no cost to riches."

"She's not here for your riddles," Costin says. "We need the amulet repaired."

The troll snorts.

I glance at Costin, wondering just how much more I'm not seeing. He seems tenser than usual. His jaw is set, but there's darkness again lurking in his gaze, something I can't quite place.

"What you need does not dictate what Morvok gives." The troll sets the book on his table. He picks up a dagger. "Come."

Costin begins walking toward him.

"Not you, vampire," Morvok denies.

I glance at Costin before forcing myself toward the troll. I give a nervous laugh and joke, "You're not going to put me in a stew, are you?"

Costin loudly clears his throat. He had told me not to make small talk or jokes, but the troll has stopped trying to kick us out of his home. So there is that.

"Humans too chewy," Morvok answers.

I want to believe he's joking, but I'm not sure. His expressions aren't exactly readable.

"If you lie, you will be dead," Morvok warns. He

reaches for an open jar of yellow powder with his free hand and sprinkles it over the amulet. He then follows it with drops of green from a vial.

I eye his dagger. In anyone else's hands, it would probably be a broadsword. "I'm not lying."

"Hand." Morvok nods at the table.

I stare at his sword and slowly place my palm flat on the uneven surface, ready to jerk back if he tries to hack pieces off me.

"If you harm her..." Costin lets his threat hang as he appears next to me.

"You want a fix," Morvok says.

"Costin, it's okay," I whisper.

Morvok moves surprisingly quick for one so large. He grabs my arm, his large hand wrapping me from elbow to wrist. He lifts me from the table and quickly slices open my palm with the tip of his blade.

I cry out in pain as my blood spills over the amulet's broken pieces. Costin grabs me by the shoulders and shoves me behind him. The troll lets go of me but instantly holds the blade to the vampire's chest, pressing it over his heart.

"No, don't!" I try to reach to stop the knife. I push the troll's arm but am unable to move him.

My spilled blood begins to bubble and steam.

Morvok tosses the blade to the side, causing the dagger to stick in the tabletop. "This amulet cannot be fixed until the magic is earned."

"What does that mean?" I look at Costin, confused. "I have never had magic, so how do I earn it?"

"Come back when you have completed the labyrinth and have seen your true face," Morvok holds the yellow powder and reaches for my arm. "Until then you do not have the worth."

I don't like the sound of that.

Costin's eyes are fixated on my blood, and I swear I see him lick his bottom lip.

"I fix," Morvok insists, curling his fingers to indicate I should give him my hand.

I lift my arm. He dumps the yellow powder on my wound. It tingles and burns along the cut, but the sensation is over quickly. The troll's magic clots the injury.

Costin grimaces.

"Uh, thanks," I tell the troll to be polite.

"What's the labyrinth?" I ask.

I reach for the amulet shards, but Morvok blocks me.

"I do not know what your labyrinth is," Morvok answers.

"It's a series of trials you must face and it's different for everyone," Costin explains before saying to the troll, "The labyrinth is too dangerous for a mortal. There must be another way."

"That is the price of this great magic," Morvok says. "Otherwise, everyone would use it."

"There has to be another way," Costin insists.

"You can throw the pieces to Draakmar as an offering," Morvok suggests. The way he says the creature's name inspires both terror and reverence.

"And that will keep the evil from rising?" I ask, hopeful.

"No, it will help Draakmar to surface, but he might spare you his fire." Morvok takes a yellow stone from the ceiling and sets it on the table. He crushes it with his thumb, griding it into dust.

The evil has a name. Draakmar.

I was right. It doesn't make me feel better to give it a name.

"Who is this Draakmar?" I ask.

The troll frowns. "Everyone knows of the great sleeping dragon Draakmar."

I think of the schoolchildren at the bridge. Maybe I should have joined their field trip.

"My education was..." I gesture helplessly. "Human."

The troll harrumphs.

"Draakmar is a fire dragon who embodies raw, destructive power," Costin says. "The original amulet was formed from one of its scales."

I frown at him. He knew all this and didn't tell me before?

"This is why you failed to protect the magic," Morvok grumbles. "You should not have been given that which you don't understand. It took many trolls several years to pry it from his back. So long as the magic was intact, he did not notice. Now that it is broken, he will come looking for that which was stolen. He will come to eat you first."

"Come on, Tamara." Costin is unhappy as he forces me to leave with him.

I try to free myself, but he holds firm and blocks me from returning. "Wait. I have more questions."

"She must face the labyrinth trials alone, vampire," Morvok calls after us.

Costin pushes me through the troll's entryway tunnel so fast I can barely stay on my feet. Something has changed in him. He's always had that domineering quality to him, but he's starting to act a little too controlling.

"Dammit, Costin, let me go," I demand as we reach the row of mud-brick houses.

"I told you to let me do the talking!" Costin hisses under his breath. His eyes are swirling red with anger. "You didn't need stories of Draakmar filling your imagination and distracting you from your purpose."

"So the evil has a name," I argue. "Does it really change anything? And I don't need you dictating what I do and don't need to know. From now on, you tell me the—"

"Eh?" The goblin's earthen jug rolls toward my feet as he struggles to stand.

I jerk my foot back to keep whatever liquid is inside from splashing on my shoe.

"Halt!" the goblin orders from the ground, lifting his finger. He holds the warning for a few seconds before collapsing back into drunken oblivion. A disturbing falsetto snore sounds.

"I don't get why you're so angry. It's not like you have to do the trials," I argue. "I mean, I didn't really think the prophecy was going to be as easy as step one: find troll, step two: fix amulet, step three: all good."

"Keep your voice down," Costin warns. "It's not safe to talk here."

I wonder if that's true or if he just wants to shut me up.

"Follow me." Costin doesn't give me a choice as he ducks between two of the dwellings.

FIFTEEN

I want my brother. I want Anthony.

I grip my phone, willing him to get in contact with me.

Anthony isn't always the most reliable, but it isn't like him to leave me hanging. He did say to text him when I came down, and he would find me.

My stomach is in knots, but I try not to panic. It's possible he partied too hard and is passed out some-where. Or maybe he hooked up with someone and is preoccupied.

"He'll answer," I tell myself.

"Who?" Costin turns at the sound of my voice. He's trying to lead me over the scary bridge, but I don't want to follow him. I'm irritated with him for not telling me about Draakmar.

Okay, sure, it changes nothing and, fine,

knowing has given my fears a more distinctive shape, but how can I be expected to fight without all the facts?

"My brother, if you must know," I answer. "Anthony isn't texting me back."

Costin frowns. "You should not be wasting your time with that right now. Anthony is probably in one of the many clubs and can't hear his phone. We don't need him."

"What is wrong with you?" I demand. "You're being more of an ass than usual."

"Me?"

"Yeah, you." I put my hands on my hips. "I'm not going anywhere until you answer my questions. Why are you so pissed at me?"

"I told you to let me handle the troll. Instead, you flirt with him, and now he's sending you into the labyrinth," Costin answers. He keeps his voice soft in deference to those close by, but I can hear the bubbling anger in his tone.

"Flirting?" I gasp at the accusation. I'm not so quiet. "I was doing no such thing!"

Several people stop their conversations and turn to look at us.

"Keep your voice down, Tamara," Costin orders. "And what was all that about beautiful mountains and troll history?"

He cannot be serious. There is no conceivable

world where I'm attracted to a troll. For one, it physically would not work. I'm pretty sure Morvok would crush me into nothingness. For second, I'm not in the habit of flirting with rock creatures with dead animals hanging in their hair.

"I'm not even going to dignify that accusation with a response," I say. "But if I was flirting with him, so what? It's not like you own me, vampire. We're not going steady. We fucked. Once. That does not mean I'm your property. I can do whatever I want with whoever I want in any position I want."

In quick hindsight, I realize that is not the appropriate thing to say to an angry vampire while trapped in the supernatural realm beneath a mausoleum. I follow Costin's eyes as he glances around. We are drawing a crowd. Some of that crowd looks very interested in my last declaration.

A hairy beast with wiggly antennas—*what the hell would you call a half ant, half dog?*—licks his lips and winks at me.

I move closer to Costin and whisper, "Get your jealousy in check. In case you forgot, I have a world to save. How about we focus on that? Now, what exactly is this labyrinth?"

He grabs me by my neck and holds firm, and his eyes swirl with anger. His face distorts, showing hints of the monster he can become. I've never seen him like this before. I feel his fingers working against my throat. With one squeeze, I could be over.

He leans in and growls beneath his breath, "Down here, I am your master. Don't make me enthrall you to prove it to them."

I tremble at the rage I see in his expression. He's never spoken to me like this.

"Keep defying me in front of people, and I will be forced to punish you." His tone lowers, and I feel his words vibrating through me. "I am the ruler of all the North American territories. I cannot be seen as weak. There are a hundred vampires in this place alone who would love to challenge me for the right, and I have no desire to massacre them all because you are having a tantrum about the truth of your mortality."

I don't move. I feel the others watching us. I want to argue, but I force the words to stay inside.

"Do you understand?"

I nod once.

"Good." He withdraws and releases my throat.

I force myself to appear calm. I can't deal with Costin being mad at me right now. If he was to storm off and leave me, then where would I be?

"You made your point," I say, hoping my narrowed eyes let him know how displeased I am by his actions. Never have I seen him angry, not like this. I've seen him irritated, and mocking, and bored, but never this.

"We need to keep moving." Instead of crossing, Costin leads me away from the bridge, cutting into a nearby tunnel where it is more private. A nearby cafe is packed with fairies hosting what appears to be a fashion show. I hear lively music in the distance and see flashes of what look to be disco lights.

"Maybe Anthony is in there." I motion toward the disco. I'm feeling very alone. I look at my phone. Where is my brother? I need him. He'll tell me how to complete this labyrinth, whatever it is. He'll make me feel safe.

"He won't be there," Costin dismisses. I don't ask how he knows.

"I don't want to be here," I whisper more to myself than to him, even though he can hear me. I put the phone back into my pocket. "I'm out of my depth. I just want this to be over."

"I am sorry I had to..." Costin frowns. He still seems irritated with me despite the half-apology.

"We're both tense," I dismiss. I know I'm giving him a pass for his behavior, but I can't deal with more drama right now. I have enough on my plate. "Let's just focus on what we need to accomplish. Tell me about the labyrinth."

"I could have convinced Morvok to find another path before it got this dangerous," Costin says. "You should not be alone in the labyrinth where I can't protect you."

"It's done. I don't think I have a choice." I don't think he understands exactly how much pressure I'm under at the moment. I am completely out of my depth. My entire life I've been told that I'm mortal, delicate, a freaking butterfly. Whoever heard of a butterfly surviving a fight with a monster?

No. Not just any monster. Draakmar, a fire dragon who embodies raw, destructive power.

A fucking fire dragon.

Of course, it's a dragon.

You're a delicate butterfly in a world of fiery dragons. The world needs butterflies, Tamara, as much as it needs dragons. Probably more. We all have our place.

My grandfather's words repeat themselves in my head. It's like he was trying to tell me something, even before he knew the full prophecy for himself. I always took the words as a warning to be careful, but maybe they're more than that. Maybe he was telling me to be brave, that I stood a chance.

Shit. I'm so scared.

My hands are shaking, and I want nothing more than to curl into a ball to hide from everyone and everything. I try not to cry. Heroes aren't supposed to cry, right?

Costin takes a deep breath as if coming to a decision. "You are not going into the labyrinth alone. It's not safe. I'll go with you."

I instantly want to say yes. But that is not what the signs are telling us.

"I don't think you should. I have to do it alone," I counter nervously. "Nothing about my life has been safe for me."

Of course, I would rather have him with me. Who wants to go into a labyrinth alone? I don't even know what this labyrinth thing really is. But it doesn't sound good.

How do you stop a dragon?

In the vision, the lava did not burn me. I have a feeling that's not going to be the case if those events really do come to pass.

I don't want to do this.

I don't have a choice.

The fairies' shouts become louder, and I press my hands against my temples to drown them out. I can't concentrate. It is all too much.

I lost Paul and Diana, but more than that, I lost the dream of a normal life that they represented.

I lost my best friend, Conrad, to betrayal. And now he's haunting me and keeping me from moving on.

I'm being forced to marry Chester. Enough said. Just picturing his face makes me want to throw up.

How can they expect me to look at that for the rest of my life?

And then there is this prophecy. With everything else going on in my life, I'm expected to go into a labyrinth by myself to do trials—whatever that means—with absolutely no protection or power, or knowledge for that matter, and save the fucking world from Draakmar, a lava breathing ancient evil monster.

As bad as the first timeline was before the reset, this one is starting to look much worse. And, at the end of all of this, everyone might be dead anyway.

"I can't deal with arguing with you right now. Please, let's just get through this next task." I don't add that the odds are I'm going to fail, and none of the other stuff is going to matter anyway. "What do I need to know about this labyrinth?"

"Have you heard of the Greeks?" Costin asks.

I arch an unamused brow and stare at him.

"Of course." Costin has the good sense to look apologetic. "What I meant to ask is, have you heard of the Greek labyrinth?"

I hug my arms across my chest, wishing I could make myself smaller. "Please tell me I'm not going to have to fight a minotaur."

"Not *the* minotaur," Costin explains. "But your version of it. I can't tell you what that is. There is no way of knowing what you will face when you accept the challenge."

"Well, this sounds fun," I drawl sarcastically.

He leans in close to me. His look says, *I told you so.*

I'm getting really tired of that self-righteous expression.

"Do you think..." I glance around to make sure no one is staring at us. "Do you think Draakmar is my minotaur in the labyrinth? Do you think I'm going to have to... fight...?"

My breath catches.

"I don't know what you'll face. Like the labyrinth in Greek mythology, this labyrinth is a test," he explains. "It represents the complexity of your personal journey. It takes the things you fear the most in your life and makes you face them. And this isn't just some metaphorical figure out your feelings type of journey. These things can kill you. There will be confusion, challenges, misdirection, powerful magic. It will be harder than anything you've ever faced. Once you go in, there's no escape button. When you're in, you're in. You either make it out or you don't."

I close my eyes and take a deep breath, willing myself to wake up from the nightmare.

"Are you listening?" Costin touches my arm. "Because this is important."

I nod and look at him. He's standing so close that I can't see anything else. I stare at his neck, watching his jaw move as he speaks.

"I can't tell you how the trials will manifest for you. Like I said, it's different for everyone. But essentially, you will face three tests that will embody strength, knowledge, and courage."

My eyes move down to his chest. I placed my hand flat over his heart. I feel it beating like he's alive. Alive. Undead. Unalive. As much as he aggravates me at times, I have to admit there's a part of me that appreciates Costin's protective nature.

"What if I can't do it?" I remain focused on his heartbeat, needing to feel close to someone. "What if I fail?"

"Then Draakmar wakes up, and the world as we know it dies."

The words are not exactly comforting. Then again, Costin has never been one to pretty up the harsh truth.

I can't help but hear Astrid's voice in my head, saying, *"It can die."*

I was five years old, holding a stray puppy that I wanted to keep, but as she said it, I knew she meant me. I'm the one who could die. That one word had become a mantra of sorts, a harsh reminder of my limitations.

I want Costin to tell me I can do it. I want him to tell me that he believes in me.

He doesn't.

"Can we find a restroom?" I ask. "And maybe a water bottle and a protein bar?"

Not that I'm positive I can keep either of those things down, but I'm stalling.

Costin looks around as if to gauge where we are. "The old subway tunnels are on the way to the labyrinth's entrance."

I nod, not knowing the significance.

"Few people dare go down there unless they're entering the labyrinth. You will be safe waiting there while I find you water. It will be easier to get there if I mesmerize you."

For the first time in my life, the idea of being mesmerized doesn't scare me. In fact, the idea of falling into oblivion where I have no control holds great appeal. I nod my head. I'm not sure I could force my legs to make the journey.

Almost instantly, I find myself slipping into that deep vortex inside of Costin. It's beginning to feel familiar, safe. I want to fall into his dream and never come out.

SIXTEEN

I stare at the tiled wall of an abandoned subway station. I have no idea how far we traveled to get here, but it's quieter than the marketplace. In fact, it's too quiet. I'm the only one here. Costin has left me with instructions not to move as he searches for bottled water.

He's bossy, and it's annoying, but I listen. Where am I going to wander off to? Following scary-ass tracks into the unknown darkness? For all I know, ghouls live right around the corner.

As a New Yorker, I know about these old subway tunnels. Usually, they are urban legends told drunkenly at bars as modern-day campfire stories about mole people and various scary entities. I never thought I'd find myself in them.

The station is a forgotten relic, sealed up and

frozen in time, deep in the bowels of the city. It's no wonder supernatural creatures have claimed them. Thick dust blankets the cracked floor, and rust crawls along the edges of metal beams that support the ceiling. It's a little sad to think some brave builders sacrificed to create such a transportational work of art only to have it bypassed for a new plan.

Unlike the marketplace, the light here comes from old fixtures. I wonder if it's magic that keeps the bulbs flickering or if some fairy in a toolbelt flies through and replaces them when they burn out. Haunting shadows fall around me and when I close my eyes, I think I hear voices—soft and faint, like ghosts from another century.

My eyes are drawn to faded letters around a spiral pattern in the tile wall. I can only make out part of a word, *Mort—*. It's strange that the design is still here. I would have expected a layer of urban hieroglyphs, the graffiti of some tagger marking his territory. It's untouched by such vandalism. I brush my hand over it, dusting it off in an attempt to read what's there and shivering at the cold I find. The paint chips against my fingers, and I pull away.

The lights flicker harder than before, and I hope they don't go out. When Costin doesn't return, I move to the edge of the platform. I listen to the darkness stretching beyond the tunnel. All is an eerie silence but for the echoing *drip-drip* of water somewhere down the line. A piece of the ceiling falls from above, clanking on the corroded steel rails below.

I hear a faint rumble coming from the dark, and I instantly step away from the platform. A breeze comes toward me, bringing with it the stale air scented of damp concrete, oil, and decay. Yellowed paper somersaults across the floor. The rumbling becomes louder, and I see a soft flash of light. I press my back against the spiral on the wall and hold still as a transparent old train stops at the station. The doors open, but I don't see anyone getting on or off. It waits as if inviting me to go in.

I don't. I'm not an idiot. There is no way I'm hopping onboard a ghost train.

Where the hell is Costin?

"I don't belong here," I whisper. "What was I thinking? I can't do this."

What if Costin doesn't return?

A long, tense minute later, the train doors close, and it leaves. Its departure appears to stir one of the green butterflies hiding in the tunnel. It comes to hover over my head for several seconds before moving to land on the spiral on the tile wall.

"I know," I tell the butterfly in annoyance. "I get it. I have to do this alone."

I'm not sure I trust Costin not to follow me.

Oppressive stillness is only broken by the sound of my feet as I look for a possible escape. A staircase leads upward into a pile of rubble at the far end of the station platform. I reach for my neck out of old habit, not finding the amulet.

My phone dings, and I jump in fright before scrambling to pull it from my back pocket.

"Anthony," I whisper, seeing it's him. I open his text, *"He"*

He?

What does that mean?

At least he's okay. He's saying something.

I try to send him a question mark, but the phone says there is no service. I hold it up, walking the length of the platform, searching for a signal as I watch the screen.

The flicking overhead lights become more intense. Another piece of ceiling falls and clinks onto the floor next to me. I look up only to find more tiles coming toward me. They rain down, striking me on the head and arms as I try to shield myself.

The stone rain pelts harder, scratching my arms as it falls. I spin in circles, looking for safety. The spiral on the wall falls away to expose a tunnel. The butterfly flies inside. I run to follow it.

The second I crawl inside, the rain stops. I look behind me to see the stone wall grinding to a close with a decisive finality. The subway station is gone, and I'm left in darkness. Not even the butterfly remains with me.

"Costin?" I whisper, hoping he can hear me like he did when I called for him during the engagement party. "I'm not sure where I'm at."

Cold air comes at me, and for a second, I think it might be him. A shiver runs down my spine. Suddenly, flames burst close by as torches are lit by an invisible force. The light is enough to show the only way forward, but it leaves most of the cavernous space veiled in shadows.

"The labyrinth," I whisper as the realization dawns on me. That is what the spiral design on the wall represents. A magical entryway into this nightmare.

The troll's parting words echo in my mind, *"She must face the trials alone, vampire."*

It would seem the labyrinth agrees.

The tunnel curves to the right, the beginning of an ancient, mystical maze. The air feels charged with energy and smells of burnt, spent magic. I can't help but wonder how many have come before me.

Taking a deep breath, I force my fear down to the pit of my stomach. The troll said I had to do this alone. I need to be brave.

I need to have faith.

I'm not sure how one finds faith. It seems to be a thing that you either have or don't, that you find or lose, but never a thing you can will into existence.

I feel so alone, abandoned. I want to curl up into

a ball and cry until somebody comes to save me. But if I give in to my fears, everything I love will be destroyed. I have to try.

I attempt to push my swirling thoughts down so I can concentrate on the task at hand. These are my trials, and I have no choice but to pass them.

As I walk by the torch on the cave wall, another appears ahead of me. The labyrinth is more than stone and shadows—it's alive, watching me, testing me. Costin warned me that it would try to deceive and misdirect me. I need to stay sharp and fight any paranoia that tries to set in.

I am alone. I have to believe I'm taking the right path.

I pray that path does not lead straight into Draakmar's lair.

My feet step steadily over the ground. My breath punctuates the silence. I keep my eyes focused ahead, watching for what may come to test me.

I continue along the curve. Torches light the path ahead. Behind me is unwelcoming darkness and a sealed subway wall. There is no going back, only forward.

I keep moving, eyes focused ahead. I wonder if the labyrinth is a maze and I must find my way through, but there is only one path spiraling to the right so far. Every so often, I touch the wall just to make sure it's real. A new torch appears to reveal that the pathway is turning to the left. I hesitate at the change and slow my steps. As I stop to watch, the path twists like a living thing, writhing and reshaping before my eyes. Yet the terrain beneath my shoes feels solid.

The ground vibrates, and a giant rock wall shoots up from the floor to block my path. I turn, but another wall blocks me. Firelight appears overhead, showing me the way.

The first obstacle.

The route behind me is closed. There is only one way to go. Up.

"You want me to climb?" I ask, half expecting the walls to answer.

They don't respond.

"Any chance I get a safety harness?"

Still no answer.

I suppose I owe my mother a thank you for all those exercise hours she made me log growing up. The sheer rock face seems to grow taller the closer I come. Jagged stones jut from its surface, and the uneven texture promises an arduous climb.

One trial is an assessment of strength. The labyrinth is testing my endurance, and the message it is sending is clear. Like in life, there are no easy paths or shortcuts. There is only onward.

I grab a handhold and hoist myself up. The torch sticking out of the side of the cliff overhead becomes my goal, and I climb toward it. I try not to think beyond the next push upward, but random thoughts still stir.

I grew up among the supernatural, yet I will never be one of them. I used to feel defective because of the power that flows through my family. However, I have accepted my mortality. At this point, I can't imagine having to learn to control fireballs or cast spells. I don't expect magic will come to me when I complete this test. Though it would be nice to have the amulet's protection again. Gods know I need it.

One torch disappears, and another takes its place. I look down, unable to see the bottom. I look up, finding an endless cliff. My muscles ache, and I'd give anything for a break.

"Keep going," I order through clenched teeth, forcing myself to breathe.

My fingers are raw and ache from gripping the textured surface. Every inch feels like it adds a thousand pounds to my body. My movements become stunted. I've lost momentum. I become frozen against the stone.

A tear slips down my face. The first task is climbing a wall and I've already failed. What good am I?

Merely mortal. Always mortal.

If the labyrinth wants to remind me just how human I am, how weak, it has succeeded.

What was my grandfather thinking? What was the wizard who wrote this prophecy thinking?

I can't save the world. I can't even climb a damn cliff.

My arms shake, and I try to reach the next hand-hold, but my fingers struggle to find a purchase on the stone, and I fall back down. My foot slips, and I hear stones crashing along the cliff face. My heart beats hard. Panic floods me. I won't survive the fall.

I try not to think of all the people I'm failing.

A faint cry comes from above. I'm too weak to look up as I cling to the rock.

"Hello?" I call out, hoping for help. The word echoes back at me.

The noise comes again. Someone sounds like they're in pain.

I manage to pull myself up another few inches.

The voice doesn't answer me, but it sounds familiar.

Anthony?

No. It can't be him. It's a trick. He should be somewhere safe. He needs to be.

The sound comes again, fainter than before but unmistakable.

"Anthony!" I yell. "Hold on, I'm coming!"

My stomach knots, and I grunt with each push upward. I force myself to ignore the pain, to keep climbing. The labyrinth is designed to mess with my head and exploit my fears, but it can also kill me. What if it brought Anthony into its game to make me suffer?

I can't lose another brother.

Desperation drives my actions.

"I'm coming," I whisper, breathless. "I'm coming."

I can't afford to think. The labyrinth will not wait for me to figure things out. It doesn't care if I feel sorry for myself or that I'm mortal. This is a test, and I can't fail.

"I'm coming."

The words become a mantra.

I feel around above my head, and my hand finds a flat surface. I somehow manage to hoist myself over the cliff's edge, having no idea how high I've climbed or how long. My limbs give out, and I collapse on the hard ground, rolling onto my back and pulling my legs to the side to get away from the edge. I suck in a deep breath, grateful for the air in my lungs and the earth beneath me. I'm exhausted and want to rest, but the labyrinth isn't done with me yet.

"Anthony?" I croak, wishing for that bottle of water.

The sound of my brother's voice is gone. I only hear my heavy breathing.

Another torch lights to show me a large cavern.

Stalactites hang from above, pointing down like fingers. Small growths cling to the walls like popcorn. The light flickers over them, seeming to give them life. I roll over and army crawl on my stomach because I can't stand. The slide of my body echoes back to me.

"Anthony?"

He doesn't answer. I collapse. It feels like the walls are watching me, and I can almost sense the labyrinth's amusement at my weakness. One trial in, and I'm already spent.

Mere mortal. Human.

The doubt surfaces. It's what they all say about me. I don't need a stupid labyrinth to prove it true.

I hear my cell phone ding. The sound causes me to jolt in fright. I scramble to pull it from my pocket. I see a text message from Anthony, "*Help.*"

When I try to answer him, the phone dies, the screen flickering to useless black.

"Anthony?" I yell. "Where are you?"

The ground beneath me thumps, sending ripples through the stone like heartbeats. At first, I think it's my chest as I attempt to catch my breath from the climb. I try to push myself up, but the stone creaks and groans before I can get my bearings. A stalactite breaks off the ceiling and comes crashing down. I scream and curl into a ball. That first one is followed by its friends, all of the stone fingers diving from the ceiling to the ground below.

I bury my head in my hands, and my body jerks with each crash. When the noise stops, I look to find the cave formations have created walls to define my path. I push to my feet before the ceiling caves in on me. My muscles are fatigued, but fear gives me strength.

Something pushes up against my foot, and I stumble. A sharp vine twists from the ground next to me. Its barbs try to snag my shirt, and I hear a rip as I pull away. Another grows with lightning speed, whizzing dangerously close to my face. Heat seems to radiate from the vines. My heart quickens at the rapidly changing landscape. I dodge another and try to run, each step a test of my reflexes.

There is no time to strategize as I struggle against the supernatural terrain. The labyrinth is determined to wear me down, making me expend every ounce of my mortal limitations. I don't know how I keep moving.

My sneaker catches on one of the vines, and I hit the ground hard. The wind knocks from my lungs, and I wheeze. For a moment, I lay there, unable to draw a full breath. Exhaustion presses in. My body screams in pain.

Rage begins to replace the fear. I may not be built

for this, and every inch of me might scream for a reprieve, but I can't let the supernatural win.

I'm hit with flashes of my life, and the grief stings. I think of Paul and Diana being chased by monsters, of Anthony and our parents being placed into the crypt wall, of the broken amulet killing Conrad. I think of Costin being forced to babysit me because of a prophecy. I don't know if he really cares or if I'm simply a diversion. Either way, I wish he was here now to save me. The supernatural world has taken so much from me.

Another thick vine curls from the ground near my feet. The temperature feels like the inside of an oven. Its thorny tip comes around to form an arch above me before embedding itself into the ground once more. I must keep going. Self-pity serves no one.

I push my doubt aside and shout, "You're not going to break me!"

Maybe it's foolish, but I want the labyrinth to know I'm going down fighting.

"*Tamara,*" a disembodied voice whispers as if taunting me.

I swipe the tears from my face, feeling the unsettling sensation of someone watching me. Let them. I hope they find the mortal in a maze fucking entertaining.

"Get it together, Tamara," I whisper. The

labyrinth is designed to distort reality, to make me doubt myself.

Another torch reveals the way as the one behind me disappears. Eerie silence is a welcome reprieve to the sound of creaks and rumbles. I propel my body angrily toward it, weaving past the last of the vines.

I'm sweaty and gross. My hands are raw. Dirt from the cave covers my clothes.

The walls groan, echoing my own insecurities, amplifying them. I keep going, doing my best to ignore the physical strain. I don't need the labyrinth to remind me of how outmatched I am, of how small and weak I always feel. It's been lingering beneath my surface since my birth.

I may not be like my family, with all their magic and power. I'm not like Costin, with his immortality and strength. But I do have one thing—no one expects me to succeed.

Maybe I don't belong in this world. Maybe I never will. But if it takes me down, it's going to be fighting.

"Tamara."

I hesitate and take a deep breath. I really hope that's not Draakmar calling out to me.

SEVENTEEN

My legs are like lead, but I tell myself to keep moving. Scratches mar my dirty arms. Knots are forming in my muscles. I brace my sore hand against the wall for support. I thought this was supposed to be a test of strength, but it feels more like a reminder that I don't belong here.

The faster I go, the faster I will find the end. I pass the torch, expecting another to appear to light the way.

Darkness remains ahead.

I take a steadying breath. What now?

The air becomes cooler, momentarily welcome against the heat as it chills my sweat. I fall against the wall for support and start to shiver. My breath comes out in white puffs. Does this mean the physical test is over, or is it the beginning of freezing to death?

The way behind me is blocked. There is only one direction to go—forward into the darkness. I use the wall as a guide as I walk.

I tell myself that I have survived worse than this.

I try not to think about him. Paul. But sometimes, in the quiet moments between chaos, I wonder if he ever senses something is missing. That there is a piece of his life, of me, that he's forgotten. It is better this way. It has to be. For his sake. For his daughter's. For my own. But even as I tell myself that, a small part of me doesn't believe it.

I must keep going. This labyrinth is only a moment in time, and soon it will be over. Tiny green lights appear like glitter over the walls. They move as if alive, insects crawling over the rock. They're smaller than the butterflies I followed before.

I withdraw my hand, careful not to touch them. The tiny bioluminescent creatures stir. They swarm into the darkness, giving the softest of lights. It's difficult to make out much, but I take a tentative step to follow where they lead.

The energy differs from before. Something's coming, and it isn't good. I focus on the darkness for a hint of what is to come. The walls move, silently shifting in the shadows as if the labyrinth is preparing for my next trial.

The swarm of insects moves faster, forcing me to quicken my pace to keep up with them or be left behind in the dark. I feel like a rat in a scientist's maze. Only the scientist is a cruel sorcerer with a sick sense of humor.

The walls constrict, and the path becomes narrow. I have to turn to the side to pass by. Breathing becomes harder as the cold air thickens.

I don't want to be alone. Not here. I mouth Costin's name, wishing he would sense me and come for me. But I know that I must face these trials unaided. There is a reason the labyrinth let me in when I was alone in the subway tunnel.

I'm moving faster now to keep up with the insects. Unease marks every step I take. And then, finally, I hear something. At first, it's faint, like someone whimpering into a pillow.

"Anthony?" I call, recognizing the sound from before.

I run to find him. The faint cry becomes louder, echoing down the narrow passageway.

Anthony's whimpers continue to grow, turning into moans. He's in trouble. He needs me.

I lift my arms as I run through the insects. They scatter around me and fall to the ground like a burst of confetti. I see a new light up ahead, and I go toward it.

Finally, the passage opens up into a vast chamber. Shadows cling to the edges, and I have no idea how deep it goes. That doesn't matter now. My eyes are drawn to the center of the room. Anthony hangs suspended in the air. His body is shackled with writhing gold tendrils of magic. They hold him by his wrists and ankles. A thick band wraps around his waist and another winds around his neck.

The magic around his neck coils and tightens, causing him to whimper and moan. My heart seizes in my chest as panic sets in. My brother's eyes are closed, his face contorted in pain. His skin is draining color as if the snare is alive, feeding off him and drinking his magic.

"Anthony!" I rush toward him, but the moment I cross the threshold into the room, the air crackles with dark magic, and the tendrils writhe faster, sensing me. They pull tighter, and he lets out a sharp cry of pain. "Let him go! He has nothing to do with this. This is my trial, not his."

The magic doesn't listen. I have no command over such ancient and cruel things. I don't know how to fight this kind of magic.

I can't lose him. Not now. Not like this. Not like Paul.

But I'm not trained for this. My parents sheltered me from the knowledge of these things. They kept me away from magic and spells. They only taught me that which they thought would help me defend myself. Mortals have no use for magic. We're not meant to dabble where we don't belong.

"Feels familiar, doesn't it?" The voice seems to slither in behind me. I don't have to turn to know it's Conrad. "Shall we watch him die together?"

"Help me get him down," I beg.

Conrad laughs. "I rather like him as a chandelier."

I should have known Conrad wouldn't help me.

"Go away. Leave us alone." I clench my teeth and focus on Anthony. I look for something I can use to reach him. I have to get him down.

"Tamara," Conrad's voice whispers as if coming from the far end of the room. Seconds later, it sounds behind me as a distraction. *"Tamara."*

"Stop it," I yell.

Anthony thrashes and moans.

"How does it feel, watching another person you care about slip through your fingers?" Conrad's ghostly form materializes close to Anthony, his blackened eyes gleaming with malice. He looks up at our brother. "Helpless? Weak?"

"Shut up," I order. "I'm not listening to you."

"That would be a mistake," he warns. "Maybe we should have the labyrinth bring somebody else? Paul maybe? Or how about his cute little button of a daughter?"

"Don't you touch them! We had a deal." I see a

rock, and I go to it. I try to push it toward the center of the room. It doesn't budge.

"How does it feel to know that you will fail everyone that you care about?" Conrad's voice is a poisonous whisper. He's always been able to cut right through me. He knows exactly where to strike.

"Shut up, Conrad." My voice is steady, but I don't feel brave. I can't let him see he is getting to me.

Conrad steps closer, taunting, "Paul was right there, wasn't he?" He points to the floor next to my feet. "Right next to you. Bleeding out. And you couldn't do anything. Just like now."

I flinch at the memory. Images of Paul flash in my mind—the sound of gunfire, the blood covering his chest, the life fading from his eyes as he died in my arms. Guilt and pain flood in.

"Anthony always thought he was better than me," Conrad sneers, circling our brother. "But look at him now. My little puppet."

The magical shackles around Anthony's wrists and ankles begin to move as if making him dance. Anthony cries out in pain. The sound only makes Conrad smile.

"Not so superior now, are you?" Conrad taunts. His eyes turn back to me as I continue my search. "You will not find anything to help him. You might as well accept it. You failed Paul. You'll fail Anthony, too. You'll always fail."

My vision blurs with tears I refuse to let fall. Anthony is gasping for breath, the dark magic constricting him more with each passing second. I can hear his fear beneath the pain. It echoes my own.

I can't lose him.

Not again.

This isn't Conrad's doing. He only wants me to believe that he has control. Conrad always liked for people to think he was more than he was. I lost perspective for a moment, but I'm in the labyrinth.

Suddenly, the air shifts. The labyrinth is closing in on me. The pressure grows, dark energy builds in the room, and a new realization dawns. The labyrinth isn't just testing my strength. It's testing my will. My choices.

This is a test of knowledge. So that means I have to know the answer somewhere deeply hidden within my brain.

I force myself to stare at Anthony. His complexion is as pale as a vampire's. I try to remember bits of conversations I've eavesdropped on in the past. This is dark magic holding him captive—old, powerful, dangerous, and very real. There was a story our grandfather used to tell us about being trapped. Perhaps it was more of a warning, a way to teach children how to defend themselves against monsters. I try to remember the details, but it was so long ago.

Conrad's spirit fades.

I know this. The magic is tied to the mind, locking Anthony in some kind of trap as it feeds off the emotional energy of its victim. I need to disrupt its connection.

But how?

"You can't save him. You never could save anyone," Conrad reappears, sitting on the ground as if watching a show. "You might as well admit defeat."

I clench my fists. I touch my neck, but there is no amulet to comfort me.

Anthony's breath comes in short, ragged gasps, and his face contorts with pain.

"You let Paul die." Conrad points upward, and the magic on Anthony's neck tightens like a noose. "And now you're going to watch Anthony die, too. You always fail, Tamara. Being human is what you're good at."

I move closer. I feel the magic shifting at my nearness. It's drawing energy from everything in the room—not just Anthony.

Conrad appears across from me, his cold eyes locking with mine. "You're not strong enough to save him. But you can end this, you know. You can make a choice. A life for a life. You for him. Tell the labyrinth you'll take his place."

I feel the weight of the world bearing down on me, the magical threat pressing in, Conrad forcing my hand. The shackles around Anthony move with life, but this time, they quiver. The magic is waiting for me to decide.

Anthony doesn't deserve this. We weren't close growing up, but I've always loved him. There was always a bond, even when he was off at his fancy school, living in the world of magic that I could only dream about. He's my brother, my blood.

My attention moves to Conrad, and my resolve wavers. I know who he is now—what he has become. The man in front of me isn't the brother I used to trust. Yet, despite everything, there's still that tug, that piece of me that clings to the version of him I grew up with, the one who shielded me from the crueler parts of our shared world. The one who kept me company when everyone else abandoned me to tutors and loneliness.

My mind flickers back to those days, to the way we whispered secrets to each other when no one was listening. He was my best friend, my companion. More than that—he was my protector, my brother. I trusted him with all my secrets. I trusted him with my fears, my hopes, all those little pieces of myself I never showed anyone else.

"Choose, Tamara," Conrad whispers, a twisted smile curling his lips. "You or him."

I try to feel that connection we once had—or that I thought we had. It was us against the supernatural world. So much about him is familiar, even though black erases his eyes and ash covers his skin. Even though I hate myself for it, there's a part of me that still loves him, still wants to help him. Despite the malice in his smile, despite everything he's done to me, I can still see the boy I loved. He has been so much of my life.

I'm so tired of pretending that everything is fine, that I can keep going, no matter what the world throws at me. But the truth is, I'm running out of steam. Each day feels like a new battle, and the weight of it all is crushing me, piece by piece. My defenses have been up for so long, but the cracks are showing. I hate that I feel like this. I hate that I can't just keep it all together.

It's not just Conrad or the constant threat of the supernatural. It's everything—Paul's death, the memory of what we had, the endless nightmares, and even the haunting presence of my family's expectations. I've been trying to be strong for so long, but I feel like I'm at my breaking point. I want to give up, even though I swore I wouldn't.

I loved Conrad and would have given my soul to help him. But that was then, and this is now.

I'm tired of crying, but the tears still come. I shake my head, trying to clear my thoughts, trying to remind myself of the truth. A cold realization settles over me, and I understand. The labyrinth wants me to decide. It's testing my loyalty, testing whether I can make the impossible choice.

Conrad's been so much of my life, whether or not I want to admit it. He's shaped who I am in ways I didn't even realize until it was too late. There's an ache deep in my chest, a pull that refuses to go away. I don't want to feel it. I shouldn't feel it. But it's there, the stubborn echo of something I once thought was real.

I want to hate him.

I want to wipe the smug look off his face. He thinks he's won. I can't remember the exact story, but my grandfather indicated that dark magic feeds on negative energy, on things like fear and betrayal. I always thought he was talking about monsters, but maybe it applies to people, too. Conrad is nothing if not a walking embodiment of all of that.

It should be easy. After everything he's done— the lies, the murders, the betrayals—it should be the easiest thing in the world to let the labyrinth take him.

But it isn't.

The boy I knew is long gone. But that doesn't make it hurt any less. It doesn't make the memories fade or the part of me that still wants to save him go away. I hate myself for it, for that sliver of hope that maybe, just maybe, he can be saved.

My eyes drift to Anthony, still struggling, the dark magic choking the life out of him. He never betrayed me. He's never tried to twist the knife in the way Conrad has. He doesn't deserve to suffer.

There is no choice.

"Take him," I tell the labyrinth as I force myself to look Conrad in the eye, my voice steady now, even though the pain lingers in my chest. "Take Conrad."

For a moment, the room goes silent. Even Conrad seems caught off guard. His smirk falters as the magic quivers and shifts focus.

Conrad's eyes widen, a flash of anger crossing his face. "You think you can sacrifice me?"

"I'm sorry, but you left me no choice." I step closer to him. "The magic wants negative energy, and you have more than enough to feed it."

The hold on Anthony loosens as the dark energy withdraws from him to slither toward the ghost. The magic recognizes the darkness in him, latching onto it like a predator drawn to blood.

"You'll pay for this," Conrad snarls, his ghostly form flickering as the magic surges around him. "You'll regret this, Tamara. I swear it."

Conrad tries to disappear, but the magic takes hold. He screams as the shackles clamp down to feed on the darkest parts of him. I force myself to watch through the knot of guilt and regret wrenching my insides.

Conrad's eyes darken, his face distorting in fury. I can see all the things he wants to say, but the threats never make it past his lips.

As the last of the magic leaves Anthony's body, I reach up to catch him as he falls. His weight pummels me to the ground. I push him off me. He's weak, but alive.

The labyrinth sucks Conrad into the shadows. The screams stop, and he disappears.

"Anthony?" I touch his face as he blinks up at me.

"Was that... Conrad?" Anthony groans as he sits up. He looks around, confused. "How did we get here?"

I want to explain everything, but I'm not sure we should take the time. "We're in the labyrinth."

"The... labyrinth?" Anthony looks around with renewed awareness. He surges to his feet and reaches to pull me next to him. "How the hell did we wander in here? You can't be here, Tamara. It's too dangerous for mortals. Supernaturals train for decades before taking up the challenges."

The light in the room fades, and the torchlight flickers at the exit.

"We should go," I tell him.

"Yeah." He's weak, but he's alive. That's what matters.

I saved Anthony. But part of me wonders if I'll ever be able to save myself from Conrad.

We leave the chamber, and Anthony stops to look at the tunnel. "Who else is here?"

I know what he means. I can't shake the feeling that we're not alone. My instincts tell me that someone—something—is watching.

"I don't know." I focus on Anthony, happy to no longer be alone. I stay close to him as we stumble forward. We're not safe yet. "Come on. We have to get out of here."

EIGHTEEN

"We need to keep moving," I say quietly, glancing over at Anthony when he tries to rest against the wall. His face is pale, but he gives a tight nod, his eyes scanning the shadows as if he's waiting for the labyrinth to strike again. I can tell he's struggling to stay on his feet.

He has been brought in here with me. I figure that means he deserves to know everything. However, I don't have the energy to tell him the whole story. Therefore, I simply said I needed to fix my amulet's magic so I could have protection again.

Every step I take is a strain, but at least Anthony is by my side. I'm grateful not to be alone. The weight of choosing between both brothers presses in on me. I know I made the right call—the only call— but I still feel guilty. I try to push the feelings down.

There's no time to dwell on Conrad's unknown fate. Not now.

Anthony stops.

"This isn't right. Something is off." He tilts his head, listening. Louder, he calls, "Who's there?"

I've felt like someone was watching me since I entered this place.

When no answer is forthcoming, I say, "It's just the labyrinth. It is playing tricks on our mind. It's trying to distract us and make us paranoid."

"No," Anthony shakes his head, tensing as his voice drops to a near whisper. "Someone else is in here with us, following us."

I stiffen in fright. Is this the next trial? What did Costin call it? A test of courage?

"I don't think there is," I say. "I've had the same feeling since I entered this place."

Suddenly, Anthony relaxes and gives a big sigh. "Costin, come on, show yourself. I know you're there."

Costin?

I don't know how I know, but as soon as my brother says the words, I know it's true. I can feel Costin's nearness, like a ripple in the air, a presence I should have realized much earlier. Has he been following me the whole time?

Costin steps into the dim torchlight. Relief floods me to see him, but it's brief. Why didn't he let me know he was following me? Why wait to be called out by my brother?

"Where did you come from? What are you doing here?" I leave Anthony's side to confront him.

Costin doesn't answer. His expression is unreadable.

My stomach drops, and for a moment, all I can do is stand there, my mind racing. Yes, I wanted him to come to me in moments of weakness, but the troll's instructions were clear. He was supposed to stay out.

"How long have you been following me?" I demand.

Costin steps closer, his face calm, but there's a tension in his eyes. "Long enough."

What kind of answer is that?

"Long enough for what?" My mind spins, trying to understand why he's here, why he didn't say anything before now, why he's been watching from the shadows.

"Hey, maybe we can have this lovers' spat later," Anthony tries to reason. "I don't know about you two, but I do not want to be trapped in here for an eternity."

"You can't be here, Costin," I insist.

My brother threads his arm through mine. I let Anthony lead me down the tunnel. I can't help but feel safer now that I'm not alone. But I'm not supposed to feel safe. I'm supposed to be tested to prove myself so the troll will fix the amulet and stop the great evil from rising.

"No, I just..." I stop to face Costin, who is walking behind us. "You're not supposed to be here. I'm no expert, but I'm pretty sure the test of courage doesn't come with babysitters. This is all wrong."

"I told you to wait for me. I couldn't let you walk into this place alone." Costin says, his voice steady, but there's an edge to it. "The labyrinth is dangerous. You don't know what it's capable of. You're not trained to be here. You're—"

"I didn't have a choice but to come in here," I defend. "Make up your mind. Am I the one chosen by fate, or do I need saving?"

"Hey, buddy, you going to drink that?" Anthony asks.

I frown at the interruption but realize Costin is holding a water bottle. He hands it to me.

"The troll was clear. He said that this is my test. My trials." I gesture around in frustration. "You've ruined everything. Now, I've gone through all of this for nothing. I killed..."

I can't say Conrad's name.

"No, Tamara, Conrad died in the fire. What happened in that trial is not your fault. Like you said, this place likes to play tricks," Anthony interjects, trying to sound reasonable and calm. "If he is really a ghost, one of us would have seen him by now."

I look guiltily away.

"She has seen him," Costin answers, his eyes steadily on mine like the challenge. "Haven't you, Tamara?"

"You know?" I ask in shock. "But you didn't say anything."

"Neither did you," Costin counters.

I'm not supposed to tell anyone about Conrad because he threatened to hurt Paul and Diana if I did. I suppose it doesn't matter now if Conrad has been taken by the labyrinth. But nothing here is what it seems, and how can I know for sure that it's safe to talk about it?

"Tamara?" my brother insists when I don't answer.

I flinch, the word hitting harder than it should.

I can't make myself say the words. How do I explain everything that happened before? How do I tell Anthony that our brother is a lying murderer? Why not let him at least have a decent memory of what Conrad was?

"I wasn't going to let you face this alone." Costin's eyes burn with intensity. "I didn't trust it. I'm protecting you."

Anthony gives a little cough. "Tam-tam, are you going to drink that?"

I hand him the water bottle.

My brain focuses on that one word. Trust.

Costin reaches out like he wants to touch me. I take a step back. My thoughts are spiraling. He doesn't trust the labyrinth? No one should trust the labyrinth. But I read something deeper in his meaning, something he's trying not to say. It's not the labyrinth he doesn't trust. It's me.

My chest tightens, confusion mixing with the lingering pain of everything I've already faced in here. First, the physical pain that left me exhausted and emotional. Then Conrad's betrayal, and facing my own doubts about my worth, and now...

Costin doesn't think I'm capable of doing this. To him, I'm just a mortal. He's like all the other supernaturals in my life. He thinks I'm some delicate creature that can't fend for myself. Everyone always thinks I need to be protected. No one thinks I'm ever good enough, capable enough, or worthy enough to make my own decisions.

Part of me thought maybe he was different.

I'm such a fool.

I hear the plastic seal on the water bottle crack as Anthony opens it. I ignore him.

"You were protecting me, or you didn't think I could handle it?" I ask.

He blinks, and for a moment, I see a flicker of uncertainty. "Tamara, this isn't about you. The labyrinth is ancient and unpredictable. You don't understand how dangerous it is."

"Out of the two of us, I think I'm infinitely more qualified to say how dangerous the supernatural world is to someone like me. I don't need you to follow me." My voice sounds more uncertain than I want it to. A million thoughts race through my mind. I clench my fists, my nails biting into my palms. "I needed you to trust me. The troll said—"

"I don't care what the troll said," Costin interrupts, gliding closer. Our argument is tumbling in circles. "You don't understand how dangerous this place is. I couldn't just stand by and let you face it alone. You're just a..."

I flinch at his words, the familiar pang of uncertainty creeping in. He stops himself from saying more. He doesn't have to. I hear that same old echo reverberating through me: I'm a delicate butterfly in a world of fiery dragons.

Mere Mortal. Human. Fragile.

It can die.

I don't care that we're standing in a tunnel in a dark labyrinth that has already tried to kill me. I feel a long-dormant rage bubbling up inside me. I'm so tired of everyone treating me like I'm nothing. I'm tired of people telling me what I can't do and doubting my abilities.

I just want to be normal. I just want to belong somewhere.

"Go ahead. Say it. I'm a mere mortal," I finish for Costin with a sneer of disgust. "Just a poor, helpless, stupid human."

"I wouldn't say it like that, in that tone," Costin defends. "But yes. You are a human. You are mortal. Those are the facts."

The words sting more than I want them to. I trusted him. I thought he believed in me, too. But now, all I can feel is the weight of his disloyalty. Conrad had betrayed me because he didn't believe in me and thought he could control my life and choices. And now, here's Costin, doing the same thing, thinking that because I'm fragile, I need him to control me without asking me what I want.

"You don't trust me." My chest tightens as the words slip out before I can stop them.

"Hey, Tamara, take a breath and have something to drink," Anthony encourages. "You're tired and overreacting. I'm sure when this is over, Costin will explain himself, and everything will be fine."

Anthony pushes the open water bottle into my hand. When I don't move, my brother nudges my arm to urge me to drink. I swallow once before pulling the bottle away.

Costin's expression softens for a moment, and he steps closer, reaching for me. "It's not about trust.

It's about doing what's best for you. This prophecy—"

I throw the bottle at Costin's head to cut him off. He easily avoids the attack by leaning to the side. The water splashes and thumps its way down the tunnel.

His words ring hollow. That's what they always say, isn't it? The ones who betray you. The ones who think they know what's best regardless of what I want.

"Tamara, you're not alone in this," Costin says. His tone might be gentle, but I see the bloodlust swirling in his eyes. "I care about you. I wasn't going to let you get hurt."

"But you don't believe in me. You don't believe I can handle it, do you? This is my trial," I snap. "It's supposed to be my test, not yours. You were supposed to let me handle it. If we make it through this, and the troll decides I didn't earn the magic needed to fix the amulet, it will be your fault the world ends."

Costin's expression tightens, but he says nothing more. He just watches me, his intense gaze filled with something I can't quite read.

"Whoa, prophecy? Are we talking about a real, actual prophecy? I don't suppose anyone would want to clue me in on what's going on here. I'm a little bit in the dark about this whole troll amulet world-ending thing," Anthony says, trying to pat my shoulder.

"You're right. We should go." I spin around and march through the tunnel. I stay out of their reach, not wanting to be touched. Under my breath, I mutter, "So help me if I have to go through another version of this freakshow again..."

I'm tired and hurt. I didn't ask to be a hero.

What was I thinking, taking up with a vampire? Of course, he thinks I'm incapable. He feeds on my kind. We're snacks to him, not equals. I'm just something to slake his desires, whether it's for blood or sex.

I don't need another person watching me from the shadows, making decisions for me.

The silence between all of us becomes a palpable thing. I try to focus all my energy on solving this stupid puzzle so we can get out of here.

"I haven't betrayed you," Costin says quietly.

I refuse to stop walking. My hands tremble at my sides, and I ball them into fists. "But you don't trust me either."

Before we can say more, the ground beneath us rumbles. The labyrinth is changing again, the walls groaning as they rearrange themselves. A narrow door creaks open. I see bits of light reflected from within.

"Seriously, does anyone want to tell me about this prophecy?" Anthony asks.

He doesn't get an answer.

I'm still shaken from the argument, but there's no time to dwell on it. The labyrinth isn't going to wait for us to sort this out. I take a deep breath, forcing myself to focus on the path ahead.

I try to move forward, but Costin and Anthony step in front of me. I frown at their backs.

"Stop it, both of you." I forcibly push between them and give Costin a pointed look. "I don't know what's waiting for us in there, but you need to stay out of my way and let me do it."

Anthony drops to the side and lifts his arms out of the way to let me pass.

Costin seems more hesitant to obey. He doesn't say anything. He just nods, his expression unreadable.

I move past them to enter the chamber first, feeling the need to prove myself. It feels like I've stepped into a kaleidoscope with fragmented light dancing across the walls, turning into soft rainbows, like those cast by prisms. The effect is mesmerizing, almost beautiful, but something about the way the colors unnaturally shift, and change keeps me on edge.

The floor beneath my feet feels solid, but the air is thick, shimmering with the kind of magic that makes my skin prickle. I step forward cautiously, but my heart is already racing. This place feels alive. The labyrinth is watching us, waiting for me to take the next step, the final step. I know this is it—the last test. The test of courage. But I have no idea what form it will take, and that terrifies me more than anything else we've faced so far.

As I walk deeper into the chamber, I feel a chill crawl up my spine. Large antique mirrors line the walls. Their smaller handheld counterparts hang from the ceiling to reflect the light, scattering it in a dozen directions. Each one catches glimpses of us, casting us into a hundred different versions as they reflect against each other. The reflections twist and stretch, multiplying until I can't tell where we end, and the illusions begin.

"The magic is stronger here," Anthony says. "Be careful."

A mirror catches my attention. There is nothing special about it other than I've seen its design before in the penthouse library. For a moment, I stand, staring at the dirty, frazzled reflection staring back. A familiar feeling creeps over me from when I was in the library the night Costin came to tell me of the prophecy. I had stared at myself for so long, watching my face blur, wishing I could step through the glass into another world, a place where I could be free from everything that weighed me down. I wanted to escape. To disappear.

Now, as I peer into the reflection, it's not just a longing for another world that stirs inside me. It's the realization that no matter how many worlds I wish for, I can't outrun the one I'm in. This time, I must face it.

"Tamara?" Costin asks. "What do you see?"

I can't answer him. The background of my reflection is not the mirror chamber I'm standing in. There is a foggy haze hiding something lurking within its depths. I watch it move around, a mere shadow against the foggy light. I lean closer to see what it's trying to show me.

The light around me starts to flicker, and the image begins to clear as the fog takes shape.

"*Yoo-hoo, Tam-tam,*" a voice calls as if from far away. I hear a slight whistle. "*This way.*"

My blood runs cold.

The world tilts before righting itself, and I'm no longer in the labyrinth. I'm standing in my birth mother's San Francisco Victorian home. I've only been there once—in the alternate timeline—but I easily recognize the eclectic space. There is a cozy air to the home, one that had made me feel as if I truly belonged for the briefest of times. The floor-to-ceiling bookcases aren't filled with ancient magical tomes but rather novels and self-help books, and there is a charming reading nook. The home is well lived in, with protective charms and totems that blend with artistic decorations. It's nothing like the perfect, unchanging decor of Astrid's domain.

It's how I remember it. Exactly. Down to the takeout Chinese food on the coffee table. We had to eat in the living room because there is no dining table. Instead, art easels fill the dining room. I stand amongst those paintings now, looking through the large archway between the rooms.

An open decorative box is placed on the living room floor. That is where Lorelai kept her vampire stakes. Costin's vampiric sister is waiting outside with her brood to avenge his death, but she never makes it inside.

No one else is here, but I feel as if they're close.

"No," I whisper. "Not this night. Not again."

I can't breathe. This is the night the amulet broke. I reach for my neck, thinking I might feel it. It's not there. I can't go back to this timeline. This has to be a mistake. My heart pounds, and I look around in panic, desperately searching for Paul.

No. No. No. Not again. I can't do this again.

I turn around, looking for the mirror portal that brought me here. It's gone. There is no labyrinth, only this house.

"Anthony?" I whisper. "Costin? Get me out of here."

They don't answer. They're not here. In this world, they're already dead.

"Yoo-hoo, Tam-tam," the disembodied voice repeats louder than before. *"This way."*

Conrad.

"No," I beg the universe, barely able to get the word out. I refuse to look toward the sound. I can't do this again. My heart aches in my chest. This is my hell.

The universe doesn't care.

"Yoo-hoo, Tam-tam. This way." The voice sounds caught in a loop as if it's waiting for me to press play on this version of the past.

My breathing sounds abnormally loud. I think of everything that's happened to me since this moment when my timeline reset—Conrad's death and subsequent haunting, Paul and Diana's life without remembering me, un-meeting the birth mother I just found. Then there is Mortimer engaging me to Chester Freemont, the worst possible option. Costin, who I'm starting to really care about, who thinks what every other supernatural creature thinks about me, that I'm delicate and incapable of doing anything great on my own. And the prophecy.

Even with all of that, I would not trade my current suffering for this version of reality. Here, I lose everything—Paul, Anthony, my parents, and even Costin. None of them survived this timeline.

"Yoo-hoo, Tam-tam. This way."

I've relived this moment in my mind a thousand

times, and I've tried so hard to forget it a million more.

If the labyrinth is sending me back here, to the time before the amulet broke, maybe it's giving me the chance to change things. But this timeline doesn't fix the past. By this point, everyone but Paul is dead, and Paul will be joining them soon.

What if I stay here? What if fixing the amulet means accepting this fate?

I don't know what to do.

If this is a test of courage, I'm going to fail. I'm terrified.

"Yoo-hoo, Tam-tam. This way."

I hate his voice, hate everything about Conrad.

"Yoo-hoo, Tam-tam. This way."

It's not going to stop. I can't stay frozen in this spot forever.

"You're in the hall of mirrors," I tell myself, my voice shaky. "This is a trial. You just have to do it."

All that may be true, but that doesn't mean this isn't real.

I wish I was normal. This is as far from normal as a human can get.

"Yoo-hoo, Tam-tam. This way."

I hesitate before slowly turning to look. The room is no longer empty. Ghosts from the past sit in solid reality, like actors taking their places within the scene.

Conrad is dressed in a style preferred by young vampires, in a silk shirt and dress pants. He always tried to impress them. He even went so far as to try to become one. Now, he looks in my direction, eyes glassy and wild like he's high on something. I turn my attention to the gun in his hand before looking at the couch where he's pointing it at Paul and my birth mother.

Lorelai is terrified. She's what I imagine I'll look like in twenty years. We share the same hazel eyes and curly hair. However, Lorelai's hair has a wild, untamed quality that Astrid would never let me get away with. Lorelai prefers a more natural style, without makeup, and favors an artistic Bohemian flair.

Paul's soulful brown eyes are tinged with fear. His wavy brown hair is messy. We'd made love earlier in the day, and I want nothing more than to rewind to that moment. He looks so handsome. It makes my heart ache.

Paul never asked to be brought into this supernatural world. By the time he learned that supernatural creatures are real, it was too late for him to turn back. Monsters have been tormenting him and his daughter since they met me.

"Paul," I say. "I'm so sorry."

He doesn't respond. I know what is to come. I have to stop it.

If this is how the amulet fixes itself, I can't live with that. There must be another way. I have to break this timeline.

"Conrad," I try to plead. I rush into the living room to stand between the couch and the gun. "You don't have to do this. It's not going to end the way you—"

"Don't mind them. I told them if they moved or made a sound, I'd shoot everyone." Conrad is still staring at where I had been standing.

I follow his gaze to find a ghostly image of my past self. I'm the only figure who's not solid. Conrad keeps talking, but I don't listen. I grab Paul to try to force him to look at me. My touch has no effect on him. "Paul, you have to get out of here. You have to run."

But where can he go? Vampires are outside. He won't stand a chance against them.

He doesn't hear me. I try to pull Lorelai off the couch. She doesn't respond. They're locked in the past. I'm having no effect.

Conrad's gun bounces between Paul and Lorelai like he's deciding who to shoot first. I climb over the coffee table and grab the gun from his hands. I point it at him. He holds his hands out like he still carries it.

"*Hey,*" the ghostly echo of my past self tries to reason, the sound airy and distant. "*What are we doing here? Come on, Conrad. Look at me. It's me. Talk to me. We're family."*

The words distract me for a split second, and the gun disappears from my grip without me realizing it. When I look back, it has returned to Conrad.

There isn't much time. I hurry out of the room, away from the scene. I can still hear it playing out. Desperate, I look at every reflective surface I can find. "Anthony? Costin? Can you hear me?"

I can't find a way out.

What do I do? What do I do?

Fuck!

I end up in the kitchen. My hands shake violently as I dig through the drawers, only to grab a butcher knife. I run back into the living room, wielding the blade.

"Remember when we were little?" my past self is trying to reach Conrad. Spoiler alert: I fail. *"Those nights on the balcony? Those days breaking the rules in the library? It was you and me against the supernatural world..."*

I ignore my past self.

"Conrad, put the gun down," I order.

They don't hear me.

I try to give the knife to my past self. I won't take it.

I go to Conrad and hesitate a second. I close my

eyes and make a weak noise as I plunge the blade into his stomach. I feel the resistance as it goes in.

I wait, too afraid to look at what I've done.

Conrad gives a short, humorless laugh and says, "Stop being so naïve. We're not family. We've never been family. Do you know what I remember? Davis shows up at the Turnblads' house, asks to inspect the kid who had a run-in with gremlins at the group home before coming to stay with them, drops off a wad of cash, and takes me like a puppy he picked up at the pound."

I withdraw the blade and blindly stab a second time. I feel it enter his body.

"Lady Astrid made it very clear that my only purpose was to take care of *you,* entertain *you,*" Conrad continues.

I try to stab him a third time, screaming as I do so.

"Be Tamara's brother." Conrad keeps playing his part. "Go to school with Tamara. Take care of lonely Tamara. Watch out for Tamara. She's gullible and easily manipulated by others. Never tell Tamara. If anything happens to Tamara, you'll find yourself back at the pound. So, because you needed a friend, I got to spend the next decade as your babysitter. Every time you messed up or got hurt, I was punished, even as an adult."

Just like the first time I heard them, his words hurt.

"You know that is not how it was," my ghostly self argues.

"Grow up!" Conrad yells, swinging the gun toward my ghost. "Open your eyes, sister."

I open my eyes, even though he's not talking to the current me. The knife I shoved into him is gone.

"Watch it." Paul's voice makes my breath catch. "Point that over here."

"I don't know what to do!" I scream at the labyrinth, helpless. Nothing I do changes anything. Tears are streaming down my face. "Stop this! You win! Stop! I get it. I'm helpless to change this moment. I'm not anything special. Fate picked the wrong champion."

Conrad keeps speaking, ranting like a madman. "And do you know what the final straw was? I find out that I'm not even in their will. Anthony was. You are. Uncle Mortimer even gets a piece. The only way I get anything is if all of you are dead, and that's because, legally, I'm next in line. They acted like I was a servant, not their son."

My past self tries to reason with him, but I don't listen. I rush around the coffee table to kneel close to Paul and Lorelai. I try to touch their cheeks and can feel the texture of their skin, but they don't feel me.

"They didn't love me. But they taught me that in this life, it's everyone for themselves," Conrad says.

"I believe you." Lorelai attempts to soothe the maniac in her living room. I had almost forgotten the sound of her voice. "I know firsthand how Davis and Astrid could be. But they're gone now. You don't have to do this. Tamara is not them."

"Shut. Up," Conrad demands. "No one is talking to you, birth mother."

"I'm not saying our parents were perfect. They weren't. No one is. They might not have known how to show it, but they loved us."

I want to tell my past self to shut up. Talking him out of his delusions doesn't work.

Paul tenses beneath my hand.

"Sit down!" Conrad says. "Or I'll shoot her."

"You can't hurt her. She's protected," Lorelai denies, meaning the amulet. "You never get what you're after. If you leave now, we'll forget you were here. Tamara has already promised you'll be taken care of."

"Right. Protected," Conrad says. "You know, I kept wondering how on earth you survived all those times. I waited until you and Anthony were high in the closet with his boy toy. There is no way you should have escaped that hallway. Even Costin couldn't escape that hallway."

Conrad continues with his evil monologue,

sounding very much like a lunatic as he speaks of his mother and the Turnblads and all the wrongs he's believed he's suffered. I know now that he's been watching them like a crazy stalker in his bedroom closet.

I grab Paul's face, and when I put myself in his eyeline, it feels like he's looking at me. I lean in to kiss him, feeling the warmth of his unresponsive lips. I whisper against him, "I'm so sorry. I can't change this. I don't know how to save you."

"Supernaturals believe they are so superior," Conrad continues, each word bringing me deeper into hell as the seconds tick past. I stare at Paul, begging for him to wake up and see me. "...when you survived all of that and the vampire attack at the motel, I knew no one was that lucky. Elizabeth agreed to handle your death personally. When she told me what happened, I realized that the necklace isn't just a story."

"*Conrad, I—*" my past begs.

I remember Conrad then aimed the gun at my head.

I try to hold Paul down on the couch, but he slips through my fingers as he tries to save my past self. "Tamara!"

Bang!

Lorelai screams.

Glass shatters. The first shot was meant for me. The amulet protected me.

I watch as Paul sweeps my ghost into his protective embrace. His hands move over my body to check for injury.

"How is this a test of courage?" I yell at the labyrinth, tears streaming down my face. "I can't do anything. I can't fix this. I can't..."

Conrad laughs and does a strange little dance of happiness. "Holy shit, it's true!"

Conrad orders Lorelai to join me and Paul. After she obeys, he says, "Give me the amulet."

"No." Paul puts his hand in front of me to block any transfer.

"It won't work for you," Lorelai tells Conrad.

I run toward where Paul is standing and hold out my arms to block Conrad.

"*She's telling the truth. Remember, I told you what our grandfather said,*" my ghost reminds him. "*Once I put it on, it bonded to me. It doesn't work for anyone else.*"

Conrad gives a loud, grumbling sigh of irritation and aims his gun.

"Kill me instead," I beg the labyrinth. "Take me. It doesn't have to end like—"

A loud *bang* stops my plea. I feel angry white heat stab through my stomach.

I look down, expecting blood. The bullet should have injured me, but I'm fine.

It is happening. Just like before. Just like my nightmares.

I hear Paul fall behind me. I don't have to look. I know what's happening. Blood is spilling out over his chest from his heart. I know his eyes are wide with shock, and he's trying to speak, but no words make it past his dying lips. All I could do was hold him as his life slipped away.

"Paul?" My past is trying to stop the bleeding. *"Paul!"*

I turn. I'm not sure why. I don't want to watch this, but I can't stop myself. I already know how this ends. I know what happens next.

My ghost cradles Paul, uselessly pressing a hand over his heart. *"Paul, baby, look at me. Stay with me. Don't leave me."*

I stand over the scene, staring at Paul's face as I try to suck back tears. He tries to speak, but only gurgles. The sound is as awful as I relive in my dreams. Lorelai is trying to help, but she can't.

It's coming. Any second.

I listen to his breathing. It suddenly stops, and he goes limp. His dead eyes haunt me.

The weight of Paul's death crushes me all over again, and I feel like I'm drowning in my own guilt. I couldn't save him. I failed him.

Pain releases inside me like a vice, crushing the last bit of my hope. The moment of losing him is as sharp and fresh as the first time it had happened. No, that's not right. I truly believe that it's worse now. I scream so loud and long, limbs shaking with the force of it. No one cares. No one can hear me. I try to hit Conrad, but he doesn't feel me.

"Is this what you want?" I demand. I don't know if I yell at the labyrinth or the prophecy or the very root of magic itself. "You want me to lose everything that matters?"

I fall to the ground to curl into a ball and hold my head as I rock back and forth. All I can hope is that this isn't real. That it will end, and I'll be back in the chamber of mirrors.

"Tamara," Lorelai's voice whispers, and I know she's not talking to me, the *real* me.

I can't open my eyes as I rock harder. I'm not brave. This is one trial I can't pass.

"*All those times,*" comes my distorted ghostly echo. "*I made excuses for you. I told people you had a hard life but were good deep down.*"

I finally open my eyes to look at Conrad. He's smirking, and I remember thinking that he watched my grief like a play. It amused him. He enjoyed it.

"*But they were right. You're broken. You're…*" My ghost sobs.

"Let's try this again," Conrad taunts. "Hand me the amulet, or I shoot Mommy."

"Don't. He'll kill us both anyway," Lorelai warns as Conrad steps forward to aim the gun at her head.

I crawl to Paul's body, stroking his cheek as I ignore everything else.

"I'm so sorry this happened, Paul." I lean over to kiss his unresponsive lips gently. This world is not right. "We only had a few days, but they were the best of my life. I love you."

"Tick-tock. Necklace or Mommy?" Conrad says.

"Here. Take it. I hope you choke on it!" My ghost throws the amulet at Conrad.

"No!" Lorelai dives after the amulet but misses.

"I loved you so much in those few days." I kiss Paul again before turning to watch Conrad.

The amulet had landed next to his feet, and he swoops it up.

Almost numb, I stare at my brother. "Do it. Put it on. Take everything you deserve."

"You should have listened to her," Conrad says. "I am going to shoot you both anyway. Thank you for making it so easy."

"Put it on," I growl at him. I don't care that he can't hear me. I want him to suffer for what he's done.

Conrad seems jittery with excitement as he places it around his neck. The red stone shimmers.

He thinks he's won, but the gloating doesn't last. The amulet shifts and changes. The red suddenly gives off a green glow and begins to buzz.

Conrad makes a strange noise as a bullet wound magically appears in his neck, and he bleeds. Next, vampire bites appear on his neck, followed by fire erupting at his feet. Every death the amulet has protected me from is visited onto him. He tries to fight it, but as the labyrinth has made all too clear— there is no fixing this moment.

I watch Conrad burn, not blinking or turning away. The amulet falls to the ground and shatters as his head turns to ash and tumbles from his body.

I don't know how long I stay there, watching Conrad die in the flickering flames. Time stands still, and all I can feel is the crushing weight of grief and helplessness. No matter what I do, it's never good enough. I can't save anyone.

"Tamara." Costin's voice cuts through the nightmare, sharp and tense. "Tamara."

TWENTY

"Tamara."

I turn at the sound, startled to hear it in this moment. Costin is watching me, his face a mixture of frustration and something else. Hurt? Pain? It's so hard to tell with him.

"How did you get here?" When I turn to indicate Lorelai's home, it's gone, and we're surrounded by mirrors.

"We never left," Anthony answers. "You disappeared into the mirror, and we couldn't get you out."

I don't understand what any of this means. The mirror revealed my greatest pain, but also what could be described as my greatest secret. Except it forced me into the memory and didn't let me do anything. How is that courage?

My brother stands near Costin. While the

vampire stares at me, Anthony peers into the mirror. I follow his gaze, and he's watching as Lorelai's home fades and turns into the scene outside my birthday fire when time reset itself. I hear soft voices from the past coming from within. I don't stare into the mirror too long, not wanting to go back inside.

Movement catches my eyes, and I see the exact same story playing out in all the reflections, as if to tell me I can't escape it.

If this is my labyrinth trial to complete, why is it showing my past to Anthony and Costin?

"I don't understand." I try to work through my confusion. "This test doesn't make sense. I know I have to figure it out, but... How do we get out of here?"

"So that is Paul," Costin states, not answering my question. I hear the jealousy in his tone. He tries to hide it, but I can tell it's there. A hand lifts to my face and brushes away a tear, smearing it on my cheek. His hands are cold, and I see the hunger in his gaze. He'll need to feed soon. I'm the most likely target here. "He does not look like he's no one to you."

I flinch. He's right. I had lied to him about that.

"It doesn't matter." It's only a partial lie, but what else can I say? "That life never happened. Paul doesn't even remember it. As far as he's concerned, we've never met."

I can't look into Costin's gaze. I don't want him mesmerizing me and forcing any truths out of me. I'm no longer sure what those truths would be.

"Is this what you're holding on to? A man you knew for a few days in a time that no longer exists?" Costin's voice is tight. "Is this what's keeping you from me?"

From him?

"I haven't been keeping anything from you," I say. "I might not feel the need to share every detail of my life, but..."

I can't finish the defense. Costin's right. I didn't want to tell him about Paul. I don't want to talk about it.

"I don't get what I'm supposed to be doing in here," I try to change the subject. This can't be a test. It feels like torture. "You should never have followed me. Everything is messed up. I don't think this last trial is working right. The troll warned—"

"Tamara?" Anthony interrupts, pulling at my arm to get my attention.

He points at the mirror, and I see story time is over. Our reflections stare back at us. My hair is a wild mess; and my face is tear streaked and dirty. I look like a banshee who's had a rough night.

"What was that?" Anthony demands.

"It's..." I feel both of their eyes on me. "It's..."

"What did I just watch? Why was Conrad saying

those things?" Anthony demands. "That can't be real. Conrad died in the fire downtown. I was there. I saw them pull his body out of the building. What is that house? Who are those people? Why is he talking about our parents' wills? I don't understand."

"It's an alternate timeline," Costin answers for me. "It happened and then it was erased when Conrad broke the amulet."

"Tamara?" Anthony says, as if wanting to hear me confirm it.

"It's true." I nod.

"I think you better start explaining." Anthony crosses his arms over his chest. I see the blue of magic rolling nervously around his fingers.

"Conrad set the fire at my birthday party. Originally, he killed you." I glance at Costin. I take a deep breath, forcing the truth out. "Both of you. Anthony, you and your friend never made it out of the janitor's closet. Costin, you caught fire trying to escape. I tried to put you out with a tapestry, but you poofed into ash. I would have died if not for the amulet's magic."

The fear remains that I shouldn't be talking about this. I've held the secrets in for so long. I guess it doesn't matter now, anyway. I can't change what's happened. I'm just a human stuck in this horrible place, exhausted and emotionally spent, and being reminded of how lacking I am.

Anthony opens his mouth to speak, but I cut him off.

"The fire killed our parents along with some other guests," I tell them. "We had a funeral for you all. I can't even begin to describe what it was like. But then the amulet broke, and it reversed time, and you were here like nothing happened. Conrad got what he deserved. I thought it was over, but then..." I gesture toward the mirrors.

"What happened between us dying and the amulet breaking?" Anthony asks. "I feel like you're leaving some important information out. Who is this Paul?"

"Conrad went on a rampage, setting explosions. Those people we saw in the security cameras: he killed one and tried to kill the other." I look at Costin. "He made a deal with Elizabeth. He'd give her access to the Devine empire if she killed me and made him a vampire. She tried. The amulet stopped her."

Costin grimaces. "My sister makes poor choices. I can't say I'm surprised."

I wait for him to say more, but he doesn't.

"I think part of her motivation was to avenge you," I offer, hoping it dulls the blow.

"I know it is not," Costin denies. "She'd stake me in the heart if given half a chance."

Anthony shakes his head in disbelief. "What the

hell is—*was*—wrong with him? Are you sure about all this? I mean…"

"Conrad tried to make the same deal with me," Costin tells Anthony. "He actually tried to sell your sister to me once in exchange for being turned." He gives a small shrug. "After that, I made it known that any vampire who turned him would have to answer to me."

Anthony presses a hand against his stomach. He still looks pale from his time being held prisoner. "When we were in the dog park, you asked me if magically erased memories ever come back. I thought you were talking about Louis, but you weren't, were you?"

I shake my head. "No."

None of Anthony's normal good-naturedness shows on him now. He looks beaten and sad and betrayed. I'm sure I'm partly to blame. I never told him the truth about any of this. If I had my choice, I never would.

"Conrad wanted me dead, but the amulet's magic protected me. Every time he sent me somewhere he claimed was safe, a fire broke out. Honestly, I'm embarrassed I didn't admit the truth to myself sooner. I wanted so much to believe in him. I thought he was misunderstood. But Conrad followed me to California, where I met my birth mother, Lorelai. It is her house you saw in the mirror. The rest of the story, you know. He tried to steal my amulet, and it killed him."

"And when I put the game on your phone, you said you didn't know what vengeful spirit you had come across. But you do, don't you?" my brother insists. "It's Conrad."

"Conrad's ghost has been haunting me since that night. He's full of so much rage." I keep an eye on Costin. What I need to say to him shouldn't be said in front of my brother.

"Why didn't you tell me any of this?" Anthony insists, tugging at my arm to get me to look at him. Then, not giving me a chance to answer, he adds, "I recognized that man with you in the mirror. He's the guy you were watching at the park—Paul. He had a dog with your name. He was with the kid."

"Diana," I say. "The kid's name is Diana. She's not even six years old. They were innocent bystanders whose only crime was trying to help a stranger in need."

I look at Costin. He hasn't moved. He looks so... hurt.

"Conrad threatened to kill them both if I told anyone," I explain. "I shouldn't even be telling you now. If the labyrinth trial doesn't actually stop him, he can still make good on his threats. You can't let him see that you know any of this. Please, I beg you."

"This is a lot to take in," Anthony says. "You're going to tell me everything."

"I will. Later. Not now." I try to touch Costin, but his look stops me. I hate that I'm the reason for his guarded expression. "Anthony, can you give us a moment?"

My brother looks around the chamber of mirrors and clears his throat. "Uh, yeah, I'll just be over here. Don't go anywhere without me. And maybe hurry."

I'm not one hundred percent sure that Anthony can't hear us, but I'm grateful for the illusion of privacy.

I wait for the vampire to say something first. He doesn't.

"Costin, it's not... I can't..." I take a deep breath. I don't know what to say. "What are you thinking?"

"You should have told me that your heart belongs to another before leading me on," he states.

"I didn't lead you on. You came to me. I was just trying to live my life and keep my head down." I give a slight shake of my head. "I never made you promises. It's not like we've talked about having a relationship. We were forced together. You barely acknowledged me before you needed me to do something."

My words aren't helping. His eyes narrow, and his face becomes completely unreadable. "As you wish."

He tries to turn away from me, but I grab his arm and hold on tight.

"As you wish? What the hell does that mean, Costin?" I demand in frustration.

"I don't know what you want me to say. You said you love him." Costin sounds accusatory.

"You know what, never mind. I don't know why I feel the need to explain myself to you. It's not like you were a virgin when you met me. I'm sure if we were to write up a list of your exes, it would be at least thirty miles long. And if vampires are even capable of love, I'm sure you loved a few of them."

I'm so frustrated, and angry, and sad. "I don't know what you want from me. I never know what you want from me. I can only assume it's sex and a free meal. What other use is a human to a vampire? It's like you expect me to just know what you're thinking. That, or you don't think I'm worthy of your thoughts. You don't respect me. You call me a castoff. You don't even trust me enough to complete a quest prophesied by powerful wizards that I am supposed to do on my own."

"I was going to remain hidden unless you needed me," Costin said. "Anthony sensed me. I wasn't planning on that."

I'm too exhausted to determine if I think it's sweet or annoying.

"I'm tired of being angry," I tell him. "I don't

know what this stupid labyrinth wants from me. I never asked for any of this. And now everything is just fucked up."

"You said you love him," he states as if nothing else I said registers.

"So what if I did? So what if I do?" I demand.

Costin's jaw tenses as he clenches his teeth. I wonder if he thinks of biting me to shut me up. I don't know that I'd fight it. Oblivion sounds pretty good about right now.

I run my hands through my messy hair, and the knots tangle against my fingers. I jerk them free. "Paul doesn't even know I'm alive. And he can't know because he's human, and his daughter is human, and knowing me almost killed them because I'm human, and I can't protect anyone from the endless amount of shit falling on my head. So, yeah, for a few days, I was in love, and I thought, *what if?* What if I could have this thing, this normal life where I finally belonged? What if I could forget about the supernatural? What if I could drain the Devine blood out of my veins and disappear and just be a wife and a mother and a human?"

"You are not just a human," Costin says. "I have known you your entire life. You were never just a human."

"You can't understand." I shake my head. "Do you even remember what it's like to be mortal?"

I can tell by his face that his humanity is a distant memory.

I see Anthony watching us from between the hanging mirrors.

I don't want to be having this conversation. Not now. I don't want to talk about this because then I have to admit that I'll never deserve a normal human life.

"You're more than just a human," Costin repeats, desperate for me to hear it.

"You barely know me." My legs feel unsteady beneath me. I don't know how much more I can take.

Costin is so achingly beautiful—eternal, immortal, powerful. I always felt superior to women who fell for monsters. Truth be told, I mocked them a little in my head. I told myself that I never understood the appeal.

Yet here I am. Torn between my memory of Paul and the reality of Costin.

I can't believe I'm *that* girl. Torn between feelings for two men.

"Admit it. You're only with me because my grandfather told you that you owed me a life debt and made you promise. This prophecy is the only reason you gave me the time of day."

"How can you forget our past?" He searches my eyes, and his gaze swirls.

"What past?"

"Do you care for me at all?" He lifts his hand to the mirror I disappeared into. "Or is this all you'll ever feel? Are you still trapped in that moment with him? Because if that is all you have, let me know now."

His words hit me like a physical blow. Paul's loss had consumed me for so long, and the guilt, the grief, had become a part of me. But standing here, having relived the alternative option where no one lives, I start to realize something. I've been stuck. Stuck in a memory, stuck in a past that never happened. And no matter how much I loved Paul, he's gone. He's never coming back.

The pain is still there—sharp and deep—but there's something else too. An understanding. A clarity I didn't have before.

"I'm sorry, Costin. Part of me will always love him and wonder what if." I can't make myself lie to soften the truth. "But what I had with him was just a glimpse at a life I can't have. I've been told I'm not special and I will never have magic. I used to wish so hard when I was little that I'd somehow come into power and be worthy of my family. As I got older, I realized coming into powerful magic was never going to happen, and I needed a more realistic dream. So, I fantasized about being normal. Everyone's voices have been in my head, telling me what I am, what I need to do, and who I need to be. The truth is, I don't know what I want."

The words feel like a release, like a weight lifting off my chest. I take a deep breath, my body still shaking, but I feel... lighter. As though, for the first time, I'm allowing myself to admit the full truth.

I study Costin. My heart is still raw from the pain of the memory, but my head is clearer now. "I won't forget him," I admit softly. "But I can't live in that moment forever."

The mirrors start to sway and shimmer. Those shimmers turn into tiny green butterflies. The answer to this last trial comes to my tired brain like a whisper from beyond. That is what I have not had the courage to face until now. I've been lying to everyone and pining for a future that can never be. I've been too afraid to talk about what happened to me.

"It's like the prophecy said." I lift my hand to stir the butterflies. They swarm around us, and I feel their magic blanketing us. "Fate cannot be changed."

TWENTY-ONE

The light from the butterflies becomes overwhelming, and I have to close my eyes to keep from being blinded by their magic. Relief fills me to know that the trials are over. I've passed. The hard part is over.

There is a tiny fear that Costin following me into the labyrinth will come with a cost. However, I've done what has been asked of me. I survived what everyone said was impossible.

A strange mix of exhaustion and adrenaline makes me almost giddy. I want to scream my victory. I feel the butterflies' magic heating my skin. I try to peek, but it hurts when I open my eyes. I feel hands grabbing mine as if my brother and Costin are both trying to keep me nearby.

Everything tingles. Pure energy flows through

my veins. I feel like I could turn my entire body into a fireball and hurl it into the nearest obstacle. I feel like I could take on the world. Or, at the very least, a dragon.

The heady sensation doesn't last long, and the magical fire around me begins to die. When I slowly open my eyes, I see we are all three back in the subway station. Cool air hits my face as a breeze comes from the tunnel over the platform. The spiral entrance that had been on the wall is gone, replaced by chipped tile and the clinging residual of a long torn poster.

I'm happy to be out of the labyrinth, but the gravity of the experience still lingers. I've admitted the truth to myself—finally let Paul go—but that doesn't erase the ache in my heart. There is no hiding the truth or taking the words back. Costin knows about Paul.

The vampire's eyes avoid meeting mine as he gazes into the distance from the platform. Until recently, I believed I couldn't inflict harm upon him because vampires were incapable of experiencing hurt. Now, I realize I was mistaken.

Anthony is quiet beside me, his expression torn as he processes everything he's learned about Conrad. I don't know what to say to him to make things better. I wish he never had to learn the truth. I wish he could just mourn the brother we lost and move on. I don't know what to say to him. I can't make any of that better.

I go to stand beside Costin. His presence grounds me in a way I can't explain. He looks as beat up as I feel.

"I can't believe..." Anthony starts, his voice trailing off as he glances at me, his eyes full of questions he already has the answers to. Whatever he is going to say dies in his throat.

"I'm sorry." I don't know who I'm apologizing to. So much has been said already.

For the time being, I'm content to stand and say nothing. The labyrinth is over. It has left me emotionally and physically drained. I take a deep breath and then another. I try to force the tension out of my body. It won't leave me.

Something heavy, almost suffocating, presses down on my senses. The air feels wrong. Suddenly, the subway platform vibrates beneath our feet. It is just a slight tremor at first, and I look at the tracks, expecting another ghost train.

"Did you feel that?" Anthony asks, his voice barely a whisper. He comes to stand beside us.

The ground trembles once more, this time with greater intensity. A loud, ominous crack reverberates from deep within the subway tunnel. It's the sound of stone being torn apart by an invisible force.

My body tenses, my heart rate spiking as I steal a

glance at Costin and Anthony. They are frozen in place, their attention sharpened by the unexpected disturbance. Anthony acts like he's about to jump down into the tunnel to check it out. Costin places an arm in front of him to stop him. The vampire holds tense, as if he's waiting for something.

An oppressive heat replaces the cool breeze.

"Do you feel that?" I ask almost needlessly, my voice barely a whisper.

The tremors intensify before either of them can respond. The ground bucks under our feet, throwing me off balance. I stumble forward, almost tumbling face-first onto the tracks below. Costin is instantly under me, catching me against his chest. Anthony jumps down to join us. We stand between the tracks, staring into the darkness as the sounds get louder.

I crouch, touching the vibrating concrete. It's slick with condensation and pulses with a slow, terrible rhythm—like a heartbeat that is far too large to belong to anything remotely human.

I feel a sense of urgency as I utter, "I think we need to get to the amulet."

I make a conscious effort to move deliberately, not wanting to attract the attention of anything lurking in the darkness. The pulsing of the heartbeat grows stronger, reverberating up my legs with an increasingly intense rhythm."

"Yeah, we should—" Anthony starts to agree.

Crack!

A fissure violently rips open the ground before us, the deafening sound echoing through the air like the thunderous blast from a cannon. I spin around, my heart racing, as another powerful tremor shakes the ground behind us, causing the tunnel walls to tremble. The lights on the platform flicker and fade. Dust and tiles fall from the ceiling, swirling in the thin remaining beams of light.

A rush of heat, intense and suffocating, seeps up from the cracks in the earth. The air thickens with the scent of sulfur and smoke, causing a sharp sting in my lungs with every breath.

Costin's eyes lock onto mine, and there's an edge of something I haven't seen in him before. Fear.

"What the hell is happening?" Anthony shouts.

"Run," the vampire commands.

"I thought the trials were over." I barely croak the words out. The heat is making it hard to draw breath.

"Run now." Costin's voice barely pierces through the deafening cracks.

Costin grabs my arm and pulls me behind him.

As we sprint forward, a new crevice fragments the ground a couple of feet ahead of us, causing the platform to split open. It's even wider than the last. Intense heat radiates from within, so scorching hot I feel it singeing the edges of my clothes. I reel back, my chest tightening, my feet immobilized with fright.

A low, guttural rumble emanates from deep within the earth. The rumbling grows steadily louder, and the vibrations stronger.

It's like the ground beneath us is alive, awakening from a slumber that has lasted eons. I glance toward the entrance of the labyrinth, but there's nothing there. No sign of what's causing this, no visible threat. But I know. I feel it in my bones, in the marrow of my very being. Something ancient is coming.

Draakmar.

The name flickers in my mind, unbidden, ancient and powerful. The name of something born long before time itself. And now it's awake.

"Draakmar is awake," I tell them, jumping over a smaller crack to the other side.

"Take her and go," Anthony yells.

Costin tries to grab me, but I shake him off.

"We're not leaving him," I tell Costin before turning to my brother. "Anthony, I'm not leaving you!"

"Get her out of here," Anthony insists.

"It's too dangerous to transport—" Costin tries to answer as a chunk of concrete crashes down from the ceiling, barely missing him.

"Costin!" My voice is thin, strangled.

His grip tightens on my arm as he pulls me with him. "Move!"

The air itself seems to pulse, trembling with each heartbeat. The deep, thrumming growl becomes louder. It's low and drawn-out, almost like a breath that's been held for centuries. It rattles my teeth.

We run into the darkness, driven by terror. Anthony blasts magic into the tunnel, lighting the way. We don't make it far before the ground beneath us explodes. I feel my body tossed into the air. My limbs flail, and I scream.

Costin catches me against his chest. My stomach lurches as he speeds me into the darkness. I want to protest but no words come out. He sets me down.

"Keep running," he orders.

I see the outline of his form heading back for Anthony. Suddenly, a geyser of molten fire shoots up from the platform, and for a moment, all I can see is blinding, searing light erasing the image of the men. Heat slams into me like a physical force, knocking me back, and I slide across the hard ground. The breath knocked from my lungs. My ears ring.

The ground shakes violently now, cracks splintering across the stone floor like a web. The temperature becomes unbearable, as if the very core of the earth has been ripped open. Lava oozes toward me like a river, glowing with the promise of orange death. I fight to get to my feet, stumbling backward as I search for Costin and my brother. Stones shatter as the lava continues to push forth. And, beneath it all, the same low growl.

"Costin! Anthony!" I scream, unable to see them. "Where are you?"

They can't be dead. Not now. Not after everything.

And then I see it. A looming shadow within the flames, massive and shifting, undulating as it glides with a slow, deliberate grace. My stomach drops, and terror claws its way up my spine, coiling tight around my throat.

Draakmar. The ancient dragon of fire.

At first, it's just a silhouette—a hulking shape wreathed in flames. Then the fire recedes, pulled inward, drawn into the massive, black-scaled body that emerges from the molten depths. Lava peeks out from behind its scales as it moves, while huge, leathery wings unfold amongst the crackle of flames, sending sparks flying through the air. I watch in horrified awe as it ascends higher and higher, almost scraping the ceiling of the tunnels with its head.

"Anthony! Costin!" I yell, not knowing what to do. I have to find them.

Draakmar's eyes open at the sound—two smoldering, molten embers that lock onto me. It's like staring into the heart of a volcano, into something that doesn't just breathe fire, but is fire. Every instinct in me screams to run. But I can't move. I can't breathe. I can only watch as the dragon's lips curl back, revealing rows of razor-sharp teeth, each one glowing white hot. A thick, heavy smoke rolls from its nostrils. The ground beneath the dragon glows, molten lava spreading in rivers from his claws, burning everything in its path.

I can't see Anthony or Costin.

I shake my head, not wanting to believe they're gone.

"Tamara!" Costin grabs hold of me from behind. I scream in fright, startled by his sudden appearance. Blood stains his face and hands.

Before I can ask, Draakmar roars. The sound so deafening, so powerful, it's like the very air is being ripped apart. The force of it slams into me, sending me staggering against Costin. I hear a pop and then nothing but the white noise of my ears buzzing. Dazed, I taste the blood flowing from my nose into my mouth. My head spins.

"Costin," I say his name, but I can't hear my voice. The heat of the fire follows us, licking at my back, searing the ends of my hair.

The vampire pushes himself up from the ground and takes hold of me. I feel myself tugged into action before he pulls me away from the dragon, breaking the spell that's held me paralyzed.

Costin's grip is ironclad, dragging me through

the tunnels. The walls blur as we transport forward in small bursts. Each time we slow, I find my legs stumbling over the shaking ground as the dragon roars.

As we put distance between us and the dragon, I try to make him stop. I'm dizzy and nauseous. I try to say, "Anthony," but I don't know if my voice is working past the buzzing.

Costin pulls me again and I finally see my brother up ahead, running as fast as he can. Anthony's arm is bloody, but he's alive. My feet slip on the uneven ground as we slow.

"I got her!" Costin's voice is distant and muffled as if I'm underwater.

We come to an opening in the wall where light shines into the tunnel. The sounds of the city come through from the other side.

Behind us, Draakmar moves slowly, like he's testing the weight of his massive body after eternities of stillness. Falling debris in the tunnel slows our progress. The sound of crumbling stone fills the air, and the entire place trembles as if it's going to collapse in on itself.

Anthony shoots magical fireballs at the creature. The defense only seems to anger the beast. Draakmar beats his wings as he surges forward.

"We can't fight it," Anthony shouts. My hearing is returning.

Heart pounding, I turn to Costin. "What do we do?"

"We get you to the troll," Costin growls, lifting me off the ground and pushing me into the city. "Now."

I peer down at them, refusing to leave them behind.

"Go!" Anthony waves his arm for Costin to go with me. "I'll try to keep him back."

Draakmar barrels forward, his massive tail slamming into the stone walls, sending chunks of rock crashing down.

"Cave in the tunnel," Costin says. "That should slow him down."

Before I can protest the plan, Costin is crawling out of the tunnel. Anthony throws magic at the ceiling, violently swinging his arms as he causes it to collapse into a pile of rubble, just as Draakmar unleashes another torrent of flames.

Screams come from part of the city. I hear structures crumbling from the quaking earth. I reach into the tunnel for my brother. Costin helps me pull him out of the hole.

Anthony clutches his stomach. He looks drained and battle worn. He leans against a wall, wheezing. "Get to the troll and kick this monster's ass!"

Anthony gives me a lopsided grin and winks.

"Get home and get everyone to safety," I order him. "If I fail—"

A deafening roar from the dragon comes from deep within the tunnel, shaking the city's very foundation. A frenzied rush of supernatural beings flee in a state of panic, desperately seeking refuge from the chaos.

"This way, Tamara," Costin says.

"Go." Anthony pushes away from the wall and disappears as he runs in the opposite direction.

Costin places a hand on the small of my back to get me to run into the crowd as we navigate our way toward the troll's cave, and our only hope is to stop this madness.

TWENTY-TWO

My legs tremble, barely holding me upright as Costin and I stagger toward the mud-brick homes. Several have caved in on themselves. The destroyed furniture pokes up from the rubble in pieces.

I honestly don't know how I'm still upright. Everything hurts. I feel like somebody punched me in the ribs. Just drawing breath causes a sharp, stabbing pain in my side that radiates through my body. My hands are bloody and raw. My clothing is singed, and I see blisters on my arm from the heat. My jeans are torn, and I'm bleeding from my thigh. It's not enough to be an artery, but it's enough to cause concern. I don't even know how that happened.

I hope Anthony is safe. I don't know if it was smart to leave my brother behind, but I can't doubt myself now. I can only hope Anthony makes it out of the underground city. If I fail to stop this, at least there's hope he'll reach our parents in time.

The drunken goblin is gone from the entrance, but broken remnants of his small jug remain. Chaos reigns as creatures abandon the city. I can still feel the tremors vibrating through the ground, but at least the air is cooler.

I pant, pain burning in my side. I stagger, almost falling, but Costin's hand steadies me. Even he looks worse for wear, with singed clothes and streaks of soot marring his usually pristine appearance. Now that there is more light, I see a bloody rip in Costin's sweater. An angry wound on his shoulder peeks at me from within. "You're hurt."

"I'll heal," he dismisses, not letting me check. I can hear the strain beneath his calm. "A rock fell on me when I tried to transport your brother."

From what I can see of the gash, it did more than fall on him. I notice that arm is hanging by his side, his hand barely moving.

"None of it will matter if we don't fix the amulet." He guides me into the entrance ahead of him.

My knees are weak, and I fall against the cold stone of the wall, using it for support as we make our way inside. My arm slides over the rock, my body aching with exhaustion. I want nothing more than to collapse, but Draakmar won't stop until he's burned everything to the ground.

I glance at Costin. His eyes meet mine, and for a moment, the weight of everything we've been through together presses down on me. Paul, the labyrinth, the dragon—everything is crumbling, and now we're pinned here with only an old prophecy and a broken amulet to save us. I feel like there is so much I need to tell him, but there isn't time.

We enter Morvok's home. The gemstones hanging from above jingle from the angry vibrations. The troll's rock body blends with his surroundings and it takes me a moment to see him sitting in the middle of the floor.

Morvok pushes to his feet, the low, guttural sound of his breathing filling the cave. He looks us over before ambling over to the stone worktable where my broken amulet still waits.

"Costin and pet," Morvok says. His voice is gravelly as he turns to face us. "Morvok did not expect you to return."

Why does everyone always underestimate me?

I'm too weary to argue.

"Fix it." My voice is raspy, but I force it out. I limp up to him and hold out my hand. "We don't have much time."

Costin joins me, slumping against the table's edge as if he needs it to hold him upright.

"You are too late. Draakmar is awake." The troll waves his hand as if to tell me to leave. "Morvok will go to sleep until the ancient one tires."

"We have to try, Morvok," I insist.

The troll's eyes gleam in the dim firelight, glancing from me to the amulet shards as if weighing its worth. He reaches out a giant hand, his fingers scraping against the stone tabletop as he gathers the dust of the yellow gemstone he'd crushed earlier under his thumb. He pushes it toward the broken amulet, still caked with my dried blood from before.

"As the pet wishes," Morvok says, reaching for the vial of green liquid. "If you have failed, we cannot try again."

"If I have failed, it won't matter. Everything will be destroyed," I tell him, holding out my hand more insistently.

Morvok holds up one of the amulet's shards to the light. The jagged edges of the broken piece gleam.

"A piece of Draakmar's scale," I say, repeating what Costin told me before. My voice is steady now, though I feel the weight of the words settle on my shoulders. I let my hand drop to the table, unable to keep holding it up.

The troll nods slowly. "Yes. It was forged long ago, a piece of his very essence—his fire, his soul, his power. Only that power can stop him."

The air in the troll's home seems to grow warmer. Draakmar can only be defeated by a piece of himself. That makes sense, but there is no time to dwell on the fact. Now is the time for action. But the amulet is in pieces, shattered and useless, and we're running out of time.

"How do we fix it?" I ask, desperation creeping into my tone.

"Your blood," the troll says, his voice rumbling with finality. His gaze locks onto mine. "Only with the blood of one who holds true power can this be mended. Morvok told you this."

My stomach knots at his words. I glance at Costin, but his paling expression is unreadable, his gaze flickering between the troll and me.

"And if it doesn't work?" I ask nervously, unsure if my time in the labyrinth will be enough. Costin followed me in, and it's not like I got a certificate of completion in the end. Nothing feels different. I don't feel like I have earned any magic. "Is there another way?"

"If it doesn't work," the troll says with a shrug, "then you are dead, and Morvok naps."

It doesn't seem like the troll had much to lose.

I feel like I'm standing in quicksand. I offer my hand again, and the troll reaches for his knife. The sight of it sends a shiver over me as I remember what it feels like to be cut, but I don't pull away.

Costin touches my side in support, bumping my sore rib. I flinch and suck in a sharp breath. I don't push him away as I meet his gaze. For a moment, the world outside fades away, and it's just us, standing in this cave, ready to make the ultimate sacrifice.

There is so much I want to say to him.

Thank you.

I'm sorry.

Don't leave me.

The blade bites into my skin before I can speak. The sharp pain radiates up from my sore hand, and my breath catches in my throat. I turn to the wound, watching my blood flow thick and red onto the broken pieces of the amulet. It pools over the jagged green shards, sinking into the amulet's cracks before trailing over the table to drip onto the floor.

The troll releases me, and I ball my hand into a fist to stop the bleeding. Morvok mutters to himself, low and ancient words I don't understand. I stare at the shards, willing them to change. But nothing happens. The amulet remains broken, the cracks still visible, and the pieces still separate.

A tear slips over my cheek, and I shake my head. I've failed. "No."

The tremors become more insistent, and I hear loud crashes coming from outside. Draakmar has made it out of the subway tunnels. I sense that he's close. Panic rises in my chest. It's not working. My blood drips from my fist onto the stone floor, useless. I stare at the broken pieces.

"No, no, no," I mutter, leaning over the table, pressing my wounded hand into the surface as I grip the stone. My eyes burn, and my vision blurs. "Come on."

"Patience." The troll takes my hand and throws powder on it to stop the bleeding. The cut burns as it seals shut. He then watches the amulet with his dispassionate eyes. "If the magic within you is strong enough, it will mend."

"I don't have magic." I turn to Costin. "I'm sorry. I've never had magic. I'm not special. It wasn't me. My grandfather was wrong. I'm not the one in the prophecy."

"All creatures have magic," Morvok says.

I look up at Morvok. "I don't understand what you mean."

Maybe I'm too tired to decipher his words, but I've never had magic. I know that for a fact.

"Human magic is connection," the troll says. "Your blood... your magic... it comes from the people you are tied to. Generations passing themselves down for centuries to create who you are. We all have magic—every human, every creature, but most forget. The amulet was forged from Draakmar's scales, yes, but it is powered by more than that. It is powered by love. By connection. The same magic that gave you the amulet for protection in the first place, the magic you feel for the vampire beside you. That is what will heal this."

Costin reaches for my hand. I glance up from the shards. The words hang in the air between us, unspoken but heavy. The connection. The magic of connection, of love, of bond. That's what's going to save us.

I take a deep breath, letting the words fill my tired body, trying to focus on that connection—on everything that binds me to this world. The love of my birth mother and grandfather, who cared enough to trade with trolls to protect me from harm. My parents, who love me the only way they know how. My brother, who will not abandon me. Paul and Diana, who helped a stranger and who I can never see again for their own protection.

And Costin. He's always been there since I was a child, ready to swoop in and protect me. I never realized it until now. When I burnt my hand, when I broke my arm, he was there. At parties, when I watched from the shadows, he was there. And now that I'm older, he's become more to me.

All the people I've fought for, bled for. The people who keep me tied to this world. *My* magic. *My* power.

I close my eyes, and for a moment, everything goes silent. Just the sound of my heart beating steady and strong. And then...

A soft hum.

I open my eyes. The pieces of the green amulet glow faintly, the cracks slowly sealing themselves together with the red of my blood. I watch the pieces click into place, the magic swirling and binding them together.

The amulet becomes whole, my blood turning the green shards into the red stone that once was. I gasp in shock. Costin's hand slips from mine.

"Costin, do you—?" I turn to him.

Costin slumps on the ground, unmoving. His eyes are closed, and his skin is paler than normal.

"Costin?" I fall to my knees beside him, shaking him. "Costin, wake up!"

I touch his skin. Vampires are normally cold, so I don't know what to make of it. He's not breathing, but vampires don't need to all the time.

A loud roar echoes from outside. I stand, torn between the imminent danger and helping Costin.

Morvok has the fixed amulet and is pressing thick silver threads around it. He holds it up to show a new necklace he has crafted. "Morvok will watch your vampire."

I hesitate before taking the amulet. "Don't let him die."

I'm not sure what Morvok's grunt means, but I hope it's agreement.

"Costin, I'll be back," I say.

He doesn't answer.

I limp for the exit as I slip the amulet over my neck. I have no clue what I'm doing, but I have to try.

The underground city is in ruins. Flames rise from the marketplace, and the air is thick with smoke and ash. I can feel the heat clawing at my skin, but I don't stop. I don't have time to be afraid.

"Draakmar," I yell, hobbling away from the troll's cave.

What the fuck am I doing? Everything in me screams that this is a mistake. I silence the voices that have always churned in my head.

"Draakmar," I yell louder, trying to follow the sound of destruction. I see a couple of the school-children alone, huddled together beneath a pile of rocks. I motion and point behind me for them to run.

Loud steps reverberate through the ground. The giant creature is easy to find.

Draakmar stands near the opposite side of the bridge, towering over the wreckage like some unstoppable living nightmare made of flame and rage. His massive wings unfurl to show his full size. Molten eyes fix on me with a primal fury. He opens his great jaws, baring those horrible teeth, with a roar that erupts from him to shake the very earth beneath my feet. Fire breath lights up the underground city, choking the air with more heat and smoke. I cough and touch the amulet, feeling its familiar strength back where it belongs. I have to believe that it worked, that the stone will protect me.

I take a step forward, terrified.

There's no time to hesitate. No time to run. This is my fight now.

I clutch the amulet in my hand, feeling its comforting weight. The warmth spreads through me, steady and pulsing like a frantic heartbeat, like it's alive. The dragon's power is inside it, a piece of Draakmar's own essence, and it's his heartbeat that I feel.

I know, without a doubt, that the dragon is connected to me now.

My heart hammers wildly, but I force myself to breathe. I step forward, my legs trembling as I hold my ground.

Draakmar lets out another deafening roar. In the split second that follows, he surges toward me, the ground cracking beneath his massive weight. His wings beat once, twice, creating gusts of hot wind that whip my hair into my face, and then he lunges forward over the bridge—his mouth open wide, fire pooling in the back of his throat, ready to burn me alive.

Oh, fuck.

Time slows.

I see the fire in his mouth, the deadly heat coiling in his chest beneath the black scales, the massive claws poised to strike. He comes straight at me, an unstoppable, furious beast of destruction. My instinct is to turn, to run, but I don't. Instead, I pull the amulet forward on my neck, and with every ounce of strength I have left, I face him head-on.

"Do it," I yell, my voice shaking but strong. "Come and get me."

The heat hits first—a wave of blistering air that scorches my skin, making my vision blur with tears. But I don't move. I can't move. The amulet hums in my hand, vibrating with energy, and I grip it tightly, planting my feet as Draakmar bears down on me.

In a flash, he strikes.

His massive body crashes toward me, claws outstretched, teeth gleaming in the firelight. But just as he's about to reach me, the amulet explodes with a searing red light. I can feel the power of it radiating through me, down to my bones, like a current of electricity surging out of my core. The light pulses outward, forming a barrier between me and the dragon, and for the first time, I see him hesitate.

The dragon's claws meet the barrier with a deafening clash, sparks flying as his attack is stopped cold. He recoils, his molten eyes narrowing in confusion. He strikes again, harder, but the barrier holds, the amulet's power pushing back against him. It hums louder now, like a living thing, like it's feeding off my strength.

I drop to my knees.

Draakmar rears back, letting out a frantic roar. His wings spread, and his massive head tilts as if studying me. For the briefest moment, I can see the confusion in his burning eyes—confusion, and something else.

Fear.

I stare up at him, heart pounding, but there's something else rising in me now. Not fear. Not panic. Power. It flows through me, through the amulet, connecting me to the ancient magic of this dragon, the piece of him embedded in the very thing that now protects me.

He pokes a claw forward as if to test what's happening. The barrier shimmers under the touch, but it doesn't break. The connection between us pulses, stronger, surging with each beat of my heart, each breath I take. And then I feel it.

I can control him.

I don't know how I know, but I do. It's like a whisper in the back of my mind, a soft voice guiding me, showing me the way. The amulet isn't just a shield. It's power. It's control.

I take a deep breath, pushing to my feet. The

dragon snorts but takes a step back. Another pulse of energy radiates out from the amulet, stronger this time, and I move toward him. He roars loudly.

"Stop it," I shout, my voice cutting through the roar of flames.

Draakmar instantly stops. His fiery eyes lock onto mine. For a long, tense moment, neither of us moves. I can feel the magic pulsating between us like a tether binding us together. My breath comes in shallow gasps, but I remain firm.

"Sit," I tell him.

The dragon lets out a low growl, but his wings slowly lower, his massive form pulling back to obey. He's listening to me.

I take another step forward, the amulet glowing brightly as I let it fall against my chest. The connection between us grows stronger, and I feel his ancient rage, but I also feel the weight of his long existence. He's been fighting for so long, trapped in his own fury. But now he's mine to command.

"Go back," I say, my voice steady with concern for the beast. "Rest."

The dragon hesitates, his molten eyes narrowing as if testing my resolve. But I don't waver. I push the command through the connection between us, through the magic of the amulet and the power that ties me to him.

Draakmar lowers his head. His glowing eyes lock

on mine, but the fire in them dims. I reach out to touch him, petting his warm cheek. He snorts and nudges my hand. I hold my breath, amazed at the moment. His wings fold against his sides, and with a final, low rumble, he turns away, his massive form retreating into the tunnels from which he came. He's slower now, almost reluctant. I watch his large body amble past.

The fires around us die down, the heat receding as the dragon moves further away. I watch him disappear into the darkness of the tunnels, the sound of his steps growing fainter until, finally, there's only silence.

I stand there, chest heaving, the amulet no longer glowing. It's done. He's gone.

I can't believe it.

The city is still thick with smoke, but there's a strange calm now that the danger has passed. I feel the weight of the battle, the exhaustion pulling at my core, but I also feel stronger.

The sound of footsteps shatters the stillness echoing around me. Figures emerge from their hiding places. Some of them begin to approach me, but I ignore them, determined to make my way back to Costin.

A sense of urgency propels me forward as I race back into the troll's dwelling.

Morvok sits on the floor reading the prophecy

book. I find Costin's unmoving body still slumped next to the worktable. Splotches of green and purple pepper his clothes like the troll threw gem dust at his shoulder wound.

"No sleep for Morvok," the troll pouts when he sees me.

"Thank you for your help, Morvok," I tell him. I give his shoulder a light pat as I move past him. He grunts in response.

I check Costin's shoulder. The gash is ugly, but the troll's magic has sealed it.

"Morvok fix," the troll says. "Vampire needs blood. The book I keep."

I scan the floor, my eyes darting around as I search for a weapon. Standing, I spot a glint of metal. I grab the troll's knife and cut my palm. I don't think as I smear blood to Costin's lips.

I watch it soak into his skin. "Come on, Costin. Drink."

His lips twitch and part, but he doesn't drink. The amulet stopped vampires from attacking me before, so I take it off and lean closer to Costin's mouth, offering my neck. He inhales sharply. I feel him move. Hands grip me tight, and the hard clamp of teeth clamp down on my neck.

Costin pushes forward and I fall back as his body comes over mine. Costin moans, and I feel the hard pull of him drinking. I try to hit his arm to tell him to stop, but my limbs fall weak.

My head is light. Darkness threatens. I'm too exhausted to fight anymore.

"Tamara?" Costin's voice sounds confused and far away. His weight disappears, and I try to open my eyes. He frantically pulls the amulet over my head, and the pain in my throat lessens. I look up at him. His bloodshot eyes focus on mine, sharp and intense. "I didn't mean to hurt you."

He helps me sit up, and I touch my throat.

Blinking heavily, I ask, "Can this night be over?"

"Where is Draakmar?" He sounds panicked.

"Sleeping," I mumble. It's not exactly true, but the dragon will be soon.

"You did it." His voice is filled with something I can't quite place. Admiration, maybe. Or something deeper.

I nod, my throat tight. "We did it."

TWENTY-THREE

I wake slowly, fighting the exhaustion that is still trying to pull me under. The bed beneath me is softer than anything I've ever slept in. I don't want to move. I let my body sink into the thick covers, cocooned in warmth and safety. The ache in my muscles is proof of everything that happened, but for the first time in what feels like forever, there's no immediate sense of danger, no impending doom chipping at the edges of my consciousness.

The dragon sleeps. The amulet is fixed. The fight is over.

For now.

The image of Chester bombards my dreams like a stink bomb thrown into the middle of a dinner party. I jerk fully awake. Maybe not *every* fight is over, but at least the prophecy is settled.

I groan at the thought of Chester and rub my eyes as I look around in confusion. This isn't either of my bedrooms. I've never been here before. As I stretch, my fingers brush against the cool silk sheets.

I let my eyes drift over the unfamiliar space around me. The room is too classy to be Chester's—thank the gods for that much. The last thing I need is to time slip into that hellish reality.

I reach for my neck to feel the amulet. The setting around the stone feels different, reminding me of the troll. The lack of dead animals and rocks tells me this isn't Morvok's place—not that I thought for a second it would be.

A small fear threads through me. What if the amulet changed time again?

The air is still and cool. Light filters in from behind dark, heavy curtains, casting long shadows across the bedroom. The ceiling is high, and the walls are lined with dark wood, giving the room depth. It reminds me of an old European castle. Everything appears antiquated yet is flawlessly preserved.

I must be in Costin's home. It feels like what I imagined his room would be in many ways. The weight of time is everywhere, reflected in the sculptures and objects around the room.

I brace my weight on my elbows to sit up, wincing as a dull pain shoots through my side. The amulet keeps me from dying, but not from injury. I push the thick blanket off my body. My muscles protest, a reminder of everything I've been through, but the pain is manageable.

It all feels like a fever dream.

The bed is massive, and even then, it barely fills the large room. Intricately carved dark wood posts rise toward the ceiling. The sheets are a deep crimson, as pulled directly out of the vampire seduction kit. They blend with the medieval feel of the room.

Cool linen fabric tangles my legs and tickles my neck. The feminine nightgown is not mine. I would never buy something with such voluminous folds. Billowing sleeves cover my arms, only to cinch around my wrists. Lace and ribbon pull against my breasts before endless folds encase my waist and legs.

"Am I dead?" I frown, pushing up from the bed. I cross to an antique mirror. The image is a little distorted, but I can see myself staring back. This gown looks like something a Victorian ghost would wear to haunt an old mansion. The amulet hangs over the gown.

My curls are wild around my head. They air-dried while I slept. I've been bathed. I don't remember doing that.

"Please let this be Costin's home," I whisper to my reflection.

I wander around. The floor creaks beneath my steps. It's like stepping back in time into the life of a man who has lived far longer than I can even comprehend.

I touch the amulet. Part of me is having a difficult time believing it's really there.

I feel safe in this room, tucked away from the world. If I don't look out the windows, I can imagine I'm far away from life. Mortimer can't find me to force me to sign the betrothal agreement. Chester's reedy laugh can't penetrate the silence. And Conrad can't threaten to kill everyone I care about.

There's a dormant fireplace across from the bed, its mantel cluttered with items collected over centuries. I let my fingers glide over them, dancing across the lip of a gold goblet encrusted with gems before lifting the lid to a jewelry box shaped like a tiny chest. Costin's rings and broaches are neatly laid out inside, and I smile.

It is his home.

To the side, a long, low bookcase is filled with thick, leather-bound books. A narrow space along the edge, about the width of the prophecy book, is empty. I hesitate before pulling one of the volumes. The cracked spine gives weight to its age with spots rubbed smooth in the binding as if it's been read many times. It's written in a language I don't recognize. I put it back, thinking it's best not to wake up any other prophecies. I've had my fill of fate and destiny.

On top, scrolls are stacked into small pyramids, tied with faded ribbons. I wonder what stories are locked away on this shelf. How many pieces of history has Costin witnessed firsthand?

And then there are the weapons.

A sword hangs above the fireplace, mounted on the wall, the blade long and slightly curved. The hilt is encrusted with rubies that match the goblet. Like everything in the room, it looks old but well-kept. Next to it is a battle axe and a spiked ball hanging from a chain. Next to the fireplace is a set of medieval armor, the gleam of polish unable to hide the nicks and dents of time. I imagine Costin has seen countless battles in some long-forgotten war.

This room—this place—it's a glimpse into Costin's life. So many centuries. So many moments.

How can a mortal woman possibly compete with that?

I'm twenty-eight. He's eternity.

The amulet will protect me from death, but I don't know what that means in the long term. What happens as I age? Will I just get older, kept alive by Draakmar's magic? Even now, I feel the dragon sleeping, its steady breath carrying it through dreams.

I did it. I controlled a dragon. I stood against a force of destruction and... turned it into a pet.

That will teach Astrid not to let me have a puppy.

I try to make myself feel better, but the fear lingers beneath the surface.

I might not know what this victory looks like in the long run, but its weight hangs heavy on my mind. I can't keep running from who I am. I'm a mortal, protected by a dangerous amulet that borrows magic from a grumpy, ancient being. I'm tied to the supernatural world in ways I never wanted to be.

No longer merely mortal, but mortal still.

I close my eyes and take a deep breath, letting the frantic thoughts tumble through me. I mended the amulet, but in doing so, I ensured I'd never live a normal life. I saved the world. I did that. What else am I capable of? What does it mean for my future? I'm no longer just a bystander in the supernatural world—I'm part of it. And as much as I've fought it, as much as I've tried to hold on to the idea that I could have a normal life, I know now that's not possible.

I can't keep running from who my family is.

I'm proud of what I've accomplished, but at the same time, I'm terrified of what I have become.

I grasp at the neckline of the gown, the fabric

constricting my throat. Tilting my head backward, I draw a deep breath.

A soft knock at the door pulls me from my thoughts. Costin comes quietly into the room. He's dressed in a simple black shirt and dark pants. Looking at him, there is no sign of the struggle we've just been through.

Long black hair hangs around his shoulders, showcasing his handsome face. He's so beautiful, achingly so. My heartbeat quickens.

What will we become now that the prophecy is done and his obligation to me is finished?

Neither of us speaks. He crosses the room, the shuffle of his boots the only sound in the quiet space. His eyes stay steadily on mine, and I see something I don't expect. I'm used to him being impossible to read, or domineering, or annoyed. But this is...

Vulnerability.

"You're awake," he says, his voice deep and rough around the edges. He sits on the end of the bed.

I nod. "Yeah."

A smile touches his lips, but it quickly fades. He stares at his hands, watching them flex open and shut as if gathering his thoughts. I try to think of what to say to him. Nothing brilliant comes to mind.

"You—" I start to speak when he doesn't.

"I—" he says at the same time.

I give a small laugh. He gestures for me to go first.

"You have a lovely home," I answer.

He glances around at the compliment. "Thank you."

We fall again to silence. I rub my shoulder, trying to work the knot out of one of my many sore muscles.

"Do you remember everything?" I watch him closely. "Time is what it should be? Everyone is all right?"

"There might be a few casualties from the dragon's stroll around town, but I think it's mostly property damage. There is enough magic down there to rebuild. They'll be fine." He must feel me still staring and adds, "Yes, time is normal—prophecy, troll, what we did in your bedroom, the subway, the labyrinth, your defeat of Draakmar."

I give a big sigh of relief, and we fall back to silence.

Finally, as if coming to a decision, he looks at me. His voice is low, almost frustrated. "I failed you."

I frown, shaking my head as I step toward him. He lifts his hand to stop me.

"I wasn't there to protect you." Costin is always so composed, so sure of himself. But now, there's an uncertainty in him I've never seen before. "I had one duty, an oath to your grandfather to protect you, to see you through the prophecy."

I shake my head in denial, taken aback by the admission. "Oh, no, Costin—"

"You faced the ultimate battle with the dragon alone, and as a reward, I attacked you and nearly drained you dry." He doesn't look me in the eye. "If not for the amulet, you would be dead, and it would be my fault."

"But I'm not dead." I momentarily forget my body aches. I go to stand before him. "You didn't fail me. Costin, you've been there for me through everything. You've protected me and stood by me when no one else would have. You've always protected me. I didn't realize it at times because I was a kid, but you have always looked out for me. You didn't fail me. You never have. It was my fate to tame Draakmar, not yours."

His jaw tightens. "I should've been there. You shouldn't have had to face that alone."

"I didn't." I kneel on the floor before him and place my hand on his. "You were with me the whole time. Maybe not physically, but you were there. I could feel it. I knew I wasn't fighting alone. Very few vampires would have gone to such extraordinary lengths for a mere human as you have."

Human connection, a mortal's magic.

There's a long pause between us, filled with so

many unspoken words. I've been guarded, closed off when it comes to admitting my feelings for Costin. But here, in this place, in the aftermath of everything, I can't keep running.

"Anthony made it home safely," he says. "Your mother coddles him in magic, but he is mending."

I sigh in relief. "I almost feel sorry for him. Lady Astrid's attentions can be worse than her neglect."

"I told them you were safe."

I glance at his shoulder. There is no indication of the wound. "You almost died protecting him in the tunnels. Thank you for not leaving him."

"He asks that I bring you home. I think he's worried about Conrad's vengeful spirit coming after you. Conrad should be drained at the moment after the second trial, so you are safe."

"You know, vampire, we surprisingly have something in common." I try to smile and lighten the mood. "Both of us have siblings willing to kill us to get what they want."

He frowns. "I do not find that amusing."

"I mean, relationships have been built on less," I keep trying. The attempt is lame and doesn't work.

"Lady Astrid asked me to send for a necromancer to collect the spirit so he can do no further harm. Elder Leviathan will be happy to have me owe him a debt. Conrad will not be bothering you again."

At that, I stiffen. "What does that mean?"

Damn. Even now, I care about what happens to him. What is wrong with me?

"His soul will be put in a place where he can do no harm."

I think of the two demons haggling over the soul in the jar.

"The necromancer won't…" I'm not fully sure what necromancers do with souls. "He won't give Conrad to demons or anything, will he?"

Costin does not look as concerned about this as I do. "I will make sure he does not."

"Thank you." The idea of Conrad being stuck in a jar doesn't sound like a great end, but then what else can we do? His rage needs to be contained before he acts on all his threats.

"Of course." He nods. "I'd do anything for you."

A small guilt lingers in the shape of Paul. Maybe, in another life, that would have been my path. But, after all the alternate timelines, I've had enough of other lives. I'll save Paul for those quiet, private moments when I let my mind drift. He'll always be a what if, but Costin is here. He's real. He belongs in my supernatural world.

"I don't know what comes next for us or if I'm being presumptuous in saying there is an us," I say. "I'm not sure how to handle all of this. But I know one thing. You've been with me through some of the hardest moments, and I don't want to keep pretending like what I feel for you isn't real."

Costin's eyes lift to meet mine, and there's a flicker of something deep in his gaze—something I've seen before but never allowed myself to truly acknowledge.

"This thing between us," I continue, my hand still resting on his, "it's real, Costin. I feel it. And I think, maybe, you do, too."

His hand shifts beneath mine, turning palm up to intertwine our fingers. The gesture is simple but speaks volumes. He doesn't say anything, but the way his thumb brushes over my knuckles tells me everything I need to know.

He's never been a man of long conversation. That's okay. Words aren't needed.

I lean toward him. My heart pounds, but it's not fear that drives the heady rhythm. It's something deeper, something real. When his lips brush mine, it's tentative at first, as if neither of us is quite sure how to proceed. Gradually, the kiss deepens. All the emotions I've kept locked away spill over onto him —fear, insecurity, relief, desire. They're all there, churning into that one perfect kiss.

He pulls back first and leans forward to rest his forehead against mine. His hand still holds mine tight. "We'll figure it out. Together."

I believe him.

My entire life, I've been pulled between the human and supernatural worlds. I've walked a tightrope between the two. No matter how hard I wish, I'll never be free of my family's legacy. The supernatural realm will always overpower the mortal in me, but I'm not facing it alone.

With Costin beside me, maybe—just maybe—I can face whatever comes next.

I push against his knee to stand. "How much time do we have until you take me back to the penthouse?"

"Never, if you so wish."

"What time of day is it?" Frowning, I look at the light coming through the curtains. "Should you be in here? The sun—"

In a panic, I stand and rush to pull the curtains closed.

He chuckles. "Open them and look."

I hesitate as I pull the thick, velvety material away from the wall to peek, careful not to let too much light in. There is no window, only bright lights on the brick wall to mimic the sun coming through the windows.

"We are underground. This is my crypt," he explains.

I let the curtain drop back into place.

"Sunrise is in a few hours," he says. "You were asleep for almost a full day."

"Then we'll leave in just under two hours." I smile as I return to the bed. His hands press against the soft material at my hips to pull me closer. "As much as I would love to avoid familial duties and stay here, I have things I must take care of."

His hands stall on their way up my back. "Tell me you are not going to agree to marry Chester Freemont."

I give a dramatic shiver. "That is one of the issues I need to address."

"And the others?"

"Anthony will tell my parents about Conrad. I think it's time I told them all the truth." It is a conversation I don't want to have, but it will help me explain why Mortimer's premonition won't come true. "I don't want to think about all of that now."

"What would you like to discuss?" His words are filled with meaning. He pulls a zipper, undoing my gown down the back with a wicked grin.

I feel like there are things we need to work out, but for the life of me, I can't think of what those might be. Costin is not perfect. Then again, neither am I.

Before I can answer, I'm lifted into the air and flipped around to land on the bed. I bounce on the soft mattress. Costin comes over me, stroking my hair away from my face.

"Stay here with me," he urges. "Never leave."

"Tempting," I whisper, lifting my head to receive his kiss. "I'm here now."

His hand glides down my body, pulling the Victorian nightgown with it. The material traps my arms to the side as he exposes my breasts. He gives my mouth a tender kiss before moving to nuzzle my throat and then caressing his way down my chest.

"Two hours is not long enough, but I will make do." His lips feel warm, like he's already fed. I try not to think about it. If I'm with him, I must accept that he is a vampire.

I feel his hard body above mine, pressing me down. I try to free my hands to explore, but he doesn't let up. His mouth continues its slow, torturous march across my chest. He is centuries old, and yet he somehow manages to make me feel like I'm the first woman he's ever touched.

I feel the brush of his cock against my inner thigh, padded by the thick material of the gown.

"Get this thing off me." I wiggle against the material to be free.

He laughs. Within seconds the press of his body is gone, and I feel a whoosh of material sliding off my body like some magician's trick to leave me exposed. Just as quickly, he is once more on top of me, having discarded his clothes in mere seconds.

There is nothing between us but my amulet and the hard length of his member moving along my thigh. He pulls my knees, lifting my legs so that he can settle between them. I gasp at the intimate contact. There is a domineering, controlling nature to him. This is a man used to getting what he wants. And no part of me wants to deny him.

He kisses me, so deep and long that it steals my breath. His hands move, expertly gliding over my skin. Time holds no meaning. I know he's not mesmerizing me, but I feel myself being drawn into the vortex that is him. And I never want to come out.

He rolls onto his back, gripping the soft curve of my ass to pull me with him. The movement draws me down onto him. We make love in measured, slow, deep strokes. I stare into his eyes, completely unafraid of him.

His hands seemed to be everywhere, touching everything. I'm oblivious to anything but him. We roll around on the bed almost as if it's a battle, pinning each other down to have our way.

Our climax builds, and the moment is bitter-sweet. I want the release, but I don't want the sensations to end. I don't want to wake up from this dream to find reality waiting for me. I want his touch to last forever.

I feel connected to him. After so long feeling alone, it's nice to have somebody there with me. I don't have to explain things to him. I don't have to worry that he'll discover the supernatural is real, like human boyfriends in the past. Conversely, I don't have to worry that he'll use me for access to my supernatural family because he doesn't need the Devine's influence. He's powerful in his own right.

I roll on top of him, needing release. He keeps holding my hips, controlling the pace. His grasp tightens. The pleasure builds until it has no place to go but to erupt inside us in a crescendo of perfect gratification. He stiffens beneath me, and I above him.

The pleasure racks through me, leaving me spent as I drop down on top of him. Our bodies still joined, I lay still, breathing heavily.

Worries try to worm their way in, but I refuse to think of them now. The future will come no matter what. After all, fate cannot be changed.

TWENTY-FOUR

I know it hasn't been long, but it feels like an eternity since I've been in the penthouse. A big bonus to having a vampire for a boyfriend is faster transportation. Mesmerizing doesn't scare me like it used to, and I actually find it convenient. One second, I'm standing in his bedroom, and the next, I'm in mine.

I see his eyes go to my bed almost longingly. Unfortunately sunrise is close, and it would be better if he didn't stay. Still, I find it sweet that he insists on escorting me to my family. I don't know what dangers he thinks might await in the confrontation, but I'm not worried. I am, however, glad for his company.

As we leave my bedroom, I'm immediately hit with the scent of flowers—roses, lilies, gardenias. Crystal vases and gilded urns are everywhere. Each one looks as if it is trying to outdo the rest. They're arranged in intricate, almost otherworldly displays. It's overwhelming, and a little surreal.

"What is all this?" I ask Costin. "The last time I saw this many flowers was... never mind."

I stop short of saying a funeral. I don't want to think of death right now. There has been too much of it.

He moves to pull a card from a vase of flowers and looks at it.

"They're for you," Astrid's voice comes from the living room as she appears on the opposite side of the flowers. "They're gifts from the creatures who reside in the underground city. Apparently, news of you two's little adventure has spread. Hello, Constantine."

"Lady Astrid," he answers.

I take a step forward, inching my way through the flower path.

"And not just flowers." Astrid is holding a drink in one hand and points to a stack of boxes with the other. Two maids carry boxes toward a table that has been set up in the living room. Unwrapped presents are piled at one end. "We have jewelry boxes, rare stones, potions, handwritten notes—some in languages I can't even read."

"They're thanking me?" I ask softly, more to myself than to them.

"For saving them." Costin appears on the other side of the flowers before I make it across. "For saving all of us."

"Thank you cards will have to be written. We're making a list." Astrid sighs. "We can't keep half of this stuff here. We'll have to transport it to the estate. Some of it is too dangerous."

Costin offers his hand like a gentleman as I step nearer. I take his hand, letting him unnecessarily guide me out of the floral maze. I'm grateful for his presence. It seems to keep Astrid on her better behavior.

"Let me see you. What are you wearing?" Astrid orders with a wrinkle of her nose.

Or maybe not.

I glance down at the clothes Costin gave me to wear. I didn't ask where he got it because, quite frankly, I didn't want to know. The white one-piece jumpsuit looks like something that came out of the disco era. I shrug. I'm pretty sure she would prefer this to the scorched, torn, dirt-covered ensemble I had on after the labyrinth and dragon battle.

Upon full examination of me, Astrid's attention instantly goes to the amulet around my neck. "Is that the same stone?"

I nod.

Costin gives me a questioning look, as if he expects me to say more. When I don't, he takes it upon himself to do it for me. "Tamara completed the labyrinth and repaired her talisman."

I glance at Costin, and he meets my gaze with pride in his eyes. Astrid makes a weak noise and waves her hand like she's unable to discuss it.

"Constantine, will you be staying?" Astrid inquires, giving a pointed glance at the floor-to-ceiling windows. "I'm afraid our guest room is not set up for vampires."

Through the windows, I see the sky is just beginning to lighten, casting faint shades of pink and orange over the skyline. The sun is coming, and I know what that means for him.

"Perhaps there's a coat closet where you might feel comfortable hiding from the sunlight," Astrid offers.

I give Costin an apologetic look. It doesn't seem to bother him.

"Thank you for the kind offer," he says, matching the forced politeness in her tone. "But you are right. It is almost sunrise, and I should get back to safety."

He turns to me and takes my hands in his. I can tell he doesn't want to leave me.

"I know," I whisper, trying to ignore the tightness in my chest. "Go."

Costin hesitates, his gaze sweeping over the flowers and gifts. His attention stops on the stacks of messages littering the coffee table. His eyes narrow slightly before coming back to rest on me.

"I'll be back for you tonight at dusk," he promises.

Before I can answer, he leans down and presses a kiss to my forehead. It lingers briefly, like a promise, and then he's gone.

"Tamara," Astrid's tone instantly changes now that he's left. She comes at me, shaking her head. "What on earth are you thinking?"

"I'm sorry," I defend. "I should have told you about the prophecy, but I didn't want you to worry. I swear to you I didn't have a choice. Grandfather George did not learn about the threat of the dragon until after he gave me the amulet, and it was too late. And I think he was going to tell us about it, but then he died and never got the chance. Costin knew about it so he came with me, and we had to go to see a troll and—"

"Tamara, stop babbling." Astrid finishes her martini and holds her empty glass out to the side. One of the maids rushes to grab it from her. My mother doesn't look at the woman, not even to thank her. "Yes, I'm not pleased about the prophecy. And yes, you should have told us. It was embarrassing to find out about it by goblins delivering a bouquet of flowers. However, that is a conversation for another time."

I'm confused. "I don't understand. Am I in trouble?"

I mean, I kind of assumed that I would be, but if she's okay with the prophecy, then what is this about? Surely she's not pissed that people are giving me gifts. Honestly, I'm more annoyed because I'm the one who's going to have to fill out ten billion thank you cards.

"Today is the worst possible day to deal with any of this. Your father left for Europe last night to personally oversee a shipment of iron weaponry. Chester and his family know you're in a supernatural city with a vampire. Fairies saw you two kissing. Those gossip whores told everybody. I thought we talked about this. You were to end it with him until a later date. And always, *always,* you must act with discretion." Astrid pauses as the maid returns with a fresh martini and hands it to her. My mother takes a sip and wrinkles her nose before handing it back. "More liquor, Rosemary. I want to taste the gin, not just guess that it's there."

Rosemary takes the glass and rushes away. It's not the maid's fault. My mother gets like this when she's annoyed. It's one of the reasons why there's a heavy turnover with the New York penthouse staff.

"Mabel, with her usual lack of etiquette and foresight, told the ladies at her club about her son's engagement. Any imbecile knows you don't make announcements before the ink is dry on the contracts. But thinking has never been your future mother-in-law's strong suit."

"About Chester," I try to interrupt.

"Don't worry." Astrid pats me on the shoulders. "The Freemonts will be here first thing this morning. Chester is a man, and about as bright as his mother. Men are easy. Play dumb about the rumors. Don't admit to any wrongdoing. Bat your eyelashes, stroke his ego, and make him feel like a man."

Gross.

"I'm more concerned about his father. I just know that he's going to use this to renegotiate some of the contract's terms. I've asked your uncle Mortimer to join us as well." Astrid stops as the maid returns with a fresh drink. She gives it a light sniff and then nods in approval. Rosemary looks only too happy to return to the gift table. "I don't want you to worry. This will all get straightened out. But afterward, you and I are going to sit down, and we're going to have a talk about what discretion means."

I catch her staring at my clothes again. Her nose wrinkles, and she shakes her head. "There is no time for you to change. They're going to be here soon. When this is over, though, I want you to burn that outfit. I never want to see it again."

I really wish Costin would come back. I should

never have left his room. I would much rather lay in his arms, feeling his kisses lingering on my skin.

The elevator dings. Astrid busies herself, heading toward it. Delivery people bring in more boxes, and she directs them to add them to the stack.

Though I tell myself, I'm not really surprised. This is what I expected. Well, that is what I expected, minus the flower garden and presents.

"I think we should talk before everyone gets here." I follow my mother, and she gestures for me to be quiet as she waits for the delivery people to leave.

As soon as the elevator closes, Rosemary says, "That was the front desk, Lady Astrid. Mortimer is on his way up."

"Yes, yes, thank you." Astrid looks around the room in a complete fluster. "Oh, this mess!"

She's not stopping to listen to me. I suppose it's best if I make my case to everybody at the same time. It'll save me from repeating myself all morning to people who don't want to listen.

It's not long before the elevator dings again, and I hear the doors sliding open.

"Ladies," Mortimer states by way of greeting.

I don't turn around as I hear the distinct sound of footsteps entering the foyer. They're deliberate, as if my uncle wants me to know his displeasure before he even begins his tirade.

I turn slowly to face him and realize he's not alone. Chester is with him.

Fuck.

Mortimer looks around the penthouse, his face set in his customary scowl of disapproval. He glares at the sight of the flowers and gifts that crowd the room.

Chester's expression closely matches my uncle's. Only his face is flushed and tight with anger. His eyes narrow when he looks at me. I think it's safe to say that he did not come here to celebrate my survival.

The intercom buzzes to indicate that the front desk is calling again, and Rosemary disappears to answer it.

"I don't suppose these are engagement gifts?" Mortimer almost sounds hopeful.

"No," I say. "They are thank you gifts for me."

"Right," Mortimer drawls. He looks at my amulet, unable to contain his scowl.

I cross my arms, already feeling the tension gathering in my stomach. I've had enough of Mortimer's superiority to fill a lifetime. "If you have something to say, just say it, Uncle Mortimer."

"Zephronis is on his way up," Rosemary announces.

The news seems to spark Mortimer into action. He approaches me and grabs my arm to escort me several feet away. I'm not sure why he bothers with trying to give the conversation privacy. When he speaks, his tone is loud and annoying. "What is this I hear about how you've been spending your time? I thought we were clear. You were to end it with the vampire. That cannot happen."

Astrid frowns and looks almost embarrassed. Chester smirks and gives me a superior look.

"Uncle Mortimer!" Anthony appears and stops at the sea of flowers. His easy smile is meant to defuse the tense situation. "I wasn't told we had company."

My brother is pale but determined to look at ease. He's clearly still recovering. Considering he'd been imprisoned and drained in the labyrinth as one of my trials and then had to outrun a dragon while caving in a tunnel with every bit of magic he had left, he looks remarkably well. It's good to see him standing upright. He crosses the flower maze, his steps careful and measured, but his gaze never leaves mine.

My brother looks at Chester and belatedly greets the annoying man with a monotone, "Chester."

"Anthony," Chester returns just as unenthusiastically.

"Anthony, sit," our mother orders as she urges the maids to clear more room for the guests.

Anthony ignores her, instead choosing to come by me. He drops his arm around my shoulder in support. He leans against me a little heavier than usual as if needing me to stay on his feet.

"Uncle Mortimer," Anthony says. "What brings you here so early? Did you come to congratulate Tamara on completing the labyrinth? It's quite an accomplishment, wouldn't you say? Not many mortals can make the same claim."

Mortimer appears flustered. "Yes, yes, of course. Well done, Tamara."

"Chester, did you congratulate my sister?" Anthony presses. I see his lips curl mischievously, and I give him a slight nudge on the side to tell him to stop. "She saved the world. Not many people can brag that they defeated an ancient fire dragon."

He might be taunting Chester, but I see the respect in my brother's eyes when he looks at me. He's proud of me.

When Chester doesn't congratulate me, Anthony pulls me into a half hug. "You did good, sis. Really good."

The elevator dings again, and we all turn to greet the wizard. The door is open, but the inside is empty.

"Zephronis?" Mortimer calls out, going to look inside. He frowns, shaking his head.

"It's nothing," Astrid dismisses. "Don't worry about it."

"Tamara, if we may have a word." Chester steps

forward, and I'm immediately struck by the desperation in his movements. "In private."

"Ah, come on, ole chap," Anthony denies him. "No side parties."

Chester's hands clench at his sides, and his face is flushed an unhealthy red. His breath comes in shallow, angry bursts. He's barely holding himself together.

Anthony steers me away from him toward the couch. I duck my head and suppress a laugh.

"You didn't think I'd leave you to face the wolves alone, did you?" Anthony whispers.

I slowly lower next to him on the couch, supporting his weight. He lets out a small sigh of relief to be off his feet.

"You should be resting," I say under my breath.

"And let you have all the fun?" Anthony chuckles. "Not a chance."

The elevators open, and Mortimer's tone becomes overly formal as he announces, "Ah, there he is. Greetings Zephronis. Thank you so much for taking time out of your busy schedule to join us."

Mortimer reaches into his pocket and pulls out paperwork.

"I have the new contracts right here," Mortimer says.

Zephronis shuffles into the living room. His presence commands attention, though he doesn't say a word. His dark robes flow as if they're made of shadows. His purple gaze locks onto mine, and then he shifts his attention to Mortimer and Chester, who are already on the offensive.

I stand and cross my arms over my chest. "Zephronis, thank you for coming."

Astrid nods at me in approval. I don't expect that expression to last long.

I take a deep breath and prepare myself for the fight that is to come. "Though I'm afraid it might be a wasted trip. I was just about to explain to everyone that I have no intentions of getting married. I'm sorry if we've wasted your time."

Anthony tries to hide a soft laugh and fails.

"Nonsense. You can't do that." Chester's voice is frantic. "You can't just call off the engagement now. We've already told people. I've already made plans. This alliance was supposed to—"

"Supposed to what?" I cut him off, unfolding my arms and stepping toward him. "Get your mother off your back about grandchildren? Get your mistresses to stop pressuring you to make them honest women?"

"Tamara," Astrid warns.

I ignore her as I keep going. It's stupid, maybe, but it feels good. "Secure your place in whatever world Mortimer's been trying to force on me? I never agreed to this, Chester. I never wanted to marry you. And you know it."

Chester's eyes flash, and he takes another step toward me, the anger spilling over. "Oh, like you're a prize. This isn't just about what you want, Tamara. This is about our families. About power. You can't just walk away from this like it means nothing. You will not make me look like a fool! When we are married, you will learn your place—"

"You're embarrassing yourself," I snap back, my voice cutting over the room.

Before Chester can respond, Zephronis steps forward with an unsettling calm. I feel a rush of energy commanding our attention. The wizard's movements are slow and deliberate, as though the world must bend its will to his.

"The engagement cannot be sealed," Zephronis declares, each word precise, like a judge handing down the final sentence.

"But," Mortimer protests, "she doesn't know what she's saying. She's just nervous. Marriage is a big step for a mortal."

Zephronis turns his gaze to Mortimer. "It is impossible."

The room goes still.

Anthony nudges my leg and winks at me.

"W-What do you mean, impossible?" Chester sputters with shock. "You said everything was ready.

Plans have been made. Agreements reached. You said—"

"I said nothing," Zephronis cuts him off, his eyes flicking to Chester with a hint of annoyance. "You were never in control of this situation."

Chester stares, open-mouthed, struggling to process what's just been decreed. "But... but I already told people!"

Mortimer pushes Chester aside and takes a step forward. Zephronis turns his full attention to him.

Though it's clear he does not like what's happening, my uncle's tone is more respectful of the wizard. "Zephronis, there must be something we can say to change your mind. My premonitions were clear."

"There is not." Zephronis's expression is unchanging. He doesn't raise his voice, and he doesn't deign to explain himself. His decision has been made, and no amount of protest will change it. Something in his tone silences any further argument.

I watch Mortimer's resolve crumble under the weight of the wizard's authority. His lips press into a thin line. My uncle, despite his power and status, stands no chance against one so revered and power-ful. He lowers his gaze, barely managing a frustrated exhale. "So shall it be."

"But—" Chester protests.

"It's over." Mortimer turns to Chester, his jaw tight. "The engagement is off."

Chester's face turns a deeper shade of red, and his fists clench so tightly that his knuckles turn white. He shakes violently, teetering on the edge of a full-blown tantrum. "This is ridiculous. You will be hearing from the tribunal."

It's all bluster. There is no way the tribunal would go against a wizard. From what I know of them, half the tribunal is probably made up of wizards.

"Perhaps you should see yourself out," Astrid states calmly. "Give my regards to your parents."

Chester doesn't move to leave. Mortimer's hand clamps down on his shoulder, pulling him back with surprising force.

"Good day, Chester," Mortimer says, his voice low but sharp. He leads him forcibly to the elevator. "This matter is settled. Tell your father I expect the paperwork for that other thing we talked about in the next few days."

Chester seems to deflate, his anger turning to a simmering frustration. "If you think we're still making that deal—"

The elevator closes and cuts off his threat.

I can't say I'm surprised that Mortimer would have made some kind of side deal connected to all of this. At this point, I honestly don't care what it was. I'm not engaged to a creep. This day is looking up.

"That was unpleasant." Astrid takes a drink and rubs her temple.

Zephronis comes toward me.

"Thank you." I reach to take his hand. I can't begin to convey how grateful I am for his unexpected support against marrying Chester.

"The alliance could not happen now." He turns my palm to study the lines. Then, balling my fist, he taps it lightly before letting go. His eyes glow as he looks at the amulet. "I was not sure you would survive. I am glad to see you prevailed."

"I'm just glad it's over." I give a nervous laugh. "I'm ready for some peace and quiet."

The wizard looks at me with pity.

I want to ask about it, but Mortimer demands suddenly, "What are you doing here?"

We all turn to him in surprise.

Elder Leviathan appears gingerly, carrying a small satchel in both hands. The necromancer is in a dark, floor-length cloak with openings for two black sleeves. The last time I saw him was at my birthday party. He gave me a creepy ring shaped like an eyeball. Apparently, they're the underworld's version of a spy cam. I have it wrapped in a washcloth and shoved deep in a drawer where there is no chance of him spying on me. If it were anyone else,

I'd have declined it, but when an elder from the Sacred Delegation gives a present, the recipient should know better than to refuse.

"Was that you in the elevator before?" Mortimer asks.

"Yes, apologies for the distraction. It's best to sneak up on the restless, and I wanted to pick this one up before it recovered from the energy drain." Leviathan answers with a small lift of his satchel. "Sorry for the intrusion. This one won't be giving you any more trouble."

I move toward him. "Is that…?"

"One vengeful spirit," Leviathan answers. He looks at the elevator. "Mortimer, if you wouldn't mind?"

"Of course," Mortimer calls up the elevator for the necromancer.

"Conrad?" Anthony asks, pushing from the couch. "I want to see him."

"Anthony don't strain yourself," Astrid orders. She waves at Leviathan to bring the satchel forward.

The necromancer carries the bag and sets it on the table beside my presents. Gingerly, he opens it and reaches inside. A red glow flashes and reflects off his face as he lifts a large, round crystal. Streaks of red dart around inside it, bouncing off the walls of the prison. I stare into the crystal's depths and get a glimpse of Conrad's face. It's like a reflection, temporarily flashing against the circular edge.

The elevator dings and Mortimer rushes over to hold the door open.

"That's enough." Astrid motions for Leviathan to put my brother back in the bag. "Please get it out of here."

Guilt fills me to see him like this, but I don't know what else we can do with him. At least he can't hurt anyone.

"Oh, Conrad," Anthony whispers with a shake of his head.

"I'll walk you out." Zephronis joins the necromancer. He frowns as he looks at the bag and then puts a little more distance between them. "That's an angry one. You'll want to be careful with him."

"I have just the place for him. He'll have plenty of company." Leviathan grins in excitement. "I'm lucky his energy is drained. Otherwise, he could have done some real damage."

I sit beside Anthony and reach to take his hand. He gives me a sad smile.

We wait in silence until they leave.

Goodbye, Conrad.

I know I should feel relief that the haunting is over, but it all just makes me sad.

"I think it's time for that family meeting," Astrid states. "Just as soon as I get another drink."

Mortimer gives me a long, hard look but says nothing. He crosses to a chair and falls into a seat with a big sigh. He pulls at his necktie. To no one in particular, he says, "Bring me a bourbon."

Anthony gives a small clap of his hands. "Any chance Howard has coffee on?"

"I'll check," Rosemary said. The maids were so quiet I'd forgotten they watched the family drama.

"Here. Sort through these." Astrid hands me a stack of messages. "I suppose we should have Constantine over for dinner soon. I need to call the country estate and have them deliver some of the blood he likes. I'll have to check your father's schedule."

Astrid disappears into her flurry of plans.

My eyes skim over the notes and the names of the creatures who sent them, all thanking me for what I did. But then, a pink slip used by the front desk to take messages catches my eye. Everyone else sent fancy stationery or old parchment. I drop the other cards on the couch next to me.

"Miss Devine. A human man came by asking about you. He didn't leave a name," the message reads.

I glance nervously at Anthony, who seems more interested in watching for coffee.

I again look at the message.

Anthony suddenly snatches it from me. He wads it up and throws it on the floor next to empty boxes.

"Stupid reporters. The front desk sends me these ominous messages all the time. They're always trying to do investigative pieces on the family. If they only knew the half of it, eh?"

I give a weak nod.

"Ignore them if you can, but if they ask about anything supernatural, the family lawyers will take care of it," Anthony continues.

I know all this, but I let him talk. I sense his need to fill the silence. Otherwise, we'd be watching Uncle Mortimer pout and grumble over the failure of his plans.

Rosemary brings my uncle's drink before handing Anthony a coffee. Astrid reappears with a refill and orders the maid to give us privacy.

"Promise me, Tamara, that you will not let Constantine turn you into a vampire," Astrid states. "If you insist on continuing that affair, I must require that promise. Vampires can be very seductive, but they aren't like us."

I touch the amulet. To transform means to die. I'm not sure he could change me unless I take the necklace off again. "I have no plans to do so."

"Good." Astrid gracefully takes a seat and shoots Anthony and me a severe stare. I feel as if we're two little kids in trouble. "All right, you two. Start talking. Tell us everything."

TWENTY-FIVE

They say honesty lifts the soul's burden or some such nonsense, but I'm pretty sure those people did not sit through a five-hour conversation being grilled by Astrid and Mortimer. By the end, Anthony and I would have confessed to just about anything to get it to stop. I'm sure Astrid will relay everything to my absentee father. Why should he make an appearance after I saved the world? He pretty much missed everything else in my life. There is no point in being bitter. That's who they are.

I left out the more intimate details of my time with Paul and Costin, but as for the rest, I told them everything that happened to me. I can't say they believed all of it. But at the end of the day, it is the truth.

I've come to terms with fate's plan. It's not like I

had much of a say. Things are as they were meant to be. Paul and Diana are safe. I don't have to worry that Conrad will harm them anymore. There is no reason for them to be on the supernatural's radar as long as I stay away.

As evening approached, a sense of anticipation built within me. I found it difficult to sleep during the day. Adapting to a boyfriend who is active primarily at night will take some getting used to.

Boyfriend. I shake my head in awe. I'm dating a vampire. Who would have ever thought?

I wait on the sidewalk outside our building. I need the fresh air, and I don't want Astrid drawing me back into the same conversation.

The chilly air caresses my skin, leaving me with a tingling sensation. The sky is transitioning into a deep purple, signaling the imminent arrival of nightfall over the city. Fall is here, and soon snow will follow.

Dusk has always carried with it a sense of foreboding for me. Nighttime is when the beasties and ghoulies come out to play. But now, waiting here, it's different. The evening feels charged—like anything can happen.

I touch the amulet, feeling safe, knowing that its magic protects me. This is not the life I would have designed for myself, but I feel hopeful about what may come.

I smile in anticipation, pulling my jacket tighter around my shoulders as I lean against the cool stone railing, scanning the darkening street.

Costin will be here soon. This will kind of be like our first official date.

After everything that's happened—the battles, the betrayals, the endless loss—I'm finally ready to move forward. I've chosen him, and for the first time in what feels like forever, I've made peace with my choice. The tension that's lived inside me for so long, that tiring pull between my mortal life and my supernatural legacy, is starting to settle. I'm not technically supernatural, but the amulet gives me protection, and the battle against Draakmar gives me respect.

The breeze picks up, and a prickle of warning crawls over my skin. A hunched figure catches my attention. He's coming toward me. My heart stutters in my chest. There's something familiar about him.

I hold my breath, unable to look away. The figure steps into the fading light.

Paul.

What's he doing here?

For a split second, I can't process it. It makes little sense. I hadn't expected him to come back. I had let him go. I chose Costin.

But now, he's here.

He looks different. There's something about him

that's almost fractured. His eyes, which once held so much certainty, are troubled. His movements are unsteady, and he's deep in thought. I hold still, thinking he might continue on like I'm a stranger.

Then his gaze locks onto mine, and I see a flicker of recognition. "T-Tamara?"

He remembers me.

How?

I touch the necklace. But the timeline didn't change. This shouldn't be possible.

My heart slams against my chest and my head spins. He remembers. "Paul."

And just like that, all the surety I had moments before starts to crumble.

Paul takes a shaky step forward, reaching out to me. "Thank goodness you remember me. What happened? One moment, life is moving on like normal. The next, I vividly remember that we were in California right after Nancy's funeral, but my calendar says I took clients." His voice breaks, his fingers trembling as they hover in the air between us. "Tamara, I don't understand. How could I forget that? Diana doesn't remember anything. I mean, she's had terrible nightmares about being chased by monsters since the funeral and actually insisted we name the dog Tamara for protection, but she doesn't remember you, and neither do my parents. When I talked to the counselor, they said she was just working through her mother's death."

"Where is she now?" I look behind him, hoping I don't see the child in the shadows.

"With my parents in Kansas City," he answers. "She's fine. I just talked to her."

The confusion in his voice twists something deep inside me. I fight the urge to tell him everything, to explain what happened, why I did what I did, why I need to let him go. But I can't move. I'm frozen, suspended between the past and the present, torn between the person I once was with him and the person I'm evolving into now.

I glance at the sky. Costin will be here soon. How do I explain this?

"Paul," I whisper, my throat tightening. I don't know what to say. The labyrinth made me give him up. It was all settled. It was fate. How can I tell him that I've moved on, that I've chosen someone else, when he's standing here in front of me, remembering us?

Paul closes the gap between us. His hand brushes mine, and I feel our connection snap into place like it never left. I can't ignore what's at stake —Costin and the promises I made to him—but Paul's touch feels like a distant memory, the ghost of a life I thought I'd left behind. I can't help but feel the pull of the possibility. He looks at my mouth and I think he might try to kiss me.

His voice is laced with desperation as his eyes search mine for answers. He holds my hand tighter, his fingers working against me as if to prove I'm real. "What happened to us?"

Magically erased memories are not supposed to return. That's what Anthony told me.

Cars move past the busy street.

"Paul, you can't be here. It's not safe for us to be seen together." I look around the sidewalk, hoping no one is watching us. I do fear for his safety, but I also don't want Costin finding us talking. I have to handle this delicately.

All the reasons why we can't be together remain true. I have the protection of the amulet, but he doesn't. It might not be today or tomorrow, but eventually, something dangerous will come, and I will lose him all over again.

"You need to go and pretend those memories are just dreams and never speak of it to anyone," I say. "Live a good, long life. Be there for Diana."

There is so much more I should tell him. We don't have a choice. I'm doing what I think is best. But the truth is I don't even know if I can make sense of this myself. I feel that old connection between us, the way it tugs at me, pulling me back to him and the dream of a normal, mortal life. But things aren't the same. I'm not the same.

"Not until you explain what this is." He comes closer still. I feel the subtle heat radiating from his body. "I still care about—"

"I... It's complicated, Paul." My voice cracks as I cut him off. "So much has happened."

Before I can finish, the air around us shifts.

"You have to go. I promise I'll find you, and we'll talk. But for now, you need to keep walking. Go home." I squeeze his hand before letting him go. "Don't say anything to anyone."

I can see his protest, but he must also see my panic.

"But you're safe?" he persists.

"I will be if you go now."

"Fine." Paul glances up at the buildings and then goes down the sidewalk the way he came. I take a relieved breath, watching him leave. He glances back at me a few times, as if fighting the urge to turn around and come back to me.

The hairs on the back of my neck stand up in warning. I start to go after him. Out of nowhere, a blur of movement darts from between two buildings. The massive figure is unmistakable. A werewolf.

"Paul," I try to shout in warning.

But it happens so fast that I barely have time to react. The werewolf lunges at Paul, its hulking body closes the distance in a heartbeat. Its dark fur blends into the shadows. Paul turns just in time to see the attack. His eyes widen in terror, and he lifts his arms to fight, but it's too late.

"Paul!" I scream as I run toward him, but the werewolf's growl swallows the sound.

In one swift, brutal movement, the werewolf takes Paul by the throat, lifting him off the ground as if he weighs nothing. Paul kicks and claws at the werewolf's massive arm as he struggles to breathe.

One second, Paul is in front of me. The next, he's gone.

The werewolf snarls, its fangs bared, saliva dripping from its jaws as it yanks Paul backward into the alley.

"No!" I scream again, my heart pounding in my ears. I give chase into the alley, but they're both gone as if they were never there. I search anyway, running the length of the building, searching behind dumpsters and trash until I reach a dead end.

I skid to a stop. My breath comes out in sharp, ragged pants. My eyes strain to see into every shadow, searching for anything. There's nothing. No sign of Paul. No sign of the werewolf.

He's just... gone.

And I didn't stop it.

My hands tremble as I press them against the cold stone of the building beside me, trying to steady myself. It's like the ground has dropped out from under me, and I'm falling into something else I can't control.

This shouldn't be happening. I made peace with letting him go. He was safe. Why did he have to come back for me?

Guilt gnaws at me, and I have this horrible feeling that I'm responsible for what's happened.

Before I can even fully form a plan of action, I feel a familiar presence behind me.

"Tamara? What are you doing in here?" Costin appears from the darkness, moving quietly. He immediately scans the alley before taking in my expression. I can't hide my worry.

"What happened?" he demands, locking his gaze onto mine. I see the swirl of his powers and I push away from the building.

"Werewolf," I manage, trembling.

Costin tenses, and he sniffs at the sky. He leaps from the ground, bounding up the side of the building like a predator, and he climbs. I watch his silhouette disappear onto the rooftop, hopeful that he will find Paul in time. I listen and watch, but I can't tell what is happening.

Costin jumps from the tall building, landing beside me. "It's all right. You're safe. It's gone now."

He pulls me into his arms. I shake my head. "No, it took Paul."

Costin stiffens. "What was Paul doing with you?"

"I don't know. He just showed up." I push away from him and gesture helplessly. "I don't know why, but he remembers what happened before the amulet broke. He came to talk to me."

Costin's jealousy is palpable, and it knots something inside me. I can't say I blame him. But I chose him, didn't I? But why does seeing Paul still hurt so much?

"He was just looking for answers," I lie. Well, it's not a complete lie.

"Are you sure it was a werewolf?" Costin frowns. "The moon is not full. They normally don't hunt in the city."

"I know what werewolves look like," I respond, a little too sharply. "I tried to stop it, but it happened so fast. There was nothing I could do."

Costin goes silent. I can't read his expression.

"It's not what you're thinking. I chose you," I say. "But Paul has a daughter. We have to find him. For her."

"It may already be too late," Costin argues.

"The wolf didn't bite him. He took him. There's a chance."

I don't know what to do, but I can't waste time. Every second that passes, Paul slips further away.

"One of Anthony's friends is a werewolf, Peter. Maybe he can help us?" I move to the end of the alley.

"Tamara."

I turn to Costin. I can't shake the feeling that Paul's disappearance is my fault. And I can't ignore the connection to Paul that refuses to fade.

Costin's eyes meet mine, and for a moment, the world goes still. I get the impression he knows what I'm feeling. He doesn't call me out on it, but he knows.

"I'm sorry," I whisper, my voice breaking. "I have to help him."

Costin studies me. "As you wish. We'll figure this out. Together."

I nod, grateful for his help and humbled I have to ask him to save my ex.

"I will take care of you, Tamara." Costin takes my hand in his, and his eyes meet mine. "Trust me."

His eyes swirl as he mesmerizes me. I don't want to lose myself. I try to protest, but the vortex is too strong, and I melt easily into it. All worry for Paul drains away until there is only Costin left.

"I will take care of everything," Costin whispers. "You can forget all about him."

To be continued...
The End

BARELY BREATHING
MERELY MORTAL BOOK THREE

Book three of the spellbinding new first-person POV romantic urban fantasy series by NY Times and USA Today bestselling author Michelle M. Pillow.

I thought I could finally breathe again. After surviving the labyrinth, I believed I was done with the supernatural chaos that has been tearing my life apart. I was wrong.

The world I've fought so hard to escape keeps pulling me back in, and this time, the stakes are higher than ever.

Costin, the dangerously irresistible vampire I shouldn't want, still haunts my thoughts.

Paul, the man I swore I would protect by staying away, is now in more danger than ever.

I don't know what I'm going to do.

Magic is shifting, enemies are closing in, and I'm starting to realize my mortal bloodline might not be as powerless as I've always believed. The truth could destroy everything —my family, my future, and maybe even me.

I've faced monsters before, but this time, the greatest threat may be the one I never saw coming. I don't know who to trust, and if I make the wrong choice, it could cost me everything. The only thing I'm certain of?

I'm barely breathing. And the worst is yet to come.

——

Prepare for an exhilarating journey of magic, power struggles, and forbidden love like never before! Perfect for fans of urban fantasy, paranormal romance, supernatural mysteries, forbidden love, enemies-to-lovers, power struggles, and heart-stopping twists. This is a must-read for anyone craving more than a little danger in their love stories.

MERELY MORTAL SERIES

Merely Mortal

Mostly Shattered

Barely Breathing

Nearly Dead

More Planned!

Visit MichellePillow.com for details!

ABOUT MICHELLE M. PILLOW

New York Times & USA TODAY
Bestselling Author

Michelle loves to travel and try new things, whether it's a paranormal investigation of an old Vaudeville Theatre or climbing Mayan temples in Belize. She believes life is an adventure fueled by copious amounts of coffee.

Newly relocated to the American South, Michelle is involved in various film and documentary projects with her talented director husband. She is mom to a fantastic artist. And she's managed by a dog and cat who make sure she's meeting her deadlines.

For the most part she can be found wearing pajama pants and working in her office. There may or may not be dancing. It's all part of the creative process.

Come say hello! Michelle loves talking with readers on social media!

www.MichellePillow.com

facebook.com/AuthorMichellePillow

x.com/michellepillow

instagram.com/michellempillow

bookbub.com/authors/michelle-m-pillow

goodreads.com/Michelle_Pillow

amazon.com/author/michellepillow

youtube.com/michellepillow

pinterest.com/michellepillow

tiktok.com/@michellempillow

threads.net/@michellempillow

PLEASE REVIEW

THANK YOU FOR READING!

Please take a moment to share your thoughts by reviewing this book.

Thank you to all the wonderful readers who take the time to share your thoughts about the books you love. I can't begin to tell you how important you are when it comes to helping other readers discover the series!

Be sure to check out Michelle's other titles at www.MichellePillow.com